THE PATRIOT'S
FATE

THE PATRIOT'S FATE

BY

ALARIC BOND

FOR LYLA MOLLIE, WITH LOVE.

Fireship Press
www.FireshipPress.com

The Patriot's Fate by Alaric Bond

Address all correspondence to:
Fireship Press, LLC
P.O. Box 68412
Tucson, AZ 85737
Or visit our website at:
www.FireshipPress.com

WHO FEARS TO SPEAK OF NINETY EIGHT?
WHO BLUSHES AT THE NAME?
WHEN COWARDS MOCK THE PATRIOT'S FATE
WHO HANGS HIS HEAD FOR SHAME?

"THE MEMORY OF THE DEAD" - JOHN KELLS INGRAM.

CHAPTER ONE

It had been a simple meal of boiled pork, onions and potatoes and, now that they were finished, Crowley sensed no one would feel the need for anything further. He took a pull from his tankard as his gaze roved around his four companions. Three he had known for many years and considered friends, even if they had been strangely distant that evening. Each had an odd, almost preoccupied, air that was quite alien, and none were drinking anything stronger than water.

"I think you would notice a few changes, were you to be there," the stranger, Liam Walsh, began to speak again. This was the fresh faced young man he had been brought to meet, and Crowley had long ago decided there were far too many words in his head. "Things have altered in many ways, and not all for the good."

"Aye, that's right, an' all," Doyle agreed. Patrick Doyle, the red haired southerner, was probably Crowley's oldest friend,

1

even if they had not met for three years or more. He was known for his lively wit, evil humour, and a steady hand with a bodhrán. And as a seamen he could be counted on: there had been times when Crowley had trusted him with his very life and had never in any way doubted his ability or judgement. But now the man was oddly subdued, as if he had finally encountered a problem that could not be solved, tolerated, or avoided.

"Back in April the British introduced free quarters," Walsh continued. "All of Queens County had troops billeted upon them. Within two days British soldiers had seized most of our arms and ammunition. Weapons we had been saving like misers were taken off us, an' anyone who had the nerve to object was not seen no more."

The others nodded in silent agreement.

"And I expect you will realise that the very army who persecutes us so costs more'n three million pounds a year; close on half the Irish revenue: we'll be lucky if it don't bankrupt the country it pretends to protect."

"Yet support for the cause has never been stronger," Doyle added. "Wherever you go brothers have been cutting down trees to make their own pike handles, and near on every blacksmith's working all hours to forge the heads."

"They can torment us all they wish, but they won't break our spirit," MacArthur said, a little pompously, Crowley thought, "and we will fight with our bare hands if we needs to."

"Indeed, we now amount to over three hundred thousand," the young man had started again. "That outnumbers the military by more than five to one. And despite everything, we still have weapons," he assured them.

"You make a strong case," Crowley agreed, reaching for his pot once more. "And I cannot say that I am against you."

"Yet still you will not join us, Michael?" Doyle's tone was mildly accusative.

2

"This is not the man who sailed with the fleet in 'ninety six," Doherty spoke for the first time. "Are you really so set under King George's belt?"

Crowley replaced his tankard without having drunk. "It is not the crown, or him that wears it that I care for," he said. "I have no love for either; you should know better than that."

"For the last few years you have been serving in a King's ship." Doyle said pointedly.

"That is true, but I swore no allegiance, and neither would I ever."

"Then there is nothing to stop you from joining with us again," MacArthur's words hung open, and there was a silence that no one felt able to break. Crowley fiddled with the handle of his tankard, suddenly unable to raise his eyes to meet those of his fellow countrymen.

"It is a hard task to explain," he said finally, his fingers rubbing up and down the dark pewter. "Most of you know me of old, and know that I have never left a friend in need."

There was a brief exchange of glances amongst the others, but no one said a word. Crowley continued.

"Indeed, those I trust are very important to me, which is why I feel unable to join in your game."

"It is hardly play, Michael," Doyle murmured softly.

"Aye, that's as maybe," Crowley replied, "and sure, I can see a time when it might be anything but. Still, there are others I must consider: others who have seen me right in the past, and I will not let down." He raised his eyes to meet theirs. "And yes, some of them may be British, but that does not make them the worst, not in my mind at least."

The four men shuffled uncomfortably, but Crowley had begun now, and was going to finish.

"You can hate a country, despise its ways, and begrudge a

history of wrongdoing. But that may be the work of a few, not all. I have found there to be good amongst the British, and that good is at least in equal measure to the bad."

A silence lasted for several seconds before Doyle asked, "If you are not with us, are you then against us?"

Crowley's expression relaxed, and a few instinctively smiled in return. "No, I will not fight you, lads. Indeed, you shall carry my heart wherever you go. But I have been on one venture such as yours, and it failed. A powerful fleet, an army of men, and we were to set Ireland ablaze, as I recall."

"It wasn't the British that defeated us then," Doyle reminded him. "It were the weather."

"Worst gales we have known, and just at the wrong time." Doherty shook his head at the memory.

"Aye, an' who would have been expecting storms in the middle of winter?" Crowley asked lightly, although this time no one met his look, and he continued in a more serious vein. "No, you are right, the British got off easy. But since then I have grown to know them better, and they are not all the stuck up fools we take them for. Some certainly know of the soft spot in their belly that is Ireland, and because they do, no plan for a French landing can be successful; they cannot afford it to be, for that would truly finish them."

The young man went to speak, but Crowley was not to be put off.

"And if they cannot allow for such a thing, it will not happen; they are a determined race, you must see that. All you may expect is misery and murder; families will be torn asunder, and the country'll end deeper in the mire than at any time in its history."

"The French are to support us, they will help form a republic," Doyle said.

"Aye, like in Holland, and Italy, and Switzerland," the young

4

man confirmed.

"I have seen the Dutch," Crowley's voice was soft, but clear. "Indeed, I have fought and defeated them. And I know they are no happier being under French domination than we would be."

"But if you were to choose between a French master, and an English?" The young man asked, his tone verging on the incredulous.

"Then I would choose the latter," Crowley said simply.

* * *

Thomas King bounded up the stone steps outside the Keppel's Head and pushed through the double doors. A slight, grey haired man was dozing behind the counter, but the lieutenant paid him no attention as he made for the upstairs room that Kate and Robert Manning had been sharing for the past few weeks. He rapped sharply on the door, which was opened by Kate wearing a long flannel dressing gown and with her hair already in papers. King took a small step back; her eyes stood out: red rimmed against a face that was uncommonly pale. He knew that her pregnancy was not progressing well, and he felt clumsy and strangely out of place in his watch coat, with the scent of the evening air all about him.

"Is it a bad time to call?" he asked.

"Indeed not, Tom; you are welcome. And I am far better than this morning."

"That is good news indeed," King replied awkwardly, entering the room. Robert was sitting at the small desk under the window and King felt mildly relieved at seeing his friend.

"What cheer, Tom?" Manning asked, turning and rising from his chair. "How was London? Did you meet with Sir Richard?"

"I did so," King replied, unbuttoning his coat and handing it to Kate. "Though it is not good news, I fear. The ship will be many months more than thought; they cannot be certain of a date."

"Will you take tea?" Kate asked.

King shook his head. "Thank you, no." Actually, a cup of hot tea would have been very welcome, but he knew his friends were not exactly well-to-do since leaving the East India Company's employ. In fact he wondered how they were able to maintain their current room, when the prospect of future employment was so poor. King had already moved from the hotel and found himself something a little less expensive. He brought his attention back to Manning. "Much of the fresh coppering has to be replaced; something about the preparation being poor, and fixings insufficient. The yard is taking responsibility, of course, but nothing can make up for the time lost."

"That won't make the captain happy," Manning muttered ruefully.

"Indeed it did not. Michael Caulfield and I were with him barely half an hour, and most of that time was filled with stories about the yard's inefficiency."

"It must be frustrating for him," Kate said flatly. She could feel little genuine sympathy for a man who might wait several lifetimes for employment, yet still not find himself short of a roof or food.

"I think he blames the yard more than is their due." King sank into the chair that Manning indicated and sighed. "It were most likely his fault to begin with; he would chivvy them so to have *Vernon* completed. Doubtless incentives were offered, and this is the result."

"Aye, you can be too keen, I suppose," Manning pondered, remembering that they had exactly two weeks rent left in their savings. Two weeks which might just stretch to three if their already meagre food bill were cut further. "So, when would you say?" he asked.

"At a guess, November, or possibly December; allowing for time to fit and work up; we will be lucky to be a-sea by the New Year."

"Seventeen ninety-nine..." Manning shook his head again, and no one spoke for the moment.

"And sadly none of this has lessened the talk of his appointment," King continued. "If anything, the gossip grows worse with news of the delay."

"But he will be a senior captain in a week or so." Kate had settled herself on the edge of the bed and was picking at her sewing.

"Sure, and an 'over-three' is fully entitled to a line-of-battleship, though it is rare for one to be given quite so soon, or as readily."

"But Sir Richard commanded *Pandora* at both St Vincent and Camperdown," Kate said. "As commissions go, it must be one of the more successful, surely?"

"There were many ships at both actions," Manning replied dryly. "And few of the other captains have been allowed such an advance; especially when not six months ago he was set to give up the Navy for politics."

King shrugged. "He has a powerful family and is being well looked after, but cannot escape the criticism of his fellow officers. And frankly, I think it is beginning to get the better of him."

"Even he has little choice but to endure it," Kate said philosophically. "And five months is not so very long. We could maybe find employment, and there is always the prospect of a berth elsewhere."

"I think that to attempt work in your condition would be foolish in the extreme," Manning said firmly. "And the chance of finding another ship quite so quickly is small; we shall just have to wait it out."

"That might not be necessary. Sir Richard did make mention of a different opportunity. There is another frigate, a thirty-eight; bigger than *Pandora*, and ripe for a captain of his seniority to command." Kate and Manning's eyes stayed set on King as he continued.

"She's the *Scylla*; she came in from the Channel Fleet a couple of months ago – likely to return there as well, but now she's having a few minor repairs attended to and is lying at Falmouth. Ralph Jenkins had her last, but has opted for a quieter life; gout, I fancy. Her premier is being given a swab, along with a fourteen gun brig, so he will be taking one of the lieutenants and some of the lads with him. Sir Richard has been offered her as a jobbing captain, until *Vernon* is made ready, or so I gather."

"Well that would be a splendid solution," Kate said, flinging her sewing down and sitting upright. "She could be at sea almost immediately!"

Manning smiled. "There may be a few details, but in essence you are correct."

"And he has to accept her first," King reminded them. "I think his heart was set on a liner. A fifth rate, no matter how powerful, is not the same."

"But he can take this now, and still have his battleship for later," Kate insisted. "Really, I would have thought there would be no discussion in it."

"Perhaps our dear captain is not so concerned about his rent," Manning murmured.

"If there is a problem," King said, his awkwardness returning. "I am sure I could maybe help."

"Thank you, Tom; there is no need at present." Manning said definitely. "And there never will be, as long as Sir Richard sees sense."

* * *

"So you are set on your way," Walsh said, when it was clear there was no more eating and little talking left to be done. "Sign on for the King and fight his enemies, even though they may turn out to be those of your own kind."

Crowley shook his head and drained his tankard. He had been the only one drinking ale throughout the evening, the others having claimed no intention of raising more in taxes for King George. Such a petty action, Walsh's comment, and the constant battering to join their cause suddenly combined to annoy him, and he knew it would be difficult to finish the evening with any degree of civility.

"I'm to sign on for the *Vernon,* if that is what you are meaning," he said, placing the mug down and wiping his mouth with the back of his hand. "She is a liner, and likely for far-flung places, so will be of no bother to you and your expedition."

"When do you sail?" Doyle asked.

"Likely a month or so; she is still in the yard, so I hears. But there is a berth for me when she is ready, and I will be taking it."

The four men considered him, and Crowley felt obliged to continue. "It isn't that I do not wish you well; you know it is a cause I have supported in the past. But that was a while back. Now I have found a home for myself in the Navy, and to my mind that is as precious as a land I have not seen for many a year. It contains men who have fought with me, and for me. I did not ask for you to force a choice, but as you have, I must go with them."

MacArthur sighed. "So be it, Michael; though it is a sad day when your friends desert you."

Crowley opened his mouth to say more, when a sudden

9

commotion from the street below made them all start.

"That's one hell of a shindy going on below," Doyle stood up and made for the window as the sound of hammering at the front door of the inn reached them.

"The press?" Doherty asked, of no one in particular.

MacArthur shook his head. "The landlord assured me not," he said firmly, while young Walsh began to look about the place, as if for somewhere to hide. "Said he paid a pretty penny to the regulating officers for immunity."

"Thieving bastards, the lot of them," Doyle replied, although there was little malice in his comment. "Come, they are in the street; there must be a place we can shelter."

The door opened slightly, admitting the worried face of a small balding man. "Gentlemen, you had better be about your way," he told them urgently.

"So tell us where we should go," MacArthur snapped. "The impress men have us surrounded, and after you gave me your word."

"The word of an Englishman," Walsh said automatically, as the door suddenly flew open, projecting the landlord towards them at the head of a column of burly men.

"Come lads, there is no need for alarm," one of them said as they filled the room. "We are simply here to offer you employment."

A naval lieutenant had followed and was smiling triumphantly. "A proper find, methinks," he surveyed them with satisfaction. "Prime seamen, by the look of it, though the yonker might take a while to show his worth."

"I, sir, am a clerk, and have no business with the sea." Walsh's face had grown paler still, and as he spoke Crowley noticed his lips were working terribly.

"Then it will be good to have a man of learning," the

lieutenant replied. "Another fine haul for King George," he turned to one of the gang. "Take their belts, then add them to the lot below. I'd say our evening's work is progressing rather well."

* * *

Sir Richard had finished dining but still felt restless and oddly unsatisfied. His father, who sat at the head of the long table, was just selecting a cigar, and did not indicate for his butler to offer the box to his son.

"If you'd kept a better eye on the dockyard Johnnies, this would not have happened." The older man was talking through regular puffs as he lit the cigar from a proffered taper, and Banks took a couple of seconds to work out what had been said.

"That is hardly fair, sir. They were under pressure for a speedy job."

"Too much pressure," his father regarded him through the smoke. "Too much hurry to be back at sea, and this is the trouble it has caused."

Banks shifted uncomfortably. The old boy was right, of course, but that hardly made matters better. Yes, he was in a hurry; he had spent almost six months in England, and hardy seen the sea for all that time. But it was not the element he missed so much, rather the chance to be in charge: in command, not dependent on anyone for favours or approval.

The spell in the country, when he had been eyeing the Reading constituency, had been a farce. He had thought being a member of parliament would be roughly the same as a ship's captain, that he could govern his borough pretty much as he wished. But the science and intrigue of politics had confused him from the start; rules and official procedure could be read up and learned in an evening, but there was so much more. Subtle allegiances, nods and winks across crowded dining rooms; he had felt completely overwhelmed by the whole circus even before applying for the seat.

His father had come up trumps, of course, as father always did. Nothing had been said; it was clear he was not government material, and a ship was promptly found for him. He had wanted a liner, or at least something a little more solid than poor old *Pandora;* and *Vernon*, with her lumbering bulk and lower deck of thirty-two pounders, had seemed the ideal solution. She would be fresh from a major refit; no crew, no officers. It should have been the ideal start to the rest of his naval career. Once he had seen her lines and walked amongst the mess and confusion that was her quarterdeck,he had felt totally at home, and the need to be at sea once more was undeniable.

But that had been more than two months ago; she was still no nearer seeing open water, and he was starting to find life in London, in his father's house, in his father's care, and at his father's expense, stifling in the extreme.

To begin with, he had taken time out and mixed with his colleagues: eaten pies at Bellamy's and drunk wine at White's, but it was the company that soon began to stick in his craw. He had already made quite a name for himself in naval circles, and no one begrudged him any of his success. But a liner, and a newish one at that, given to a man still wearing the single epaulette of a junior captain – that was just too much for his fellow officers to take. Many of them had progressed through interest; the subtle old boy's network that gave positions to those who could afford them, but there were limits to what family connections, and good old fashioned funding, could provide. Or so it seemed. The longer Banks stayed on shore, the lower his standing would fall. It made little difference that he was due to achieve his seniority in a few weeks time; he was doomed now, and possibly for the rest of his professional life, to be marked as the man whose father had bought him a battleship.

"Have they given a date?" the old man asked, leaning back in his chair.

"Three months," there was a catch in his throat. "And another, at least, for the coppering. Then we can start to fit her out."

His father shook his head but did not speak. Banks closed his eyes; he knew himself to be a worthy ship's captain. He had commanded *Pandora* credibly enough through two notable fleet actions, and won the praise and admiration of admirals and commanders-in-chief. Yet all the old man could see was a small boy who could not get his ship into the water.

"What about that frigate?" his father asked finally.

Banks pursed his lips. The frigate had indeed been mentioned more than once over the last week, and was an option, he supposed. She was British built, at Rotherhithe, and of the Artois class, a design that was popular and well proven. But despite all that was in her favour, she was still a frigate; he had loved *Pandora*, but no one could pretend her to be anything other than a scout and message carrier. This new one was a thirty-eight, of course; far greater fire power, and from a firmer, stronger, platform, though she would doubtless show a good turn of speed when required. But she could never stand in the line of battle, and might be wiped out with a single broadside from a ship like *Vernon*.

"I will see her," Banks said slowly.

His father considered him. "Good of you, I am certain."

Banks shook his head. "I meant no ingratitude, but had my heart set on the liner."

"Well the liner is yours should you want to wait for it, or you can have the frigate now. I can give you that option but no more. And no more when this is done." The man was now staring at him quite intently. "You may regard the smaller ship as a temporary measure: there is a term for it, I believe?"

"A jobbing captain," Banks replied.

"Indeed, and that is how the Navy may regard you. And you have every reason to hope that *Vernon* will be ready on your return, I have no doubt?"

"Her or another. Of course I do not know how long the temporary command should last, but if successful, I would then be eligible for a larger ship."

"Well, be it short, or long, I urge you to make the most of your time."

There was something in the old man's tone that drew Banks's attention.

"I am not saying your service to date has been anything other than exemplary; indeed, you may well have progressed to your present position without assistance from me. But this is where that help must end; otherwise you would never rightly know what you could or could not achieve on your own. You must also understand that there are those who will happily credit your success to my connections, rather than any skill you might possess."

Banks lowered his head; he certainly understood that.

"So, view your frigate and, if she pleases, take her. And place her in swap for a larger in time, should you so wish. But that is now totally under your control; I will have no more to do with your career."

Banks went to speak, but his father stopped him.

"I am well aware of the frustrations of living at home. With your mother gone and sisters married, this is not an easy household, especially for one so used to being in charge. Well, you have that command now; partially because I think you deserve it, and partly because that is the correct way of things. Stay and await your liner, and show the world you are worthy of her, or opt for the frigate, and be at sea before the summer is out. That choice is yours, as will be all the others from now on."

14

* * *

They had been taken back to the Rondy, a building the impressment men were using as a base for their operations. Crowley and the other Irishmen were put in one small cell, along with seven other unfortunates who had been picked up at the same tavern. The adjoining room was lit by two lamps that hung from the ceiling and gave a modicum of light, some of which found its way into the prisoners' area. Three men were there already when they arrived, so it was clearly going to be a crowded and uncomfortable night, especially as the gang had set out once again almost immediately.

"A bunch of Irish, or so I hears." An older, grey haired man dressed like a clerk regarded Crowley and his fellows once they were safely locked up. "Don't make the best seamen, but I suppose you'll do," he said, before squirting a narrow stream of spit and tobacco juice that landed just short of the nearest man's feet.

"You'd know about being a seaman, then, would you?" Crowley asked.

The man snorted. "Not me, matey, I gets a regular wage, and sleeps in a warm, dry bed. Wouldn't catch me on the briny," he pulled a face. "Not for as long as I got this job, anyways."

"I'm not a sailor," Walsh, the young man, spoke quietly. The clerk considered him.

"No, I can sees that. An' you're Irish, so we don't get much lower, do we? But that don't mean we can't take you an' all."

"'E may be a freeholder, or an apprentice," Crowley said. "Don't you check, don't you even ask?"

The man's face was suddenly pressed close to the bars, silhouetting him against the lamplight. "Or don't we care?" he asked, and moved away.

"Well this here is a seaman," Doyle shouted after him. "And he got a berth already." He pointed at Crowley.

The clerk swung back with a look of mild concern. "You signed on?" he asked.

Crowley shook his head. "No, but I'm bound for the *Vernon*, just as soon as she is clear of the yard." He felt in his pocket and brought out King's letter from a few weeks back. "Got word from a lieutenant in my last ship," he said. "Confirms my berth."

The man took the paper nearer the lamp and looked at it quizzically for a few seconds before thrusting it back through the bars.

"I may not be no scholar, but I knows a protection when I sees one, and that ain't even close. Besides, *Vernon*'s likely to be months more 'fore she's aready. An' with Sir Richard plum-face Banks in command, heaven knows where they'll send her." he considered the Irishmen once more, and the smirk reappeared. "Whereas I know darn well where you lot are bound. Got a jaunty little sloop for you, all set up and ready for the orf. It'll be the Leeward Islands, nice warm climate, an' plenty of flies for company. Reckon you might last a year; that's if yer lucky. Main thing is, you'll be a world away from England. England an' all the troubles your miserable little country's causing 'er at present."

Walsh snorted. "The trouble is all one way, if you asks me."

"Well I ain't askin' you," the man yelled suddenly, slamming his palm against the bars, making the metal ring, and them all start slightly. "An' I ain't gettin' into no discussions where you gonna be servin'. The high an' mighty Captain Banks'll have to find 'iself another arse-wiper; you're for the 'Indies, and sharp: ship sails with the mornin' tide." He moved back from the bars, grinning once more. "You'll be there by Set'ember, and dead by Christmas."

Crowley looked away. He longed to smash his fist into the clerk's fat face and had the reach and space enough between the bars to make a credible job. But there were two gormless louts sitting in the gloom not six feet away, and he knew that any satisfaction he may draw would be more than outweighed by the punishment they would dole out. Instead he looked away and caught the eye of MacArthur, who had clearly been studying him.

"So this would be the splendid British Navy you're so soft on?" he asked quietly.

Crowley snorted. "You ain't seeing the best example," he said.

A tap came from the front door, not loud or demanding, just enough to attract their attention.

The clerk turned. "They're back early, must 'ave got lucky." He gave a slight chuckle, winked at his two companions, and sauntered out of the room.

"Looks like we have company," Crowley grunted, but the other men's eyes were alight and eager.

"That's just what we was hoping," Doyle muttered.

Crowley was about to ask further when there was a shout, closely followed by the sound of the door being pushed back against the wall. Then the outer room was suddenly filled with the bulk of several heavy men, all carrying short wooden staves and advancing towards the cell. A brief fight broke out, but it was decidedly one sided, and in no time the two guards lay senseless on the floor.

"Where's the Oirish?" one, a lightly bearded brute, shouted in a broad accent.

"Irish be damned, Jackie," a smaller, slightly better dressed man with strangely cropped hair told him brusquely. "We'll let 'em all go, there's none of them that wants to be here."

The clerk had lost much of his swagger and was being held against the back wall, while one of the men pulled at his belt. His trousers slipped and a bunch of keys fell clattering onto the stone floor. Within seconds the cell door was opened, and Crowley and his friends began filing out.

"Give us a moment, lads," the smarter man told the others. "We gets clear and you can make you're own way as you wish. Press is a good three streets off b'now, an' not expected back for a spell."

The other prisoners muttered their thanks, and one took a purposeful kick at the prone body of a guard as Crowley and the Irish were bustled out into the dark night.

"Stick together, lads," they were told, and the men slipped their clubs back into their clothing. The bearded man winked at them in the soft evening light. "We got a bit of a walk ahead of us, an' don't want you fallin' in with no trouble."

CHAPTER TWO

Lieutenant Peter Chilton had not held a commission for more than a few months and yet already was in charge of one of the finer frigates in His Majesty's Navy. Admittedly it was a harbour command and an unofficial one at that; he knew he would relinquish her as soon as a more competent, or at least a more experienced officer was appointed. But for the moment, all one hundred and forty-six feet of her hull, each of her twenty-eight, eighteen pound carriage guns, plus the additional twenty-four pounder carronades, and every one of her fifty or so regular seamen and junior officers that remained of the crew were his to direct. He strode about the quarterdeck, revelling in the space that was entirely his for the prowling. Forward, at the break of the forecastle, a group of men were busily engaged cleaning and polishing the bell. Once that was done they could turn their attention to the galley chimney, which was due for a sweep, and should be cool enough by then: a good officer checks on such things. Part of the main deck was being re-caulked and a team of painters were working on a stage over the larboard side, touching up the broad yellow-ochre stripe that ran the length of her hull. The rich smell of tar and oil based paint filled Chilton's nostrils, giving the very air a scent of workmanlike efficiency. By the time the new captain came aboard, he intended having the entire ship shining like a new pin.

Just as he was imagining the scene, Marshall, the lieutenant of marines, came up on deck. He was a good ten years older than Chilton, at least thirty-one, and carried himself with all the swagger that age, experience and access to a notable private income can give a man. Chilton watched him surreptitiously as he took the morning air to the windward side of the quarterdeck. Although apparently of the same status, Marshall was actually inferior to him in rank, and yet boldly shared the quarterdeck, and even took the coveted sheltered side, without the courtesy of reference or formal acknowledgement. It was a small matter, but Chilton was inclined to sensitivity, and Marshall's domineering ways never failed to gall him. But then, he told himself, it was probably the only annoyance in his life at that moment, and was certainly not enough to dispel the feeling of goodwill that had been present in *Scylla* pretty much since Captain Jenkins and the two more senior lieutenants had left.

The captain had been the first to go; Lieutenant Chilton supposed it should have been a sad occasion: a man who had spent his life at sea, leaving it for the last time. But Jenkins had been a miserable blighter, at least for the brief time that Chilton had been aboard, and probably for always, if the stories were correct. Gruff to the point of bloody-minded, Jenkins had bitten the heads off officers and men alike, giving scant encouragement or regard, and absolutely no credit for good work. But when presented with anything that fell even marginally below first rate, a new energy took hold of him, and whoever was responsible would be stamped down upon, almost literally, with glee and gusto until there could be no doubt that the wrong had been put firmly to right. Chilton supposed it was Jenkins's condition that made him so; certainly the advanced stages of gout were not known to be pleasant. This failed to evoke any sympathy in the younger, healthier man, however. In fact, the occasional cry when the captain knocked a clumsy foot or bashed one of his gammy legs actually became the source of a good deal of silent satisfaction.

Once clear of his presence, the ship had enjoyed three days of relative holiday before the lieutenants departed. She was moored in the harbour, with little for a tired and homesick crew to do but wait until the time when they would be paid off or transferred to another vessel. There was no official wedding garland hoisted, but that did not stop women and a good deal of illicit drink coming aboard, and for a brief period the scenes of revelry and indulgence were enough to totally distort a young man's mind. At the same time, the first lieutenant was set on marking his promotion to commander, and regularly held receptions in the recently vacated great cabin, consuming much of the stores that Captain Jenkins would later send for. The second lieutenant was to follow the first as premier of the new brig they had been promised, and both celebrated their elevation with some of the finest meals, and prettiest young women, Chilton had ever seen.

Then they left in a flurry of handshakes and goodwill, taking quite a number of the lower deck men with them, leaving only a few to be transferred to *Ardent,* the liner currently working up a few cables away, and Chilton to his current role of ship keeper. There was much talk of a new man coming; the regular victualling boat was often alive with stories of officers seen viewing the ship from ashore, or coming down *post-chaise* and immediately ordering cabin stores, or sending for possessions. But so far there had been no official notice, and they had not been bothered. *Scylla* was a fine ship: well built in a British yard, and with plenty more serviceable years in her. Still, whoever came would have much to do before she saw the open sea again. There was nigh on a full crew to find, as well as a good few junior officers, and a fair amount of sorting of stores and equipment. She would be a clean ship, though; that was certain, at least for as long as Lieutenant Chilton had command.

"Another fine day."

Chilton brought himself back to the real world to find Marshall addressing him from the starboard bulwark.

"Indeed." The lieutenant was about to take a step forward but stopped himself. He was of superior rank; it was Marshall's duty to approach him. Consequently the two remained a good ten feet apart, and shouting slightly in the morning sunshine.

"I trust all is now well with you?" Chilton asked. "There has been no relapse?" Marshall had claimed to be poorly for over a week, and had spent much of that time lounging in his cot.

"Very fine fettle, thank you," the marine replied, "though at the time I was a little concerned." Marshall's symptoms had been rather vague and mysterious. Mr Clarkson, the surgeon, was in London and unable to attend him, so no diagnosis had been possible; but from the fuss the marine made it was thought to be something between consumption and the plague.

"You have plans for today?" Marshall asked; Chilton shook his head.

"There is plenty of routine maintenance," he replied. "And I would like to take advantage of this sun to air the sails."

"Would that I were as busy. My sergeant keeps the men occupied, and we will no doubt be transferred to the shore if the ship remains at ease for very long. But there is precious little for me to attend to until then."

Chilton felt scant sympathy for the man. Presumably he had been detailed to stay in the ship, possibly it was even some form of mild and private punishment; but Chilton refused to believe that a professional officer could remain idle and apparently bored for very long.

Marshall had turned back and was once more watching the anchored shipping. As junior lieutenant it was amongst Chilton's duties to instruct the men in the use of small arms. He had minimal experience of hand-to-hand fighting, and was just about to suggest that Marshall held a drill that afternoon when

Betsy Clarkson appeared on the deck below.

Chilton watched her as she made her way towards him, avoiding the caulking team and their comments with a quick and easy response that drew respectful laughter from the men. Then she nimbly mounted the short ladder and greeted the quarterdeck in general with a vibrant beam that was equal to any salute in the young lieutenant's mind. She could only be twenty-five at the most, a good fifteen years younger than her husband, although her golden hair and fresh, clear complexion made her appear even younger. He cleared his throat as she approached, but it was Marshall who spoke with her first.

"Splendid morning, Mrs Clarkson." Marshall was not wearing a hat, but had he been so, Chilton felt certain he would have doffed it in a ridiculously flamboyant manner. The woman stopped on her way to Chilton and regarded the marine with obvious approval.

"Why yes it is, Mr Marshall. We are having a fine summer."

Chilton felt somewhat piqued at being denied his conversation, but would be damned if he was going to move now.

She turned and addressed Marshall. "I was wondering," she said, seemingly forgetting all about the naval lieutenant standing alone on his part of the quarterdeck, "my husband has sent word that he will be in London a while longer. I thought it might be a good time to spring clean our quarters; there is linen to wash, and the floor deserves a proper scrub."

Chilton winced as he heard the deck of the gunroom being referred to as a floor, but remained silent as she continued.

"Would it be so very much of an inconvenience were I to hang some of the laundry from your ropes?"

Marshall laughed. "My dear Mrs Clarkson, it would be no trouble at all." He looked pointedly to the foremast shrouds where a collection of seamen's washing was currently flapping in the breeze. "Indeed, a change of clothing might even spice up the view."

Now that was pushing things too far. Chilton gritted his teeth; it was bad enough for Marshall to give permission for something that was not his concern, but to make lewd jokes about a lady's laundry...

Mrs Clarkson did not seem in the least embarrassed however, or even annoyed; instead she laughed openly in a way that Chilton found oddly attractive.

"Oh, you need have no fear. I am very used to being aboard a ship, and will not discompose any man with my undergarments. I was thinking of some bed sheets, towels and hangings, nothing more."

Marshall bowed to her gravely. "I am sure that whatever you wish to air will be most acceptable, Mrs Clarkson. And if you would care for any assistance in your quarters, I would be happy to oblige."

Their eyes met for a moment and Chilton had the impression he was suddenly witnessing a very private conversation. Then she thanked the marine almost formally before turning to Chilton, giving him a brief but sunny smile, and leaving the quarterdeck.

Marshall strode slowly over towards Chilton and stood next to him for a moment. "Well," he said, turning finally. "It appears I might not be quite so much at a loose end as I had thought."

* * *

Crowley woke on a strange floor, and it took several seconds before he recalled the events of the previous night. His room was small and quite stuffy; enough light from the curtained window showed him that Doyle, Doherty and MacArthur were still sound asleep. Of Walsh there was no sign, but then Crowley would not have expected him to bunk in with his fellows. He pulled himself up and yawned. Doyle, to his left, murmured, but it was MacArthur's eyes that opened, and a slight smile spread across the man's face.

"Slept past the dawn, Mike. We must be gettin' old."

Crowley could only agree, and rubbed at his face; he certainly felt anything but young at that moment, and was not used to lying on quite so hard a surface.

"Come on, lads, let's be about." MacArthur seemed far more supple, and was even standing as he brushed down the creases in his trousers and tucked in his shirt. Doyle moaned again, and Doherty grunted, then groaned, as MacArthur began to open the door against his legs. Light from outside flooded in, making them all pull themselves up, and Doyle began to cough heavily.

"There's a man who is missing his share of fresh air," Crowley said, glad to see someone in a worse condition than he felt. Doyle rolled his eyes, but was too taken up with the spasm to comment. Doherty yawned, and nodded at Crowley.

"He does this every morning," he said. "Won't get a sensible word from the old wreck until past breakfast."

"How long have you been staying here?" Crowley asked.

"Just over a week. Place belongs to a cousin of the baker in Athy. When the time comes, he'll be a godsend."

"When the time comes?" Crowley mused. "Sure in any uprising it is good to have a deal of bread about you."

"You wouldn't be taking the Micky, now?" Doyle asked, before the coughing recalled him.

"Not I," Crowley assured them all. "But when the soldiers make their call there'll be a bit more needed than the help of a baker."

"The man was one of the earliest to test the triangles," Doherty said seriously. "It were Lake's idea; he was the British general who took over from Abercromby. He tried them out in

County Kildare first."

"Triangles?"

"Aye, it is a marvellous invention; a large piece of wooden scaffolding that can be set on any green for all to see. A man is bound to it and beaten with the cat-o-nine tails while all the town are rounded up to watch. They carry on until someone cracks; if he don't peach on his mates, it's likely someone else will to spare him the pain."

"Do they always talk?" Crowley asked.

Doherty gave a brief snort. "We're here, ain't we?"

Crowley's eyes fell as the other man continued.

"Baker, fisherman, farmer, mercer; there's few who haven't allied themselves to the cause. I'm tellin' you, the country's ripe for rebellion. If there be help from the Continent, so much the better; if not, we can do it on our own."

"And leave yourself open for the French to walk in anyway?" Crowley asked.

"That's as maybe, but we don't see them as the enemy. They were the ones who showed us the way: there is much they can teach us about running our own country."

"And those of others they have invaded." Crowley grunted. Doherty went to reply, but Doyle was still coughing heavily, so the two moved out of the room and in to a warm, bright kitchen that had been barely lit the night before. The bearded man from the previous evening was there. He had been introduced as Jack Douglas, and now stood before a metal range. A pan of bacon was started to make itself known as the smell and hiss of breakfast filled the morning air.

"Sit you at the table, Michael," Douglas said without turning. "There's no tea, but you'll find fresh milk in the jug and a slice if you wish."

Crowley sat at the worn wooden bench and cut the heel

from a loaf that lay on the table. Doherty joined him, along with Doyle, his red hair spectacularly awry and still coughing intermittently. MacArthur returned from a trip outside and settled himself also, muttering a brief grace as he helped himself to milk. The bread was quite hard, but would be welcome for all that, and when Douglas topped it with a chunk of hot, dripping bacon, it made the best breakfast Crowley had eaten for a long while. Walsh came in just as they had finished and Doyle was collecting the plates.

"I've checked with yer man; all should be ready in a few days," he said, taking off his coat and folding it. "Last thing they are awaiting is the powder, and that is expected the day after tomorrow." He placed the coat down carefully and took a seat at the table. "So then I went down to Collins at the quay, an' nothing has changed from last night. He's ready whenever; we should be fair for Thursday."

"Do we go at night?" MacArthur asked.

"And risk being arrested as smugglers?" Walsh laughed. "I think not." Douglas passed him a plate of bacon and he dipped some of the bread in the fat as he spoke. "No, dawn, first thing, along with the fishermen. We'll probably follow them out as far as we can, then make a start for France."

"Where is it you are heading?" Crowley asked, then instantly regretted the question. Suddenly the eyes of every man in the room were on him, and he felt himself lean back slightly under their combined glare. "I mean, it is nothing to me..."

"No, we can tell Michael," Doyle said slowly. "He may not be with us, but there'll never be a man less likely to turn."

"Brest," Walsh said softly.

"It must be nigh on two hundred miles to Brest," Crowley murmured, when he had digested the information. "Long way for a fisherman. And there'll be a weight of Navy ships blockading when you arrives."

"We're none of us afraid of a little discomfort," Douglas told him. Crowley could accept that of his friends, who were seamen through and through, but wondered quite how Walsh would take to being chucked about in a small boat for a day or more. He was about to enquire further, but the younger man was there before him.

"First, there is something you might find interesting. I have been making enquires about your ship. She's the *Vernon*, is she not? Being refitted at the government docks, and currently coppering further down?"

"Aye that's her," Crowley said doubtfully.

"Well she'll be there a while longer," Walsh said evenly. "They have more work to do than was thought; word is it will be months afore she sees water; some say the spring."

"Spring?" Crowley shook his head. "That's not what I've heard," he said.

"Well, you can take a view; I might have it wrong, though I'm pretty sure of my story. Main thing is, Portsmouth ain't the place to wait, not when the press is about. You could think about headin' somewhere else."

"Aye, a spell inland, maybe," Doyle agreed. "Or take up with a coaster?"

They were right, holding off a few weeks for *Vernon* was one thing, but the time had already stretched on far longer than that. And if he did really have to wait until the following year, he should at least find somewhere a little safer. Shipping with a merchant was not in any way a guarantee against being pressed, but the money was far better than any the Royal Navy paid, and he was starting to feel the lack of funds.

"Or come with us, Michael." MacArthur said as if in revelation. "By next year you could be back in England. See the country put to rights, then choose where you want to sail, and who to sail with."

Crowley grinned. "I have to give you credit for trying. But my mind is made up."

"Made up? Now how would that be?" Doyle had total control over his coughing now and stared hard at Crowley. "You know not when you will go, and little more where. An' you as any understand the way the yards work. Chances are high it will be six month or more afore your ship is ready, and then what? Spend the rest of the war rubbing against a lee shore on blockade? Do that if you wish, but in the meantime you can choose between staying with your friends and supporting a just cause, or being taken by the press and ending up in some Godforsaken hulk until someone else decides on where you are bound, and who you will fight."

"I'm not sure, I have to think."

"Send a message to yer man, if you will." Doherty suggested. "Ask him how long the ship will be. He'll fill you in, no doubt."

"Aye, that is a thought." Crowley reached into his pocket and found King's letter. He unfolded it on the table and looked about. "I'll go now, if that suits?"

"Beware the press," Walsh cautioned. "We can see a message gets delivered."

"No, I'd better do this in person," he said, and folded up the letter once more. "And if it is as you say, well then, maybe we should talk some more."

* * *

The frigate was by no means a certainty, but the round trip from Portsmouth to see her would take all of a week, so King had felt justified in giving up the tiny attic room and leaving his sea chest and most other belongings with the Mannings. The captain's carriage had collected him and Caulfield from Exeter's post stop the day before; and now, as he bounced along on the final leg of the journey, he was starting to feel mildly excited. It was mid-afternoon: there would be plenty of time to view the ship in daylight, and Banks must have been impressed to have sent for them in the first place. He grinned at Caulfield who, despite the rigours of mail coach travel, seemed just as eager and ready as him.

"Sir Richard said to be sure to meet him at the hotel," King shouted above the noise, as the carriage swung round and began the long, narrow decline towards the harbour. "Probably doesn't want us digging about his new ship afore he has had a chance to view her first."

"We have yet to see if she is to be his," Caulfield reminded him. "Besides, he has had time enough to inspect her properly."

The Marine Hotel came into view on their right as they headed for the town quay, and Banks was already there to meet them as they jumped down from the carriage.

"A good journey, gentlemen?" he asked, shaking their hands, and smiling readily.

"Very fair, sir, thank you." King replied. "A little trouble near Bodmin; the road is yet unmade and leaves much to be desired, I fear."

"It is being attended to," Bank assured them. "They are building a mail station here as we speak; the coach will be calling direct from London in no time."

"Indeed?" King could see little relevance in how the mail was distributed, but was struck by the energy and life that seemed to flow from his captain; a dramatic contrast to the last time they had met.

Banks nodded enthusiastically. "Were we to be based hereabouts, there should be few problems with communication," he said, then turned away from the carriage with its snorting horses, and began striding down towards the quayside. "Come, there is much to do, and more to see."

King and Caulfield exchanged glances, before hurrying after him, hoping the coachman would have the sense to collect their belongings.

"A touch eager, perhaps?" Caulfield muttered as they went. "I think the ship may have pleased our dear captain even more than we had thought."

* * *

Banks had every right to be impressed. *Scylla* was in fine fettle; a small amount of work had seen any minor defects put to right, and Chilton, the only remaining lieutenant, seemed to have the right idea with regards to routine maintenance. There was further work to do, of course; the ship had to be manned: almost an entire crew found, stores taken on board, and a wealth of other details needed attending to before she could be taken to sea. Banks was also aware that *Scylla* was not yet his; by even inspecting he was taking a liberty with the usual protocol. But then he wanted her, he wanted her so very badly, and the reaction from King and Caulfield, the two men he felt closest to as far as service matters were concerned, only confirmed his longing, and changed it into something that was very nearly painful.

"How does she sail?" he asked Chilton, who had been present through this, and his earlier, inspection.

"Well, sir," Chilton was a relatively new lieutenant, and felt awkward discussing the merits of the ship with her potential captain. "She'll show a fair turn of speed to any of the class, and with the wind on her quarter there are few who can catch her."

Banks felt his enthusiasm grow, but was careful to keep his feelings hidden. It was very much as he had suspected. He had studied the lines before leaving London, and to all reports *Artois* ships were good in most weathers. She was also solid; he reached out and felt one of the knees as he stood on the upper deck. It was not the all out bulk of a line-of-battleship, but the warm oak was certainly substantial, and felt massive when compared with *Pandora's* timbers.

"There's some weight there," King was looking at the nearest eighteen pounder carriage gun. He was right; the piece was a little shorter than a thirty-two, and the shot would obviously be lighter, but it was powerful enough for anything a frigate might choose to fight and, when backed by the twenty-four pounder carronades, they would have a broadside to be proud of.

"Would you care to view the great cabin, sir?" Chilton chanced. Banks shook his head; he had already seen what would be his quarters on the first inspection, and he knew King and Caulfield well enough; they were as smitten as he was. To investigate further, only to find his father was unable to secure the ship, would be frustrating in the extreme. There was already a personal risk taken in sending for the two officers; discovering that *Scylla* was not actually available would make him a fool in both their eyes.

"Thank you, no, Mr Chilton. We must leave you to your duties."

The young man touched his hat respectfully and stood to one side as the three made to return to their boat.

"There was just one more thing," the captain said, turning. "What officers are aboard?"

If Chilton was thrown by the question he did not show it, and Bank's opinion of the lad improved further. "All of the standing officers, sir. Most, bar the carpenter, have been with her since she launched. Surgeon's still appointed, but ashore at present, an' there are a fair few petty officers; a master's mate, the quartermaster and three midshipmen."

"Marines?"

"Lieutenant Marshall, sir. And Sergeant Rice, with thirty or so privates."

"Detailed, or are they aboard?" Banks asked.

"Aboard sir, there is a shortage of accommodation ashore,

an' we had a few runners when we first came in."

"No sailing master?"

"No, sir. Mr Seabrook retired at the end of the commission."

"Surgeon's mates?" Banks might have guessed that King would ask that question.

"We only had the one, and he went to *Ardent*. Surgeon's wife is used to helping out. She is not trained, but very good with the men, and they respect her."

Banks didn't particularly like the idea of women in a ship, but at least there was room for King's friend Manning, as well as quite a few of his own followers, by the sound of it.

"Here she is now, sir," Chilton said unexpectedly, as he noticed a figure at the far end of the upper deck. Banks turned to see a blonde woman carrying a large bundle of blankets walking towards them.

"This is Mrs Clarkson," Chilton said as she drew closer. "Sir Richard Banks, *Scylla*'s new captain."

Banks cleared his throat and the woman smiled politely, her laundry limiting further contact.

"Mr Chilton is rather premature, madam," he said. "Mr Caulfield, Mr King and I are merely inspecting the ship; nothing is official or in any way certain."

"Well, she is a good one," Mrs Clarkson said, looking into his eyes in a way that Banks found oddly disturbing.

"So I see," he said stiffly. The woman was clearly in no way intimidated by him; it was as if she could see beyond his rank and title, and look directly at the man beneath.

"An' lucky, though I don't much hold with luck myself," she continued. "I think you makes your own, don't you, Sir Richard?" She grinned, and Banks blushed slightly.

"It is not something to which I have given much thought," he said, feeling just a little foolish.

" That is probably sensible," she beamed. "It don't do to get too deep with such matters."

The men laughed awkwardly and Banks studied the woman with a little more care. Mrs Clarkson noticed the attention, but did not turn away. "Anyways," she said after the briefest of pauses. "I hope you like what you see."

* * *

With her three masts and bluff bow, the lugger appeared little different from the numerous small craft that plied the South Coast of England. She might be used for fishing, or one of a hundred other tasks, and when they left Portsmouth with the morning tide and in brilliant sunshine, Crowley and his men drew little attention. By noon the weather had started to grow unseasonably cold, and a steady rain began that continued throughout the night and all of the following day. What wind there was stayed with them, however; and the rain finally eased off as evening fell, just as they sighted the French coast and commenced the final run in toward Brest, shelter, and warm, dry beds.

Crowley shifted uncomfortably on the wooden thwart that had supported him for the last two days. Beside him Walsh drew his damp greatcoat more tightly about his body and lowered his head once more. Walsh had been horribly sick for most of the journey, yet hardly complained, even though he probably felt about as bad as was possible. Crowley knew better than to try and speak; when a man is sea-sick he has little need of conversation; but he longed for their final arrival in France, as much for Walsh as for himself.

They had already sighted several British line-of-battle ships, the main bulk of Admiral Bridport's blockading force, and the lugger's captain turned to join the coast further to the north in order to avoid them. Now as the light fell they altered course once more and were creeping towards their goal, with Ushant just visible to starboard, and the grey smudge that was the

French mainland tantalisingly close off their larboard beam.

"That would be part of the inshore squadron," Doyle spoke from the bow, where he was perched alongside Collins, the short-haired man from the Rondy who had turned out to be the boat's captain. He was more than competent, having guided them this far without incident, and was still calmly controlling their destinies. Crowley has assumed they would be dropped somewhere a good distance from Brest and the attending British fleet. A ten or even twenty mile trek would have been well worth taking to avoid the danger they were now about to run. But the captain was experienced and had clearly made this trip many times before. Besides, after two days in an open boat, he was probably just as keen as any of them to find warmth and shelter.

Crowley peered forward; he could just make out a frigate and what looked like a brig cruising silently in the half light.

"There's shoal water hereabouts," Collins spoke softly, without turning back. "Take her closer to the coast, Jackie; we'll give King George a wide berth."

Douglas, who had been solidly steering since morning, pressed the tiller across and reached for the nearest sheet to adjust the mizzen lug. The boat tilted as she changed course, but the on-shore breeze was dying and the sail would not draw.

"We're losing the wind," Collins muttered, as he was similarly unsuccessful further forward. He looked about, gauging what was left of the breeze. Ahead and beyond the British, the dark outline of rocks marked the seaward limit of the channel they were aiming for. The brig was the closest to them; she stood less than half a mile off their starboard bow and still held the wind as she crept forward, presumably at the very edge of the shallows. "The current will carry us in," he continued, meditatively. "Though I'd be happier not to dawdle so."

The lugger slowed further and began to wallow. The falling of the breeze could not have come at a worse time, and was still not effecting either of the British warships; Crowley could see the nearest more clearly now as she continued to bear down on them.

"Will they give us any trouble?" MacArthur asked from amidships. Collins shook his head.

"Probably not. They'll take us for fishermen and leave be, unless the cook fancies serving lobster for supper."

But the brig was clearly determined, and even shook out a reef in a topsail as her wind finally began to fail.

Crowley noticed the manoeuvre with unease. The very nature of a blockading squadron was to keep watch over the enemy. For that patience was the key, speed and any risky manoeuvring usually being unnecessary. Yet this brig was placing herself in danger in order to draw close to them: not even a strong tide, impending nightfall and the lack of wind was enough to keep her off.

"She seems set on speaking with us," he said, then instantly regretted the statement as Walsh raised himself from his stupor and looked about.

"Is that the British?" he asked.

"Aye," Crowley murmured, "and a little nearer than we would like."

They watched in silence as the brig crept further forward, her sails now flapping impotently. Then, with the very last of her way, she swung round and presented her larboard beam.

Crowley braced himself, and sure enough a pinprick of fire shot out from her hull, followed by a slight splash half a cable ahead of the lugger. The dull boom of the shot reached them as the men released a collective sigh, and MacArthur crossed himself.

"They're serious," Collins said, then stirred into action. "Out sweeps, boys; there's no point in dilly-dallying. King George clearly wants a word, and I am not in the mood for conversation."

The boat tipped as the four long oars were rousted out and set into the rowlocks. Crowley took up position at the larboard stern, with Doyle next to him to starboard. By mutual consent Walsh was not involved, but with MacArthur and Doherty at the other two stations they had enough experienced men to power the small craft. Crowley began to pull, setting a fast but steady pace. Manning the sweeps was a clear indication that they were on some clandestine mission, and the British were bound to take action. There was a small headland to negotiate before they could turn and make the final run into the main harbour. That would mean closing slightly with the waiting brig, and Crowley knew the Royal Navy would not stand idly by and watch them escape.

"There's movement on the bigger ship." Walsh was pointing back at the frigate, which was now almost invisible in the gloom. Despite the rigours of rowing, Crowley could just make out preparations for launching a boat. He dug his oar deeper into the water. The lugger was moving steadily, but nothing like as fast as a light naval cutter with a ten man crew. If the British were serious about catching them, the chances were strong that they would.

The sound of another shot reached them as they worked; the splash of it erupted off their bow.

"Starboard your helm; take her to larboard, Jack," the captain ordered. Douglas brought them round until they were heading straight for the nearby French coast.

"Are you to beach her?" Crowley asked. He could see that a boat, somewhat larger than a cutter, had been swayed from the frigate, and knew it would soon be setting after them.

"No, she'll ground long before we are in safe reach of land,"

Collins said glumly. "We'll hold this course for a spell, then take her back to aim for Le Conquet." Jack, at the tiller, helpfully pointed over the starboard bow, although none of the rowers could turn as far as to see.

"There's a small harbour there," Collins continued. "We should be able to find shelter until King George decides to leave us be."

Another shot came from the brig, this time falling alongside. The smaller warship had turned slightly; either the current had brought her round, or she had anchored and attached a spring. The vessel was all but in darkness now, but the time for warning shots was over and the men could imagine the main armament being run out. They were at extreme range for her popgun broadside, but even one hit from a light ship's cannon could be enough to account for the lugger. Doyle was muttering on his left, while Crowley closed his mind to everything bar the job in hand.

The sudden ripple of light from the brig's hull blinded them all for a brief moment. Crowley instinctively ducked, even though there was no sound of shot passing overhead. A body moved in the darkness; it was Walsh. He was seated next to Jack at the tiller and had stood up to face the broadside as it came down on him.

"Way off," he said with grim satisfaction.

"Maybe so," Collins clambered back past the rowers and also took up position at the stern. "But we're going to have to change course now, lest we want to stay here permanently. Take her across, Jack."

The boat turned again; the British were now almost totally invisible, and Crowley hoped in his heart that they had missed the manoeuvre. Then another single flash of light, smaller and further away from the direction of the brig, made them all look round.

"It's the boat from the frigate!" Collins shouted. "The bastards must have crept up on us."

Crowley gritted his teeth. The British would have to be going a fair pace to have covered such a distance; it was probably a longboat, with as many as twelve men rowing. They alone would be enough to swamp the lugger with her tiny crew, except that she would also be carrying marines, and obviously had a small cannon mounted in her bow.

"Come on, put your backs into it!" Collins's voice had risen and Crowley knew instinctively that they were very near to being taken. He leant back, raising the pace and feeling the others follow his lead. The lugger moved quickly enough but was heavily laden; the British boat was certain to be the faster. Another flash of light from the brig, but no fall of shot. It was even possible they had pulled out of her range. Crowley was considering this, and the state of his arms and back, which were starting to complain, when the cannon in the boat fired again.

Now that was very much closer. No one could say where the shot went, but the sound of the discharge followed almost immediately – probably no more than a cable separated the two vessels. Fortunately there was no moon; the Irishmen could see nothing from where the flash had come from, and could only hope that they were just as invisible to the British.

Walsh went to speak, but was quickly hushed by the rest of the crew. The sound of the oars groaning in the rowlocks was bad enough; anything louder and they would be revealed for certain. Crowley's face was running with sweat. A foolish thought occurred: after the many dousings with water he had experienced over the last two days, he was probably the cleanest he had ever been. He felt the urge to laugh out loud rear up unexpectedly and tried to think of other things: of what had brought him to this sorry position, of his time and friends aboard *Pandora*. Then his mind naturally ran on to King and how he would react to hearing of him being arrested as a suspected rebel. He cursed to himself; he really should have waited for *Vernon*. Why, at that moment he might be safely ashore in England: safe, warm, dry and in bed. But then an inner voice told him that all was not lost; besides, *Vernon* would not be ready this year or more, and hadn't King's lodgings been empty, with the man nowhere to be seen?

Another stab of light, this time closer still; they must surely have them by now. His eyes were recovering from the flash but still he noticed movement out there in the dark. Yes, the British were closing on them. He could hear the splash of oars and the shout of someone calling the time.

He sighed, still straining at his sweep. This was it: he was old and wise enough to know when a fight was over; there was no point in resisting a boat full of British seamen and marines. He and the others could make any manner of excuses, but their very presence would implicate them well enough. Walsh was probably a known member of the brotherhood. The boat would be searched, their stores discovered, and there remained the small matter that the British had obviously been waiting for them, and in all likelihood already knew what they were about. But even then, Crowley could not feel downhearted. When the French frigate he had been in was taken by *Pandora*, things had appeared bad, and yet it was by that very avenue that he first met with King and the other Englishmen.

A brief lightening in the sky made him wonder for a second, then there was the sound of shot passing high overhead, and a series of splashes in the water to their stern. Crowley went to twist round on his thwart, but stopped when MacArthur from behind cried out in alarm. The man was right, he must keep the pace going, however much he might wish to turn and see.

"It's the fortress," Collins grunted in a half whisper. "Over on the headland, near the entrance to Le Conquet. And they have their eyes open for once."

A French shore battery certainly altered the equation considerably. Heavy cannon mounted on a stable platform, their shot would be devastating against any size of vessel and should carry a considerable distance. Even the brig was dangerously close, and must pull back or risk being wrecked. A flash of light followed; the boat's cannon was speaking again, but already it was farther off, and once more they could not detect the fall.

Crowley felt the breath ooze from his body and he gripped the oar more firmly as his hands began to shake. He continued to row, but knew the pace to be slower, and that the tight order they had maintained until now was beginning to relax. There was no further sound from the British boat; even if the Irishmen were not rowing quite so hard, they must certainly be growing closer to the harbour entrance.

"Nearly home, lads," Collins murmured as if to confirm his thoughts. The man's voice was once more fully controlled, and even a little jubilant. The French battery fired again, an uneven series of shots, one of which passed dangerously close, but the British boat must have been in greater danger, and a ragged, ribald cheer went up from the men around him.

"Shall we carry on to Brest?" Walsh asked from the stern.

"I'd say not," Collins told him. "Our friends may have beaten the bastards back, but they knows we are about, and it won't take much to send another after us. We'll take her in to Le Conquet. There we can shelter for a spell and choose the night we finish the trip. What say you, lads?"

Another tired cheer, and Crowley leaned back on his oar, raising the pace once more for the last leg of the journey. Le Conquet or Brest, it all made very little difference to him; he was just glad to be clear and looking forward to being back on land.

CHAPTER THREE

"HMS *Scylla*, if you please."

The wherryman collected Rose's sea chest, sweeping it up and onto his shoulder in one swift and easy movement. The midshipman went to follow him down to his boat when a voice came from behind.

"Hey, belay that!"

They both looked round to see another midshipman standing on the quay.

"Appears we are bound for the same ship. There's a victualling lighter about to set off," the lad told Rose. "I'm taking that; you may as well join me."

Rose looked uncertainly at the man, still holding his chest. "Do you mind?" he asked, cautiously. The wherryman rolled his eyes, but dropped the chest back down gently enough and sauntered away.

"Otherwise, you could have sent a signal to the ship," the lad informed him as Rose lifted his belongings, far less expertly, to his own shoulder. "But this way will probably be quicker."

"What about your chest?" Rose asked him.

The lad grinned. "Already aboard," he said.

The lighter was indeed ready to go; Rose just had time to swing the chest on, then jump after it, before they were leaving the quayside. The lads moved aside as the boat's hands set sail, then perched themselves more or less comfortably on the low bulwark.

"Name's Barrow," the second midshipman said, when they were settled.

Rose gave his name, and wondered for a moment about offering his hand. But then Barrow, a fresh-faced lad who looked a few years older, didn't behave as one to stand on ceremony. "I'd chance you are new to the ship," he said.

"First posting for several months," Rose agreed. "Was in *Pandora*, with the same captain. She paid off in the fall of last year. There's been nothing since. By the time Sir Richard sent for me I was all in hock and about to set a course for home."

"Hard times, that's for sure," Barrow grunted. "I passed my board in May but lieutenant's berths are as rare as hen's teeth."

"You're commissioned?" Rose asked in awe.

Barrow snorted. "I've passed, but yet to be employed; until someone sees my true worth, that is," he added.

Rose pursed his lips. His guess at the lad's age was about right. No one can stand for lieutenant until they are eighteen – or that was the theory at least: he had met a couple who were a good deal younger. It would be two full years before Rose would be eligible and, as a relatively friendless soul, he doubted whether anyone would make an exception in his case.

"What was your last ship?" Rose asked him.

"*Victory*," Barrow said with just a hint of pride. "I was helping Jervie out in the Med squadron. He was most grateful."

Rose grinned. "Clearly."

"I came back with a capture to sit my board; made friends with the prize master, a lieutenant called King who asked me along to this one." He indicated *Scylla*, which was now less than a cable off. "Rather than starve, I thought I'd come. You must know a bit about her captain."

"Sir Richard? He's the only one I've served under, but I was always treated well enough, and the men speak highly of him. Made me decide to stay in the Navy, if that be any guide."

"You had another choice?"

"My parents' farm; they'd have me back sure as a gun."

"Better grub, I'd warrant."

"And less chance of drowning," Rose agreed, warming to both the lad and conversation.

"So the captain sent for you?" Barrow reminded him. "Must have caught his eye then."

"Oh, we were famous together."

"*Pandora*," Barrow said, as if suddenly remembering. "Wasn't she the jackass at St. Vincent?"

"Aye, then we transferred to Duncan."

"So, you were at Camperdown?"

"I was."

"See much of the fight?"

"Only what I could through a gun port."

They were nearing the ship now and their lighter was hailed as both lads stood to take their first close look at *Scylla*.

"She's bigger than *Pandora*," Rose said.

"Aye," Barrow agreed. "But smaller than *Victory*. Let's hope she sees as much action as both."

* * *

King could hardly keep himself from smiling. He was dressed in seaman's duck trousers and a plain cotton shirt, doing work that could not by the widest stretch of credibility be called enjoyable; yet, once more, he was a lieutenant in His Majesty's Navy. More than that, he had been appointed to one of the best frigates the old boy possessed and was serving with men he knew, liked and respected.

They had been hard at it since first light: seven hours with just a brief break for breakfast, and there was a wealth of tasks to finish before any of them slept. But still the feeling of satisfaction and fulfilment was all but overpowering. With every hoy or lighter that came alongside, another important commodity was taken on board, be it beef, spirit, powder or men; and, as the ship settled deeper into the water, a new life seemed to develop within her.

She was coming alive; more than that, due to the input in so many quarters, she was almost being born again. Whatever had been before would be forgotten, and a new HMS *Scylla* was appearing to start an unspoiled life under a fresh command. And King was part of that process – an important part. With every decision or order a piece of himself was being given to the ship and, in return, a portion of *Scylla* passed back for him to keep for always.

The two new mids had just joined them and were already helping with the stowing of the bread that had captured the attention of the lading team for the last half an hour or so. King had not seen Rose since *Pandora* had paid off: the lad had grown several inches; and Barrow, the able second in command of the privateer they had sailed back from Lisbon, was now through his lieutenant's exam. The midshipmen they had inherited from *Scylla*'s previous crew were all pretty experienced, so even if they filled the remaining spaces with dolts and newbies, they would still have the makings of a first rate midshipman's berth. And there was Adam Fraiser, calmly making notes on the manifest as each successive net of biscuits swung aboard. Fraiser was an exceptional sailing master, as well as being one of the soundest men King had ever served with. The lads could have no finer role model. Johnston had also joined them as boatswain's mate; it was his first taste of authority and, as a known deserter who had changed his name on at least one occasion, King should have been concerned. But the man possessed all the skills and experience necessary, and he had responded to the call and promotion eagerly enough. In fact he was already proving himself worthy of both. The only slight cloud on the glorious horizon was Crowley.

They had left on more than amicable terms; the Irishman had been keen to sail with King once more, and would be waiting, he promised, for the time when *Vernon* was ready. King could not be certain what had happened in the meantime; three messages sent to The Star, the Portsmouth inn which acted as an unofficial contact point for many seamen, had gone unanswered. He had even asked Manning to look for him in person, but no one there, or at any of the other usual haunts, knew of his whereabouts. Perhaps the delay in getting back to sea had been too much; maybe he had taken another berth, or chosen a completely different tack; but any of the myriad of possibilities that King had considered were wiped away by one consideration: it was unlike Crowley to break what both parties had clearly understood to be a firm undertaking.

King shied away from the thought once more, and focused his mind on the current problem of the boatswain's need for tallow. The man was in front of him now, respectfully waiting for either an answer or a miracle: it would be several days before the yard expected delivery.

"You'll have to make do with slush," he told the man. "My compliments to the cook, and could we raid his store? I'm sure he is collecting enough, even on petty warren provisions." The man touched his hat and moved away, leaving King to think once more about the Crowley situation. Yes, it was a puzzle, but not one that he was going to let spoil his mood. A chorus of laughter broke out from forward. One of the biscuit-filled nets had caught the wind and sent a hand bowling over onto the deck in a cloud of dust and flour. The man was not hurt and clearly appreciated the humour as much as the rest. Despite the hard work they seemed a happy crew, and King could really ask for nothing more.

"Message from the captain by the bread barge, sir." Rose had crept up on him unawares and went to touch his hat. Both were bareheaded however, and the midshipman was forced to rather foolishly knuckle his forehead in the seaman's manner.

"Thank you, Mr Rose." King returned the compliment with a grin and opened the folded sheet. "Sir Richard has been invited to dinner," he said, turning to where the first lieutenant was studying a watch sheet. "He won't be with us until the evening."

Caulfield looked up. "I think we can manage, eh, Tom?" he said. "Though if he brought a dozen hands with him when he returns I would welcome it."

King strolled across and spoke more softly. "We are still light then?"

"I'd say by about forty trained men," Caulfield confided. "Chilton's been gone on his recruitment drive a couple of days now; he may bring back a handful of landsmen; with the country as it is, we cannot hope for more."

"Besides, it is seamen we want, not a bunch of tin miners filled with dreams."

Caulfield snorted. "Hush now, most of the crew's from round abouts: you'll offend those that we do have."

"Come on, you blackguards, put your backs into it!" The voice of Sergeant Rice cut into their conversation. The marine NCO was in charge of eight privates who were working the mizzen fall. The men were stripped to the waist and clearly tired, but with the ship so short-handed, there was little chance of relief at present.

"I suppose there is always the quota," Caulfield continued. "Local assizes meets beginning of next week; we are first in line and should raise a few there. They might be fishermen, not proper seamen, but they'd do at a pinch."

"It all rather depends on when we sail."

48

"Aye, were there the time I'm certain we could raise the men eventually." Caulfield shrugged. "But then that is just what Sir Richard is finding out. And if they've asked him to dinner, they cannot be in so much of a rush."

"That's right, take a nap, why don't you?" Rice growled. The last of the bread was now aboard, and the marines were standing down and drawing breath. The sergeant regarded them with apparent disdain. "The more I look at you lot, the gladder I am I had daughters." The comment drew the expected response from the men; they had heard it, and many similar, countless times before.

"Bob Manning coming soon, is he?" Caulfield asked, unexpectedly.

"Aye, he should be on the next mail. And he's bringing Lewis, do you remember, master's mate from *Pandora*?"

"Oh yes, Lewis, the tarpaulin; takes a lot to haul yourself up from the lower deck. He had all the makings of a first class officer as I recall." Caulfield thought for a moment. "We'll find a space for him for sure, but you'll forgive me if I wish he were still a regular hand."

"It is a strange situation, a want of seamen and a surplus of officers," King said. "'Though not to be surprised at, I'd suppose."

Caulfield turned back to the watch sheet and shook his head. "Well, it is a problem I shall solve one way or another, though for the life of me I cannot say how at present." He looked up and caught King's eye as he continued. "'Tis a pity you did not hear from that man Crowley; he would have been mighty welcome."

* * *

Caulfield was not the only one to feel regret. Crowley was watching the small British brig as it ambled about the shallow waters on its endless patrol. He was standing on the southern

49

shore of the harbour mouth. To his right, on the opposite headland, was the shore battery that had granted them safety, and behind, the small village of Le Conquet. It was there that Doyle, MacArthur and the others would be sating their long withheld desires on French wine, tobacco, and doubtless other pleasures that King George did not tax. They had reached harbour the previous evening, and the lugger was now safe from all but the most determined of landing parties. She would remain so until a particularly dark night or favourable wind made the close blockade the Royal Navy favoured more difficult to enforce. A short trip around St Matthew's point, and they would finally reach Brest. The recent brush with the British had in no way endeared the race to Crowley, and he had heard enough stories over the past few days to totally re-think his view on the people in general. But still, as he watched the jaunty little brig, well set up and beautifully handled, and the graceful light frigate beyond her, so similar in line to his old *Pandora*, he could not deny a faint longing for the time he had spent in His Majesty's service.

The night was growing dark; it would be foolish to remain longer, especially as the place was known to be a haunt for deserters. Crowley had already started for the dim lights of the village when he noticed a figure walking towards him. He slowed, instantly suspicious, then recognised the slender form of Walsh.

"Taking a walk are you, Michael?" the young man asked, genially enough. "I'd have thought you to be with the others in the tavern. Sure I knew they could drink, but not quite to such an extent."

"They've been missing it a fair while," Crowley said evenly, as Walsh fell into step with him.

"You never did give it up when you were in England," Walsh observed.

"I could not be so dedicated," Crowley admitted. "A penny

or so of tax is neither here nor there, as far as I am concerned."

Walsh said nothing for a while, and Crowley actually began to feel guilty for not being as committed as his friends. Then an anger rose up inside him. He had not asked to be involved in their mission; in fact, his objections had been raised from the start. It was just a queer combination of circumstances that had led him to France; there was nothing for him to feel bad about.

"It were a close call last night," Walsh said after they had been walking a short while. "I thought our goose was caught. Caught, plucked and fully roasted."

"Then we were of the same mind," Crowley agreed.

"It was as if they were aware of us," the younger man persisted. "Why would that be, do you think?" he asked innocently.

"I have no idea."

"I was wondering if you might have something to do with it."

Crowley stopped suddenly. "You are suspecting me?" he asked flatly. "You think I peached on my mates?"

Walsh had taken a couple more steps, and had to turn back. "The opportunity was there, right enough," he said. "There was ample time when visiting your friend the British lieutenant. And the allegiance you hold to King George's Navy is well known."

"So your logic suggests that I betrayed you?"

"You must grant it a possibility."

"And in doing so, put myself in danger at the same time? The British were firing on us and cared not who they might hit, or had you forgotten?"

"To be truthful, Michael, I know not what to think," Walsh conceded, and the tension relaxed somewhat. "The others will not have a bad word said against you, and that would normally be enough for me. But then we live in times when brother is often set against brother. And frankly, I am not sure where it is that you stand."

"I owe no allegiance to any country," Crowley said, his tone quite soft and even, "and frankly despise those who do. There has never been a clump of grass, a rock, or a tree that has meant more to me than a person."

Walsh watched him in silence as he continued.

"It is people who matter to me. So I stand for my friends, be they British or Irish. And I'll tell you now, I would cheerfully betray any cause if I felt that one that I regarded as my own was in danger. But never, ever would I speak against a friend, and certainly not in favour of a project such as yours. Or any other merely political ideal, come to that."

The other man considered this for a moment, then began to move on once more. "I had thought as much, but am thankful to hear it from your own mouth. There would be many who might think the same, but say otherwise."

"I am not amongst them," Crowley told him, walking alongside.

"I see that, and am glad."

They were nearing the village now, and the lights from the tavern were in clear sight.

"Douglas and Collins will be staying here," Walsh said. "They can manage the boat right enough on their own. We will be leaving in the morning for Brest: it is only twenty-five kilometres away. With luck we should be there in time for dinner. There is much news that has to be shared, and not all of it good. I would rather do it there. There is also a man I want you all to meet, who may do the telling better than I."

"And then?" Crowley asked.

Walsh paused for a moment as if relishing the prospect. "Then there is the biggest group of ships that has been put together for quite a while, and they will be sailing for Ireland. Ireland and freedom. I hope you will join us Michael, really I do." His eyes flashed, suddenly bright. "We need all the honest men we can get."

* * *

The majority of the officers berthed in the gunroom, a space slightly smaller than the captain's quarters directly above it. The quarters were subdivided into eight cabins, with a central communal area for dining. In larger ships it would have been known as a wardroom, with a smaller gunroom below, for lesser officers. In a frigate these lower ranks, which included the gunner, berthed outside the gunroom and had alternative, less salubrious messing arrangements. Traditionally the gunroom officers formed a tight family. Their cabins were admittedly tiny, but as all bar two were for single occupancy, and in one of those the second tenant was a cat, the lack of space was no great problem. Besides, it was usually more comfortable to sit in the dining area, where the mess table made as pleasant a place to read as to eat, and company was usually to be found.

King had finally come to the end of a busy day and was tucking into a large plate of mutton that a steward had brought him. The meat was fresh, a welcome change from the usual sea diet of salt beef or pork; and King, with no one to talk to, found himself wolfing the food down with a young man's appetite. He pushed the plate back once he had finished and considered calling the steward for a pudding; but he had eaten on an empty stomach, and the haste had given him mild indigestion. Instead he sat back in his chair, belched quietly, and then yawned. Really he should go straight to bed, but he felt like some company. Caulfield would probably join him shortly, or Fraiser; either one were good for conversation. King decided to wait for them and, in the meantime, enjoy the peace and solitude; both rare luxuries aboard a ship of war.

But his time was soon interrupted. Almost before he had closed his eyes and tried to think of anything other than the problems of the day, a murmur of conversation from the surgeon's cabin caught his attention. He had yet to meet Mr Clarkson, who was currently travelling down from London; his wife was aboard, of course, but there should be no one for her to speak to in their quarters. And one of the voices sounded male.

He wriggled uncomfortably on his chair as the talking changed to a whispering that ended abruptly in laughter. It was definitely two voices; one was a woman's and must belong to Betsy Clarkson, unless Mrs Porter, the boatswain's wife, was in there as well. The other, well, King was reluctantly certain it belonged to a man. And, being that Mr Clarkson was absent, he could only conclude that whoever owned it really should be somewhere else.

But who was it? Chilton had been sent off on a recruitment drive and would not be back for several days. Caulfield and Fraiser were on the quarterdeck. Dudley, the purser, was ashore, and the final cabin was currently unoccupied. That only left Marshall, the lieutenant of marines.

King raised his eyebrows and puffed as another chorus of giggling made itself heard. He was not unduly surprised; Marshall was as cocky as he was vain: King could have guessed that the lure of a pretty and temporarily available young woman would be too much for him to ignore. But such a thing was not encouraged in any commissioned ship, especially during wartime. Women were not even officially allowed on board, although they might be carried at the discretion of the captain. Once there they had to behave themselves, or risk being put off at the next port.

King also sensed that any case of marital disharmony could only grow and fester, even when Mr Clarkson returned and all were apparently put to rights. Such tension must disrupt the ship, and just at the wrong time, as she was settling down to a new regime. There can be few secrets in a wooden frigate; it would not be long before something was noticed or overheard, just as he was doing now. Then questions would be asked and folk were bound to talk and speculate; it would be hard keeping such delicious gossip quiet, and right now all their energy was needed getting *Scylla* up to standard.

He stood up a little uncertainly. It was a difficult situation and one he was not truly fit to handle. He could order the lowering of a topgallant mast when storms were expected, and might usually be relied upon to set the ship's position to within tolerable limits. But this went far beyond the realm of seamanship. Marshall was his inferior in rank; it would be quite in order for him to rap on the door and demand an explanation. But there might be a scene, and he would have to think quickly; the marine was an eloquent man and was bound to have some reasonable explanation, one that would be perfectly innocent and leave King looking the fool.

Another peal of laughter broke out, followed by what sounded very much like a slap. King swallowed, and looked about. There was no one else in the gunroom; he was quite alone, as clearly Marshall and Mrs Clarkson felt themselves to be.

So, it would be a case of his word against theirs, and this early on in the commission, it was a confrontation he did not relish. Perhaps it might be better to leave things as they were; it could only be a momentary fling: an affair that would die away to nothing as soon as Mr Clarkson came back to claim his rightful place. Besides, did King really have any business interfering with such things? He might be better to choose discretion. And telling himself he was in no way dodging the issue, he rose and quietly made for his own cabin.

* * *

In the midshipmen's berth the entertainment was far more innocent. The boys, and with the possible exception of Barrow they might all be called so, had just finished an especially tiring day and carried appetites worthy of men twice their age. The middle-aged marine servant who acted as a combination of steward, housekeeper and surrogate parent had drawn the same meal as that of the officers, and the smell of fresh mutton was there to greet them as they tumbled good naturedly into the small room.

"My, that smells good." Barrow made straight for the pewter pot and peered within. "No salt horse there, what? God bless Peter Warren!"

"Peter Warren?" Parfrey, a twelve year old volunteer who had joined that afternoon, asked cautiously.

"It's a jape," Rose said kindly, "a play on words; when in harbour we are issued with petty warren rations."

"Don't listen to him," Barrow said, dipping a finger in the stew. "Mr Warren's the butcher who supplied this mutton; and it was a splendid beast, I'd chance."

"Come on gentlemen, we 'aven't got all night," the marine steward was also keen for his own supper. "Form up and I'll serve out; then you can spend all day talking if it pleases you."

The lads clattered down on to the benches that ran either side of the table, and the marine reached for the pile of plates. Rose collected a handful of forks from a locker and threw them down in an untidy pile in front of the lads. The more experienced amongst them collected one apiece and pressed the tines through the canvas table covering, cleaning the head of any debris left over from the previous meal, while the marine passed out the plates until there was one in front of each. He regarded them seriously. "No foolin' now," he cautioned. "Sergeant Rice 'ears you makin' a noise, and it'll be me who's for it."

The lads smiled angelically back, and soon they were left alone.

"So?" Barrow said, looking about. "This is our first proper meal together; what's it to be?"

"Do we say grace?" Parfrey asked.

"Can if you wish," Barrow shrugged. "But there is more fun to be had elsewhere. "I'd say we try a spot of... All change!"

At the words he, and several of the other, older boys immediately slipped off their bench, and began crawling under the table on all fours. They emerged on the other side, sometimes to an empty place, sometimes to one that was filled, but shortly to be emptied, whereupon they began to devour the food in front of them. Most had managed two or even three forkfuls before the cry of 'All Change' went up again, and the process was repeated. The new lads caught on quickly enough, and soon the evolution was even working quite smoothly, although some confusion, when eight adolescent bodies met under a table while trying to pass in opposite directions, was inevitable.

The stew was finished in no time, and the lads beamed at each other, panting exaggeratedly and wiping nonexistent sweat from their brows. It had been an excellent meal.

* * *

Fraiser entered the gunroom just after King had fled to his cabin. He also heard the talking, but took far less time in coming to a decision. Instead of taking a seat and calling for his supper, he made straight for the surgeon's cabin and rapped firmly on the door. There was a sudden silence from within, then Mrs Clarkson's voice gave out a hesitant "Yes?"

"Sailing master, madam," Fraiser said, in a firm tone. "You have company in there, I believe."

"Bugger off, Fraiser. We're busy." It was the marine lieutenant's voice, as he had expected and, despite Marshall's seniority in rank, the man had no business addressing him so.

"Mr Marshall, kindly present yourself, sir."

The sound of movement from within was unmistakeable. Fraiser waited, but the door remained closed.

"Mr Marshall, I insist that you exit this lady's cabin immediately."

Suddenly Marshall's face appeared at the partially opened door. "What the devil do you mean by this?" he asked, glaring down and into the older man's eyes.

"You are in a lady's cabin, sir," Fraiser said, his voice barely louder than a whisper. "Kindly remove yourself at once."

"We are doing nothing untoward, and this is not of your business."

"Very well, then I shall inform the captain," Fraiser went to go, but Marshall called after him.

"And tell him what? That Mrs Clarkson and I are playing a game of *vingt-et-un*? Hardly a criminal offence, I'd chance."

"Not a criminal offence, Mr Marshall," Fraiser said, "but one that will certainly see you off this ship. If you were to play a game with Mrs Clarkson, you would have been better to do so at the gunroom table."

Marshall considered him for a moment. "Very well," he said finally. "We shall do so in future."

"There will not be the opportunity," Fraiser said firmly. "You shall leave this ship without delay."

"I shall what?" Marshall stepped out of the cabin. He was dressed in a plain shirt and britches, and his hair was not dressed and hung in a tangle. "You stupid old fool; you are naught but a sailing master; how dare you presume to order me about?" The marine's complexion had grown dangerously red, and he all but spat his words. "I am your superior and could buy and sell any warrant officer a hundred times over. You have absolutely no authority in this matter, and certainly none over what I do in my free time. And in addition you have made an outrageous suggestion that has upset Mrs Clarkson deeply; I insist you apologise." Marshall's face was barely inches away from Fraiser's, although the older man met his glare with quiet composure.

"There will be no apologies, unless you see sense and choose to offer one," Fraiser said, his words clipped and firm. "I have found you carrying on in a commissioned ship of war. Worse than that, a fellow officer's wife is involved. The matter shall be taken to the captain, or you will leave this very evening; it is your choice, and you must make it straight away."

Marshall considered Fraiser for a second, then a quizzical look played upon his face. "You're serious, aren't you? I cannot just walk off a ship to which I am appointed."

"Mr Marshall, you can do exactly that; hand in your papers if need be, but go, and go now. There will be time to appoint a new man in your place."

"You jumped up, Jesus bothering nonentity..." the marine stopped, mouth open, desperately searching for words.

"I have right, and the law on my side," Fraiser continued smoothly. "And the Lord as well, since you choose to include Him."

Marshall continued to stare at the man, then suddenly pushed past, out of the surgeon's cabin, and across the gunroom to his own. He went inside, slamming the frail door behind him.

"Steward, do we have some food?" Fraiser asked suddenly, turning away from the half opened cabin door and ignoring the sound of a woman's sobs from within. The gunroom servant appeared, rather too readily he thought, and placed a bowl of steaming stew on the table.

"And I'll take a cup of tea, if you please," Fraiser said, seating himself, and pulling the bowl towards him. He began to eat and continued, even when Marshall bellowed for his servant. He was just finishing his meal as the two of them bustled out of the cabin, out of the gunroom and, in Marshall's case, off the ship.

CHAPTER FOUR

"We are for the Irish station," Banks said; and, strangely, the statement brought no immediate reaction. All of the officers present had been expecting a posting to the Channel Fleet, and it took several seconds for them to properly register the news. "Admiral Kingsmill is at Cork, and we shall be based there, though we are bound for Dublin first with despatches and to be briefed," he continued, taking advantage of their surprise. "*Scylla* will be travelling alone, but I believe it likely that further reinforcements are to be sent to join us shortly."

Banks looked down from the head of the table. Of the four men before him, three he knew well; only Chilton stood out as the newcomer and, as he had only just returned from his recruiting drive, still remained something of an enigma. The captain unfolded the orders he had received that morning; they carried far more background information than was usual, but then Evan Nepean, the secretary to the Board of Admiralty, was known to have an interest in Irish matters.

"I think at this point it may be worth a brief résumé for those who are not fully aware of the current state of affairs," Banks said. "You may well have heard of the rather ragged uprising a few months back." He raised his eyes and looked at each in turn. Caulfield, he knew, had Irish connections; Fraiser was a Scot; and it was not inconceivable that Chilton or even King held sympathies. Should he notice any sign of support in these, or any of his officers for that matter, he would have them exchanged without delay. The Irish situation was difficult enough; it was vital that he trusted everyone: there was no room for subversive tendencies or misplaced ideals.

"The attempt was ill organised and inconclusive," he continued, studying them still. "This was partially due to our agents infiltrating the illegal organisation known as the United Irishmen, and partially to the firm hand taken by the military. A series of arrests were made which raised the tension and precipitated a spontaneous revolt that was relatively easy to put down; although not without bloodshed, of course." The men were meeting his gaze with nothing other than total attention, and Banks continued, quietly relieved.

"We think that the rebels had been planning something a little more elaborate, very likely involving French forces. Similar expeditions have been staged in the past; I know that most of you will be aware of the attempt in 'ninety-six, when enemy ships came as far as anchoring in Irish waters. That attempt failed, and I am proud to say that our last ship had no small hand in the matter, which incidentally may well have influenced my Lords of the Admiralty when selecting *Scylla* for this task." He paused; there was no harm in reminding them of previous success. "So May's rebellion was defused, although feelings still run high, and it is considered that another attempt, possibly with assistance from the French, is likely." To Banks, the Irish's apparent fascination with rebellion truly was surprising. Why any nation should wish to decline the presence of Britain, with its wealth, power and intelligence, was something of a mystery.

"There are at least two squadrons of enemy shipping thought to be in the general vicinity; one of them, commanded by Commodore Savary, left France when news of the May uprising was received. They are known to be carrying upwards of a thousand troops, which, though not an especially large force, will probably attract support from the civil population.

We have yet to discover where they are bound; they may even be half way to the 'Indies by now, but if Ireland is their destination a landing must be avoided at all costs."

He studied the men again and then relaxed. "So, gentlemen; are there any questions or comments?"

Only Chilton, who was unused to his new captain's strange habit of inviting his inferiors to hold an opinion, looked in any way disconcerted. Caulfield was the first to speak.

"You mentioned support, sir. As I recall the Irish station is not blessed with many ships; when can we expect assistance?"

"True, they have only one liner plus a handful of frigates and some smaller stuff in the south," Banks agreed, "hardly sufficient to protect a country as large as Ireland. But then the Admiralty is fully aware of the situation, and hopefully the Channel Fleet will stop any sizeable force venturing too far. Privately I would expect at least one flying squadron to be despatched to reinforce us without delay, and there may be others joining on a more permanent basis."

Fraiser was the next to speak, and did so with his customary quiet assurance. "The crew, sir. There are many Irish amongst them."

"Indeed, Mr Fraiser," Banks said, picking up the thread. "And all must be watchful. In some ways we are in a far better position than the Army; an enemy at sea is clear and indisputable; whereas on land there is no telling whom you can trust. But that does not mean we are immune to sympathisers amongst our own. If you have doubts or suspicions you will report them to me without delay. And clearly any act that could be looked upon as sabotage will be dealt with in the firmest manner."

He waited, but no one was keen to add further. "Very well, gentlemen; our orders are to sail at the earliest opportunity: can you give me the current situation with stores, Mr

Caulfield?"

The first lieutenant cleared his throat. "Yes, sir, we are fully victualled in all bar fresh water, although the remaining tonnage required can be taken on in a morning. We are also awaiting candles and tallow from the renderers, but would have sufficient should you wish us to proceed. Fabric and frame are in good repair, with only regular maintenance, and some small attention to the forecastle caulking required. And standing rigging is now complete, with running to be likewise by the end of the morrow. The outstanding problem is men." He allowed himself a brief sigh. "Despite Mr Chilton's gallant efforts we still remain forty able down, and could probably find a place for that many landsmen if given the chance."

Banks leant forward in his chair. "I think I can put your mind at rest. We have been awarded a draft from a seventy-four, currently being paid off in Torbay. There should be fifty prime hands with us by the morning after next." The officers' look of surprise and relief was like a tonic. Banks savoured the moment, even though it was probably the last favour his father would grant him.

"They will indeed be welcome," Caulfield murmured. Banks glanced up; all the lieutenants were actually smiling like a bunch of lads, while Fraiser assumed an expression of smug approval.

"We have also had news of a replacement for Mr Marshall," Banks continued, oblivious to any affect that mentioning the man was having on at least two of his officers. "We are to receive a captain of marines, a Mr Westwood, in addition to a replacement lieutenant. Also a further fifteen private soldiers and a corporal."

"That will be quite a force, sir," Caulfield remarked.

"Indeed," Banks eyes fell for a moment. "It is possible that *Scylla* will be involved in operations ashore, and provisions are being made to see that we are properly equipped." There was a moment's silence; all were well aware that any land based action was likely to be difficult and deadly; their force of marines, though large compared with the usual frigate's compliment, was minuscule in military terms. And, if they were deployed, the very fact would be a sign of failure: an indication that the enemy had been allowed a firm stronghold and that every available resource was needed.

"It is indeed strange that Mr Marshall chose to leave so suddenly," Banks said, collecting his papers together and considering for a moment. "Problems of a family nature, I understand, but still..." He was clearly hoping for some response, some thread of information, but received nothing but blank stares in return. Even Fraiser, usually one with particular concern for his fellow man, showed a remarkable lack of reaction. But then Banks was conscious that Marshall had made very little impression on him, and he supposed the others felt the same. Yes, rather a nonentity, he decided; and, that being the case, it was probably better that he had gone, even if taking on a replacement this close to sailing was inconvenient.

"Very well gentlemen," he said, bringing himself back to the subject in hand. "I am sure we all have plenty to keep us busy; if no one has any objections we will aim for Wednesday's morning tide: I will signal to that effect."

* * *

Egmont had been a decent ship, of a proper size, and with a lower gun deck stuffed full of thirty-two pounders, an armament worth talking about. This *Scylla* was nothing more than a row boat in comparison, and her eighteen pounders, what they were pleased to call the great guns, were almost an insult to a man accustomed to handling true weaponry. As a quarter gunner Surridge was used to having overall charge of four of those monsters. And he had trained men to use them, trained them in such a way that they did not lose their heads or cry for mother when the shot started flying, or their mates got snuffed about them. He could probably do so again, even on this piss poor little gig, if that was what King George intended: Surridge, or Suggs, as he was known to the men, wasn't inclined to go against authority as high as that. But he didn't have to like it, and even now, from what he regarded as a position worthy of respect, Surridge could still cause trouble on the lower levels should he choose to do so.

He'd drawn one of the coveted hammock spaces at the end of a row. It was almost next to the galley, which was convenient, as Surridge hated chewing tobacco but was fond of a night time pipe, and handy for the heads. But in *Egmont* he had wangled a cabin – not a true one admittedly, it was more a partitioned off pen; the carpenter had made it to house a gentleman's fag when they were shipping a bunch of gentry coves back to England. Surridge had claimed it as soon as the party left, and it was an indication of his character and position in the social hierarchy of the ship that he had done so over the heads of several petty officers superior to him. He'd liked that cabin, both for its space, and the recognition it gave of his true worth. To go back to sleeping amongst other men, and in a ship that hardly warranted use of the title, was not Surridge's idea of advancement. Besides, he had been looking forward to a decent cruise ashore. With three years' wages in his pocket he should have been able to spend a happy week or so in the Torbay brothels and tap houses, and to find his plans so drastically altered had thoroughly spoiled Surridge's day.

He walked down the berth deck where others from *Egmont* were also finding their way about and commenting on the situation. There was Cox, a former miner who had been a gun captain; and Joshua the negro, one of the servers, and strong enough to haul a thirty-two back almost single-handed. It would be an education to see how they took to the pop guns they would be using. A gawky midshipman was calling out names from a sheet of paper; presumably they were setting out the messes. Surridge caught the eye of Cox, who acknowledged him good-naturedly.

"Whatcha think, Suggs?" he asked. "Bit more space than the old girl, eh?"

Surridge sneered and looked about. Admittedly the lack of guns on the berth deck gave generous room for the two hundred or so men who would be sleeping there. But no artillery also meant no proper divisions; messes would be spilling out into one another; there would be a lack of privacy and no shortage of draughts.

"I been in frigates afore," Surridge grunted. "She'll be cold, damp, and constantly on the move."

Cox shrugged. "Maybe so, but given the choice between 'er and the *Egmont*, I'd choose 'er," he said. "No smell of wet rot, an' you got more than an even chance of seeing port."

Surridge took a furtive glance about, then spat generously on the deck. Cox looked his surprise, which bolstered the quarter-gunner's mood still further. "B'now I should have been deep in the arms of Nellie Lake," he confided. "Biggest apple shop in the West Country, she has."

Cox opened his mouth to comment, when his face became fixed on something beyond his friend's shoulder.

"You there," it was a lad's voice, but not without authority. "Wipe that up!"

Surridge turned to see a midshipman glaring at him, and pointing to the spittle on the deck. "What's that?" Surridge demanded.

"I said, wipe that up," the lad repeated. "An' you call me Mister Rose."

"Rose?" Surridge's eyebrows twitched and a faint look of

scorn appeared across his grubby face. The midshipman's uniform was slightly too small for him, emphasising his age, and making the surname seem even more appropriate.

"Mister Rose," the boy insisted, still pointing at the spittle.

Surridge smirked, and extended a bare foot. He wiped the spot with his sole, smearing it into the deck, then regarded the boy once more as if he was assessing him for a minor task.

Rose's face was mildly flushed. "What is your name?"

"Surridge." The man paused. "*Mister* Rose."

"Very well, Surridge. "The next time I catch you behaving like that it will be a report to the lieutenant."

"I'll remember," Surridge's expression was not quite a smirk, and certainly nothing that could be officially regarded as insubordination, but he noticed the glow on the boy's face had increased, and knew that the lad would remember as well.

* * *

Throughout the next day *Scylla*'s men worked. The last of the water was taken in, along with a further, unexpected, and very welcome consignment of fresh vegetables. Then the tallow finally arrived, together with several barrels of oil, what seemed like a lifetime's supply of candles, and even some soap, all of which was instantly claimed by Mr Dudley, the purser.

Amongst the hands there was a good deal of confusion at first. The men were of vastly differing backgrounds and intellects. Some, mainly those new to the Navy, found pretty much everything confusing, and could not be expected to remember much beyond their own names, while the experienced hands blatantly ignored their correct messes and gravitated to previous mates, much to the despair of their divisional officers. But by the evening a few were becoming familiar faces; small routines, such as the division of spirits at noon and four, had become established; and at least some semblance of sense and cooperation was starting to appear.

The senior officers were reasonably pleased, in fact, and as they all met in the small ship's gunroom and ate their first meal together there was quite a convivial atmosphere.

Robert Manning had joined them that afternoon, and was present as a guest of King. By luck he had come down part of the way with Mr Clarkson, and so had had plenty of time to become acquainted. They had yet to work together, of course, but it was clear that the fair haired, slightly hesitant surgeon knew his stuff, and the two had the makings of a good professional relationship.

Captain Westwood had also boarded that day. A pleasant, well educated man of middle years and delicate features, he was far more refined than the bumptious Marshall they had grown uncomfortably used to, and soon became accepted by all. Westwood's subaltern was Lieutenant Adshead, a considerably younger and almost frail little man, serving his first term at sea. Adshead was not quite so easy; he came across as somewhat nervous, and was inclined to stammer. He also had very fair skin that had already burnt horribly in the English summer and would not serve him well should *Scylla* ever be sent for tropical service.

The surgeon's arrival meant that his wife finally released herself from what had become almost continual occupation of her cabin. Both her self-imposed exclusion and Marshall's departure was understood by those who knew or guessed the reason, and politely ignored by the rest. In the case of Mr Dudley, the purser, whose life was neatly divided between keeping track of his constantly changing stores and the well being of Sophie, the gunroom tabby, it was possible that neither had even been noticed at all.

But now they were all together; even the cat was surreptitiously present on Dudley's lap, and they seemed to have the makings of a full and happy gunroom.

"Wine with you, sir!" Westwood raised a half filled glass to Chilton, who had been one of the quieter contributors throughout the meal. "You have served in *Scylla* before, and shall have a wealth of stories to tell, no doubt?"

Chilton sipped at his wine a little uncertainly. "You are speaking of her sailing manners, sir?"

Westwood laughed. "Lord, no; I have singularly little knowledge of such things, nor the need of it." He beamed good-naturedly to the company in general. "I was meaning more her history; she has shone in battle, perhaps?"

"I regret not," Chilton replied. "The occasion never presented itself. Though of course I am sure that she would have, had it done so," he added clumsily.

"You were with the Channel Fleet, I collect?" Caulfield asked.

"Indeed, and were once ordered to join an escort for an India convoy back to Portsmouth; apart from that we spent much of our time polishing the French coast – without actually touching it, I am thankful to say."

"Blockade duty can be deadly dull," Caulfield conceded, amidst the polite laughter. "Let us hope our current role will show a bit more life."

"It would be good to see a little action," Chilton mused; then, noticing a faint look of concern in Fraiser's eyes, he hurriedly added: "Not that I am wishing for bloodshed, of course."

"On the contrary, it should be the desire of every serving officer," the young Adshead replied, as if reading from a book. "We are at sea to fight; to do otherwise would be a waste of our talents."

"Well, I for one have no need for combat," Clarkson said. "And I think you would feel the same were you to attend the results."

There was further laughter, and King noticed how Clarkson's wife, who had been attentive to her husband's every wish since his return, squeezed at his arm after he had spoken. The two exchanged what might have been a secret look, and King wondered briefly at her nerve.

"No, a bloody war and a sickly season," Westwood joked, and glanced at his deputy. "Is not that what you are after, Gerald?"

"It is the better way for promotion," Adshead confessed, then blushed dramatically at the roar of laughter that followed his comment.

"In that case, you will pardon me if I seek to retain my present rank," Fraiser replied.

"And I," Westwood agreed. "Long may your chances of advancement be thwarted," and the laughter returned yet again. Then he focused on the sailing master. "You are new to the ship, sir?"

The Scotsman nodded. "Aye, I last served with our present captain, alongside Mr Caulfield, Mr King and Mr Manning."

Westwood looked with interest. "So, we have a team ready built? Capital! What ship?"

"*Pandora*," Caulfield replied. "A light frigate."

"I regret I have not come across her; did she see action?"

"Oh, yes," Fraiser confirmed. "Enough to satisfy even Mr Adshead's desires."

The young man, who had suddenly developed a keen interest in his dessert fork, blushed again but did not look up.

"We fought the Spanish at St Vincent, and the Dutch at Camperdown," King admitted, and Westwood beamed with approval.

"And now you are to fight the Irish?"

"Hardly that," Caulfield, said quickly. "Were the Irish to be

71

supported by the French, it may well come to action, but that would be another matter entirely."

"Do you think so?" Westwood asked. "My brother is currently stationed in Dublin. There are few Frenchmen to be had, but the Irish seem happy enough battling it out with each other. Since May's rebellion was put down, they've been mainly warring between themselves: Catholic against Dissenter, worker against farmer, that is the rule. And the United Irishmen are united in name alone; by all accounts they are an ill-disciplined bunch and have little interest beyond pillage and plunder."

"The troubles continue?" Caulfield asked.

"They do for now, but slowly things are easing. I gather the pitch-cap has much to do with it."

"Pitch-cap?"

Westwood shrugged. "It is a cruel device, to be certain. A man's head is coated with a mixture of pitch and gunpowder. When ignited there are few that will not speak, and many who cannot stop."

"Barbaric," Fraiser said softly.

"Indeed," Westwood met his eyes. "But when brother is fighting brother such measures are needed if they are to put a stop to the process."

"But you said things were easing," Caulfield persisted.

"So I believe," Westwood agreed. "My brother was involved in a recent flogging campaign; it left most praying for the King and cursing any who say otherwise. There are croppy hunters by the score, and the magistrates are half hanging any who show signs of dissent. I should say a few more months of such action will see all put to right for the next hundred years or so. That is, if the Frogs don't interfere; then we may well find ourselves fighting them as well as the Irish, and I for one do not relish such a prospect."

"I don't understand," King interrupted. "The rebels have no navy; surely an enemy at sea can only be French?"

"In theory, yes." Westwood regarded him. "But this talk of an invasion fleet, do you believe that to be entirely manned by Frenchmen?"

"In the main," King said a little uncertainly.

Westwood shook his head. "I should be surprised," he replied. "The French cannot afford to waste any more able-bodied men; they have lost a good few on the invasion force that Admiral Nelson dealt with. An army sent to assist the Irish in their revolution would be largely made up of foreigners. And of those, the Irish dissidents, of which there must be a fair few, would make up the majority."

There was silence for a moment as the room digested his statement. Westwood, realising he might have broken the mood somewhat, shuffled in his seat. "But let us not dwell on such matters now; this has been a pleasant evening. What say we round it off with song?"

The suggestion was quickly adopted, and soon voices were raised that filled the small room and could be heard throughout most of the ship. King joined in readily enough, although there was something in Westwood's remarks that had bothered him. It was quite true; many patriots had sailed with previous invasion attempts: why, even Crowley had been present in the French frigate that *Pandora* had fought and captured on her way down to Gibraltar. But then Crowley had not been a true nationalist. The man was more of a stateless drifter, one without a home or a cause to support. King knew that his friend had found both in the Royal Navy and was glad; even though, as he had now decided, Crowley must have chosen to join another ship rather that wait and serve with him. But it didn't stop King from wishing Crowley was with them in *Scylla*, nor did it quell the faint and undefinable feeling of unease that stayed with him for the rest of that evening, and even late into the night.

* * *

"So, dearest?" she dabbed at her face. "You have yet to tell me, how did you find London?"

The cabin was dark and cramped, although they had managed to install a small table at which Betsy always sat. It was next to the canvas wash stand and had a strip of mirror above. A lantern hung overhead on which William Clarkson would occasionally bang his head; but, as it gave his wife light to attend to her appearance, he was content for it to remain.

"London was as London always is," he replied. "I gave in the paper at Surgeon's Hall, and met up with Daniel Brown – you will remember him from Haslar?"

"Oh yes, Daniel...." Indeed she did remember.

"We spent a pleasant couple of days together, and then I travelled on to see mama."

"Well, I trust?" Betsy was applying powder to her nose even though they were about to retire. She was one who flushed easily, and the memory of Daniel had caused just such a sensation. It was fortunate that she was in the exact position to remedy the problem.

"Well enough, though her knee still pains her."

"And your father?"

"He is splendid, thank you."

There was little more that needed to be said. Betsy had complied with the common rules of politeness, which had been duly acknowledged by William. His parents had never approved of her, and consequently she held little feeling for them. Of course nothing was ever spoken out loud, but each party knew the situation well enough.

"Well, I am glad that you are back," she said, turning and smiling up at him.

"And I equally so," he rested his hand on her shoulder. The hair he loved so much was only half tied; some strands were loose and flowed down her back in a golden torrent. Daringly he ran his fingers through them, before finally smoothing and making all right once more. "You were not terribly bored?"

"Oh no," she said lightly. Turning back she freed herself from his touch. Her hair was now in a perfect mess and she began to tease it back into place with the handle of her brush. "No, I found enough to occupy myself, thank you."

"The new men seem fine." He spoke more softly, as sound was very likely to travel between the frail gunroom cabins.

"They do," she agreed.

"I should say Westwood is quite well educated," he continued. "And a captain of marines; that is a rare thing for *Scylla*. The others appear a good bunch, and I certainly approve of Robert Manning: potentially a brilliant surgeon, I think. All in all I'd say it were an improvement on the last set."

She tensed, hoping his mind would not follow on to the previous officers. "Yes, I think this will be a happy ship," she said.

"Adshead may be a bit light." The surgeon had taken off his jacket and was unbuttoning his shirt. "Not like that Marshall, though I confess I never really took to the fellow."

"He meant little to me," Betsy said evenly as she started to apply yet more powder.

Clarkson accepted her statement readily enough. "I expect you had little contact with him," he said.

They had a bed, one of only a very few in the ship. The carpenter had made it during their first commission; it was almost four feet in width, but it folded up neatly if required, although it was rare for the gunroom to be totally cleared during action. Clarkson had clambered in and was settling himself while his wife finished her toilette. He waited as she continued to play with her long blonde hair: tying it up, only to release it once again to try a different style. It was a habit she had taken to relatively recently, always the same routine and always last thing at night. Of course she had no idea how much the procedure frustrated her husband, and did not notice the times when he had actually fallen asleep waiting for her to join him. On that night, though, he was determined to stay awake: they had been apart for almost two weeks, and with the ship working up and all the confusion of a new crew, he felt the need of comfort and physical intimacy.

"Will you be long, my darling?" he asked eventually.

She looked up, and at him through her mirror. "Long? Why I shouldn't think so." Once more the hair was released, floating down onto her bare shoulders in a way that almost caused him physical pain. "But do not wait for me, dearest. I shall be certain not to disturb you when I do retire."

* * *

They caught Wednesday morning's tide. After nine weeks in harbour, a significant change to her crew, and being fully victualled for a good ninety days *Scylla* was more than ready to return to her natural element. The westerly wind was firm and all the senior officers, together with most of her crew, were on deck to witness the event. The last remaining anchor was now clear and being fished on the forecastle while topmen, already aloft, were carrying out their work competently enough despite the novelty of a fresh ship and colleagues.

"Lay out and loose!" Johnston, new to his position as boatswain's mate, had a voice that carried and was revelling in the chance to use it. He glanced across to King, who was officially officer of the watch, and received a simple nod in reply. "Stand by – let fall!"

"Man topsail sheets and halliards!" Other voices were raised now, and Banks noticed that the men responded well enough.

"Tend the braces!"

"Sheet home and hoist away topsails!" the calls continued, further fresh canvas appeared, and *Scylla* was slowly transformed from an inert lump into a thing of grace and beauty. Gathering speed, she slipped effortlessly between Pendennis Point and St Anthony Head, easily skirting the low waters around Black Rock.

"Take her sou' sou' east," Fraiser's usually gentle voice rang loud against the growing breeze. The ship heeled slightly as the sails filled, then settled on to a steady course that felt remarkably stable to those used to the stagger and buck of a jackass frigate. The air was now filled with the deep scent of open water, and Banks was smiling at all about him as the wind increased and the deck took on an even greater incline.

"It has been too long, Mr Caulfield," he said, his voice cracking as he raised it to counter the wind. Caulfield grinned and was about to reply when a rogue gust caused him to grab at his hat. He pressed it more firmly on his head; then, admitting defeat, swept it off and trapped the thing under his arm. Banks noticed the action and both men laughed out loud. Barrow was ready with the log; *Scylla* might be smaller than his last ship but it was already clear she would be no slouch. King marked off the traverse board and replaced it in the binnacle. The spray was rising, giving a sting to the air that was at once both painful and stimulating, and the ship's motion began to relax into something more regular and almost rhythmic. But all on the quarterdeck were oblivious to such insignificances; the ship oozed strength and power, she was well armed, fully manned, and would be perfect for the job in hand. There was still a good deal of summer left, and clearly a battle to be fought: none of them could ask for more.

CHAPTER FIVE

Theobald Wolfe Tone was not an especially impressive individual. The son of a protestant coach builder, or so Crowley had heard, his pale skin and fragile frame spoke little of manual work, and more of time spent in the courtrooms of Dublin where he had practised at the bar. Their paths had almost crossed several times in the past. Once, just over two years ago, Tone, under the auspices of Adjutant-General Smith, had sailed with a fleet that mounted an invasion of Ireland. Crowley only saw him twice in passing before their departure. It later evolved that Tone's ship *Indomptable* had actually anchored in Bantry Bay and came very close to landing troops, whereas Crowley's frigate was amongst the many separated from the main fleet in one of the worst storms of the century. Crowley finished up in the hands of the British aboard *Pandora* while Tone returned to France where he continued with his quest for revolution.

They were to come close to meeting once more the following year, this time at the Texel. By then Crowley had become a regular and trusted member of *Pandora's* crew, and Tone waited with the invasion fleet that *Pandora*, alongside Admiral Duncan and two worn out liners, stubbornly blockaded. The Scottish Admiral's bluff and a decisive battle eventually saw the end to Tone's plans, and the much vaunted army that had been ready to free Britain from the yoke of Monarchy was absorbed into other forces.

And now here he was again, this time in a small and rather shabby village hall, preparing to speak to men who had volunteered to join yet another attempt on behalf of Ireland. Men who were in the main Irish, and all doubtless already inflamed with the desires and ambitions that Tone was about to further arouse. Crowley shuffled uncomfortably on his wooden bench: there was, he knew, little for him in such an endeavour. The past two years had changed him greatly; he now held scant feelings for his home country, and hardly cared if it were under English or French domination. But fate had taken him thus far, and he was reconciled at the least to hearing what the man had to say. If, as he suspected, it was just a bundle of empty rhetoric, he would leave it at that. MacArthur and the rest could carry on alone; he would bide his time in France, where at least there should be a better chance of avoiding conscription. Then, come winter, he might make his way back to England and discover if *Vernon* was ready for him to return to the sea.

The buzz of conversation began to subside, and men started to grow attentive as Tone stepped up to the small platform and stood before them. There was no announcement, no introduction; every man present knew who he was and what they were there for, and all were content to let the process begin. For a moment Tone paused and surveyed the room as if it were an obstacle to be overcome, then his shoulders dropped, he relaxed, and began.

"Gentlemen, I thank you for coming here tonight, when I am certain there are greater pleasures awaiting you close by." There was a murmur of laughter from the front of the audience; the hall was situated between a brothel and a tavern, and Tone smiled briefly. "I certainly do not intend to waste your time, however. I have important things to speak of, some of which may come as a surprise. Others you may know already, though I beg that you allow me to say them, as there might be some who are maybe not quite so clever." Again the laughter, although now it held more of an expectant quality. Crowley watched, appreciatively; the man had primed his audience well and would be worth listening to.

"And to the last group, the ones who know me not at all, and to whom the idea of taking back a country from English rule would rate as nothing more than a waste of time and maybe lives; to them let me say this: I am in total agreement with you."

The atmosphere was suddenly tense. Some thought they had misheard, or that the great Wolfe Tone had undergone a transformation not seen since Saul started off on the road to Damascus. And others, the majority, simply leant forward to hear every last word of what this strange little man might say.

"I have no illusions about the country of my birth," he said, looking to the left and right as if for confirmation. "In truth, the land is not especially fertile and, although it may be pretty in parts, I have seen landscapes in the Americas and elsewhere that would surely put it to shame. But then, one loves one's country no less for having a lack of romantic feelings about her. And when we speak of a country, do we mean the ground, the scenery or the weather? Or are we talking of the people it contains: the Brotherhood of Affection that I have been pleased to be a member of these five years or more? Men who, though dissident in their own beliefs, are wise enough to throw open the doors of Parliament to include all faiths and every religion. Men who cannot stand by and see the humble worker trodden down by rich English landowners and magistrates. Men who care enough about their brothers to take up arms, if need be, to see that such atrocities cease."

Crowley looked about him. In the main the audience were sitting upright, their fists clenched, some even with faint murmurs rising in their throats as Tone continued. In the space of two minutes he had mined and smelted the ore, and was now patiently forging an alloy from the various individuals present. Soon, no doubt, he would be casting out revolutionaries, all as inspired and sincere as any leader could wish for. More than that, these very same men would then go out and preach the word to others. It was a masterly performance: Crowley even found himself sitting more erect as he continued to watch and, despite himself, he was impressed.

* * *

They were now well clear of the Lizard peninsular; but the wind was still set in the west, and to reach Ireland *Scylla* was having to beat stoically against it. Chilton was almost at the end of his watch and had spent much of the time talking to Parfrey, a volunteer who had yet to reach even the lowly rank of midshipman, and was still becoming accustomed to being at sea. King came on deck early and acknowledged the pair as they stood next to the binnacle. He wandered across and collected the traverse board, inspecting it by the dim glow of the overhead lantern. They had tacked two hours ago, and were due to do so again. It was midnight, but the moon was bright, and there was enough light to see that *Scylla* was quite alone. He sniffed at the breeze; the wind showed no sign of changing. Until it did, they would make very little progress, and the effort would start to take its toll on the men and equipment.

"We have a fresh crew and will be tacking using all hands," Chilton told the lad with the air of one who had offered many explanations over the last few hours. "So we usually try to wait until the change of watch. That way we may retain men from the old watch for the manoeuvre, rather than allow them below, only to be summoned back later."

The lad nodded wisely enough, but then he would probably have done so if the lieutenant had stated they were about to raise a crocodile to the main top. King caught Chilton's eye; both men were close enough to Parfrey's position to remember the total confusion of being at sea for the first time. The marine private tending the hour glass was peering at it intently, and some of the watch below were already starting to come up on deck.

"Do you wish to tack her?" King asked. Chilton hesitated and King continued. "It is a clear night and nothing hereabouts, I think the captain will trust us. Will you take the honour?"

"Very well," Chilton reached for the speaking trumpet just as the bell sounded for the end of the watch.

"What is your name?" King asked, turning to the volunteer.

"Parfrey, sir."

"You have witnessed the ship tack before, I presume?"

"Oh yes, sir, several times. Though I was below at four bells, so never at night."

King smiled. "It is little different, and you will not see as much; some matters must be taken on trust."

The lad absorbed this very seriously.

"Are you aware quite why we are tacking, Parfrey?" King persisted, and the volunteer silently shook his head.

"Wind's coming from the west, which is where we are bound, making it impossible to travel straight in that direction. Consequently the ship is close hauled, that is sailing as near to the wind as she will lie."

"I see, sir," the lad said, and King looked at him doubtfully for a moment.

"So, while we are making a small amount of progress into the wind, it is at the cost of moving significantly to one side; currently it is the north, as we are on the larboard tack. The larboard tack is..."

"When the wind comes across our larboard side, sir?" Parfrey asked.

"Indeed. Were we to hold this course for too long we should eventually be in danger of running into the southern coast of England. And so we have to tack, to change direction; in this case we want to reverse the present angle we are holding to the wind, so that we make as much distance southerly as we have to the north. On both tacks we are gaining a small amount of progress to the west so, in effect, the ship is sailing into the wind.

Parfrey's face cleared as if he had been struck by a mild revelation. Chilton called for all hands to make ready, while King continued more softly.

"Tacking is preferable to wearing, as we wish to keep what ground we have made, but will mean turning our bow directly into the wind. It is a little more complicated, however; we must maintain enough way, or forward movement, to continue until we are settled on the opposite course."

"Ready about, stations for stays!" The men, who were in the main experienced enough, responded immediately and began taking up their positions without undue confusion or comment.

"Ease down the helm."

The wheel began to turn while the *Scylla*'s jib sheets were eased off and the spanker boom gently brought amidships by the afterguard.

"Helm's a-lee!" The fore and head sheets were then released, allowing her bow to swing into the wind.

"Rise and tack sheets!"

"Haul taut, mainsail haul!"

Parfrey and King watched as the evolution continued until the ship was riding comfortably on the starboard tack, with all sails filled and her stem once more nosing into the swell. "It is complicated," the lad said finally.

"It would seem so," King replied. "But I chance you are a quick learner. Watch all you can and never fear to ask. I should say you will be tacking *Scylla* yourself before we see England again."

"That soon?" Parfrey asked, his face the picture of wonder. King shuffled uncomfortably.

"It may be a long commission," he said.

* * *

Within half an hour it was clear that the speech was coming to a close. By now all the audience were as if on fire; any would have cheerfully taken on the might of an English army single-handedly, and the murmurs of support were very nearly growls. Tone held up his hand for silence, which was given instantly. Then he spoke again, this time in a far softer timbre so that most had to strain to hear.

"You know of the uprising in May." A brief groan went about the room, ending the second Tone's mouth opened to speak again. "Many chances were lost, and many men died needlessly. Since that time the repercussions by the British have been brutal and barbarous. Five hundred alone were massacred in Kildare when they were ready for surrender, and there has been torture and suffering beyond the telling." He paused to allow the dreadful truth to be absorbed, then continued.

"And now they are saying it is over. Telling us they have quashed the revolt. More than that, boasting of having quenched the spirit that caused the rebellion in the first place. They say that Ireland has no life left in it, and can continue as a British colony; a provider to the mother country, and a breeding house for their slaves and servants." He paused again, as if absorbing the anger and energy from his audience.

"But I tell you this is not true. I tell you that even now there is a force alive in Ireland, a force provided by the French that has joined with our brothers to produce a mighty army." His voice rose as some began to cheer. "And I tell you that, even as we speak, they are heading for the capital of our fair country."

Now men were positively screaming, but Tone was shouting back, loud above the uproar, delivering his point home as a carpenter might hammer in heavy nails.

"I tell you they have already routed the British in one

mighty battle: no fewer than six thousand were sent packing by less than two thousand French and Irish brothers."

There was hysteria now, and the only man in the room apparently unaffected was Tone himself. Even Crowley was standing, standing and shouting with the others.

"And now the victors have sent for us. They know that with our help they can take the entire land. Take it, and wipe every memory of the English from its shores. Take it and free our country from the yoke of oppression. Take it, and deliver a homeland back to those brave souls who will rise to fight for her. Take it, and be free. Now who will join us?"

* * *

The wind backed with the morning, and Fraiser was finally able to set a course that would allow a reasonable distance to be covered without undue strain on *Scylla's* men or fabric. The captain came on to the quarterdeck shortly after first light and remained while the ship awoke about him. The decks, already passably white, had been treated to further attention from holystones, and were now steaming in the first of the morning's sunshine. Hammocks had been turned out and the scent of breakfast was in the air as the hands ate. Banks was about to follow their example when Captain Westwood, accompanied by Lieutenant Adshead and a marine private, came up on deck. Westwood approached Banks as he stood with Chilton, who was once more officer of the watch. Banks briefly touched his hat in reply to the marine officer's salute, and was about to turn away when he sensed there was something more.

"Go ahead, Mr Westwood," Banks said genially. "I hold few rules about speaking on the quarterdeck."

"Thank you, sir. I was wondering if you would permit a spot of target practice?"

The captain looked his surprise. "For the men, Mr Westwood?" he asked.

"No sir, I was thinking of myself and Mr Adshead."

"Indeed?" It was customary for marine privates and NCOs to engage in firearm drill, usually when the great guns were being exercised, but almost unknown for officers.

"Pistols?" Banks asked. Then, because the morning was pleasant and he was in the mood added, "do you intend to fight a duel?"

"Hardly that, Sir Richard," Westwood laughed. "But I have recently taken delivery of a new piece from an Italian gun maker, and I would wish to put it to test."

"Then I will gladly permit, Mr Westwood, and trust you will tolerate an audience?"

The servant was duly despatched, returning shortly afterwards with a wooden target holder and a cloth covered case that he placed on the deck.

"A rifle, sir?" Banks asked, when he saw the size. A gentleman might carry a long arm for hunting, but for one of commissioned rank to hold anything other than a pistol was almost unheard of.

Westwood looked up from opening the case. "More than just a rifle, sir," he said. "I have yet to prove this piece but, if the reports be true, it is truly remarkable."

Banks and Chilton looked with interest as the lid was opened. Inside the lining was quite rudimentary; apart from the firearm there was none of the usual compartments for flints, wadding, and powder, just two heavy metal flasks that looked quite plain and utilitarian. Banks supposed them to be for ammunition, although they appeared unusually heavy and would be awkward in use. At first sight the rifle itself looked conventional enough: roughly four feet in length, with a rounded and bulbous metal butt that would definitely not be comfortable to hold. Westwood picked up the piece and examined it while the other officers, and two nearby seamen, watched on. There was little or no decoration, rare for a gentleman's firearm, but apart from that Banks could detect little to excite comment.

"What say we load, her, eh, Coleman?" Westwood asked. The marine private reached into the case and withdrew one of the metal flasks. "Took three men half the night to charge two of these," The marine officer said, as he rested the fore end on the case, unscrewed the metal butt from the rifle and removed it. The private took the part from him and offered one of the flasks in its place. There was a faint hiss as the thing was fixed in position.

"An interchangeable butt?" Banks asked, mildly confused. The replacement seemed very much like the one Westwood had removed; and, once fitted, the rifle was apparently no different.

"It comes with three," The marine captain explained. "Each will allow twenty to thirty shots, but it is better not to leave the piece fully charged."

Banks said nothing, even though Westwood's explanation made little sense. Carrying ammunition in a rifle stock was not unheard of, but he did wonder that so many balls of a reasonable calibre could be held in one of the metal butts.

"Gaskets are greased, sir," the private muttered.

"Very well, Coleman; target if you please." Westwood held the rifle vertically and looked across at Banks with just a trace of doubt. "She came by a circuitous route and was only delivered recently, so is not tested. I have heard the very best of the maker, but you will not judge by first impressions I trust?"

"No indeed." Banks had just noticed that the hammer held no flint. It may well be one of those newfangled percussion weapons, although Westwood was not attempting to fit a cap, neither was he loading the piece with powder or shot. The marine private had attached the large wooden target holder to the taffrail, and a paper bullseye flapped gently in the breeze.

The target was less than twenty feet away; hardly a test for any weapon, but nothing was said as Westwood lowered the rifle, took aim and fired.

There was no flash, no smoke and the noise was far less than that of a standard musket, but the target was penetrated credibly near the bull. Westwood beamed.

"Hardly a recoil," he said. "And the shot is almost instantaneous; no delay for the pan to ignite, or even a cap to fire."

"Very impressive, Mr Westwood," Banks said politely.

"But does it have range?" Chilton, who was also an interested spectator, asked.

Westwood had raised the rifle once more. "She's credited with one hundred and fifty yards, sir," he said. "That is for accurate shooting. And a ball should penetrate an inch of oak, or the body of a man."

"Fair performance," Chilton said appreciatively. Westwood was lowering the piece once more and, without making any attempt to reload, fired again. Another shot could be seen on the target, slightly off this time, but still a reasonable hit.

"I say," Banks said, amazed despite himself. "It repeats."

"And will continue to do so," Westwood replied, with just the trace of a smirk. "There is a magazine of twenty balls here," he said, pointing to a metal tube running along the stock towards the hammer. "And upwards of thirty charges in the butt."

"And what is the charge, sir?" Chilton asked.

"Air," Westwood beamed. "It is a *Windbüchse*; deadly and accurate, yet powered by nothing more mortal than the wind! Will you take a shot, sir?"

Banks shook his head. He had a credible eye, but was not going to risk his dignity by shooting a strange firearm on his own quarterdeck.

"Mr Chilton?"

The young lieutenant was less reluctant, and eagerly collected the weapon.

"Hold it upright," Westwood instructed. "You will feel the ball roll into the chamber." He turned to Banks. "It is not only fast and convenient, but this method of loading allows for a prone marksman to retain his position."

Banks pulled at his chin speculatively. Westwood was correct, a man could stay relatively hidden while maintaining an astounding rate of fire. There would be little risk to him while reloading, and the lack of smoke and flash would mean he was almost invisible to the enemy. Chilton had the rifle now and was holding it cautiously.

"The butt is a touch large," Westwood explained. "Though the lack of recoil means that placement is not so essential."

The lieutenant took sight for several seconds then fired. The target was hit, a little lower than before, but still within the bull. Chilton grinned at Westwood. "What an astounding thing, sir. Sure, there is no flash and hardly a kick at all; it is a sharp-shooter's dream!"

"All of the force of the charge is directed at propelling the shot; there is none lost through the pan, and no chance of stray embers blinding the firer or robbing him of his night vision."

"I should like to see its penetration," Banks said. "And there may be issues with the loading; you said it took some while to compress the air."

"Experiments are in hand to produce a larger device that several might operate; similar to a ship's pump, so a detachment of men might be accommodated at one time. The intention is for them to load the charges overnight, or just before action. As to the penetration, for a ball to carry accurately it must hold a fair degree of force. The first ten shots are reckoned to be the better, beyond that the range and penetration grow less, although they remain able to stop a man. And, of course, a fresh butt may be inserted at any time. Sure a musket may be more powerful, but this is almost as effective and, considering the higher rate of fire, must be considered the more deadly weapon."

"Highly impressive, Mr Westwood." Banks conceded. "I assume the government knows of such an invention?"

"Indeed, sir. It is currently issued to regiments of the Austrian Army, and the Americans are also considering adoption. The British Army are holding trials and I would hope to see our marines carrying them in action before so very long."

"How typical that the Army should have them first." Adshead snorted.

"First or last, I simply hope we will not be missed," Westwood replied. "A weapon such as this could surely change the course of the war, and I consider it vital that we are not left behind."

* * *

A bunch of gentry coves playing with a toy gun. Surridge viewed the spectacle with disdain from the forecastle to where he had returned following his morning ablutions. Officers might fancy themselves as fighting men, but a true scrapper didn't need gewgaws or trinkets to get the job done. Surridge had never actually been in action with the enemy but was the veteran of countless private brawls, and he was confident that he could handle himself well enough with maybe the occasional help from a cosh or knuckleduster.

But he was off watch and wasn't going to waste time in fruitless musings. Besides, Surridge was not a happy man; he had a headache, which was rare for him, and his throat felt dry and rough. His tongue was also strangely swollen and there was an unpleasant taste in his mouth. The cause was obvious to anyone with even half a brain; he had a bad case of 'fat head', it was what came from sleeping in an airless berth full of common hands. Surridge stomped about the crowded forecastle with a face like thunder; he would not go below, as it was the cause of his current problems, but equally did not want to remain in the fresh morning air, even if doing so might allow the symptoms to disperse. There were still some while before his watch would be called, he had nothing constructive with which to fill the time, and, for Surridge, a bad mood and a loose end was a dangerous combination. Even as he stood there, while annoyingly contented men worked or relaxed about him, the quarter-gunner felt well known symptoms of repression and anger build up inside. Experience told him that his temper was ready to explode, and he longed for a cause, a justifiable reason to release the pent up emotion.

Rose was the unwitting provider. He happened to be in the vicinity with Johnston, the boatswain's mate. They were carrying out a check of the bowsprit gammoning that had been giving concern when Surridge came lumbering across the deck. The lad stepped back and into the seaman's path, giving a short cry of surprise as the ox-like bulk struck him. He was spun round, landing against Johnston, who caught him almost instinctively, and both glared at Surridge as he continued on his way.

"Steady there!" The midshipman called back, brushing himself down.

Surridge stopped for a moment but did not turn.

"Where are your eyes, man?" Johnston asked, reaching to collect Rose's hat. "Be more space aboard if we'd shipped an elephant."

"You got a problem?" the man was looking back now, and neither Rose nor Johnston liked the light in his eyes.

"You're a lumbering oaf, Surridge," Rose told him as he replaced his hat. "Watch your step in future."

"An' have the grace to apologise when you don't," Johnston

added.

Neither felt the need for more and were about to return to the gammoning when Surridge lurched forward. Despite his temper the seaman knew better than to threaten the lad in the dandy blue uniform, even if a clean hard fist in the face would arguably have been well worth the throwing. Instead it was the boatswain's mate who drew his attention and the focus of his wrath. The man, Johnston, had annoyed Surridge several times already and, being new to his post, could probably benefit from being taken down a peg or two. With a movement swift enough to belie his heavy build, Surridge grabbed the petty officer by the shirt front and dragged him close. For a moment he enjoyed the look of shock on the man's face, then closed his eyes as he cracked his own head down on Johnston's skull. The smack of bone on bone was delightful: a delicious release, and as Surridge, still holding Johnston's shirt, felt the body go limp, all the frustrations and disappointments of the last few days were magically resolved.

CHAPTER SIX

"I've examined Johnston," Clarkson told King, the divisional lieutenant responsible. "He has a fine lump to his frontal lobe, but nothing more."

"He was probably blessed with a skull as thick as his skin," King grunted. He had known Johnston in previous ships, and even under a different name. The man had been a persistent deserter for many years and King had hoped the recent elevation to petty officer rank would cure his errant ways. It was clear Johnston had done nothing to instigate matters, yet still King felt mildly disappointed to hear of the fight so early in *Scylla*'s commission. "Can he take up light duties?"

The surgeon considered this for a moment. "In a day or so, maybe," he said finally. "I'd like to keep an eye on him a while longer."

"Very well."

"Then there is Surridge," Clarkson continued.

"Surridge?" King was surprised. There would be some official action to be taken, of course, but he had not thought the man to be injured.

"Yes, potentially more serious, I'm afraid." Clarkson was referring to a small piece of paper. "My assistant, Mr Manning, examined him and his report is not good. You certainly won't like it and neither will the captain."

Actually King could not have cared less what was wrong with Surridge. In the space of a few days the quarter-gunner had already made his presence aboard *Scylla* painfully evident. There had been several bad reports, and an awful lot more gossip. King secretly wished whatever damage the man had caused to himself would be permanent and enable his dismissal as soon as they reached Ireland.

"He has the mumps."

"The mumps?" Now that definitely was more serious. While the condition might be not dangerous in itself, there had been instances when entire ships had been all but disabled while their crews succumbed to the illness.

"The man's parotid glands are heavily distended, and he complains of nausea and headaches."

"Striking Johnston on the head might have caused the latter," King said, hopefully.

"Very likely, although not the swollen tongue. Also he appears to be in a particularly sour mood, although I gather that not unusual in his particular instance."

"What have you done with him?"

Clarkson looked up from his paper. "Done with him, Mr King? Why he is in bilboes on the punishment deck awaiting judgement at your orders."

"But the mumps, surely the condition is infectious?"

"Oh yes, highly. In fact they are likely not to grant us entry to Dublin, have they the mind."

"Well, should he not be in isolation?"

"Ideally yes, though I would suggest that any quarantine we might arrange now would be somewhat belated. The condition is infectious long before the first symptoms appear, and Surridge has already been active in the ship for several days. Any man who has previously suffered will be immune, and those that have not, well, I would say that contagion is already extremely likely. Besides, whatever provisions we make, absolute isolation is impossible; this is a fifth rate after all."

King thought for a moment. The mumps might have come to the ship through a variety of different avenues; Chilton's draft of volunteers, the men from *Egmont*, or it could even have been present in the original crew. It was a nuisance, but no more, he supposed. Unless they were very unlucky no one was going to die, and most should avoid the more unpleasant complications. In fact the majority of the crew may even be safe; it was in the midshipmen's berth and amongst the volunteers third class that those without immunity were more likely to be found. But that would not stop the older hands worrying. Seamen were inherently gullible; it only needed one blab with a modicum of medical knowledge, some tattler to regale them with a few horror stories, and they would all be thinking of nothing else.

"The young can expect the condition to pass within ten to fourteen days," Clarkson continued. "The same with older men, although any complications are more likely to come about there." He hesitated as a thought occurred. "Tell me, Mr King, have you had the mumps?"

A cold feeling ran down his spine. "I believe so," he said. "Many years ago, when I was young."

"Then you have nothing to fear," Clarkson was positive.

"But, are there not unpleasant side effects?" King was now starting to worry: it might have been measles rather than mumps.

"They need not concern you, Mr King. And the less we talk of such matters the better. I am not adverse to the opinion that illness can be acquired through thought; indeed I have witnessed it myself on a number of occasions. No, this is simply something we will have to ride out, hoping that all is passed by the time we see action." Clarkson considered King again. The man's face appeared mildly flushed, although there was no sign of undue swelling about the ears and neck. "You are quite certain about your medical history?" he asked.

King went to speak but no sound came, instead he nodded emphatically, before adding a feeble, "Yes."

"Good." Clarkson considered him once more. "Then I had better inform the captain."

* * *

Banks had dined well but alone, and came on to the quarterdeck to benefit from the afternoon sun and perhaps a little company. The wind was blowing light but steady, cooling what had been another baking day, and, as he stood breathing in the soft air that had just the faintest tang of pitch he felt relatively at ease.

They had made slow progress. Even now Fraiser did not expect them to raise the south-east coast of Ireland until the following evening. Then there would be nothing more taxing than to follow the land north until they reached the mouth of Dublin harbour, a slow cruise in pleasant weather; there were worse ways of spending a hot summer. Such journeys might be long or short, and totally depended on the weather. Banks had been a naval officer long enough to enjoy the present without undue concern for a future that was beyond his control. And the present, for him, was actually quite rosy.

He was certainly pleased with his ship; *Scylla* had already fulfilled many of his expectations. She was a good strong sailer, with perfect manners and just the right amount of weather helm to make her both a joy to command and a first rate sea boat. She might lack the all out might of a seventy-four, but he had already decided that her speed and manoeuvrability, combined with a fire power that was by no means meagre, would outweigh any prestige that standing in the line of battle might bring. Besides, he had been fortunate in already partaking in two fleet actions. The majority of naval combat was single ship engagements, and he was confident that *Scylla* would hold her own with any of her size, and even some larger.

Sure, she had a few minor idiosyncrasies; there was a small but persistent leak on the forecastle deck that no amount of paying or re-caulking was able to stop, and the gammoning to the bowsprit was slightly loose and really should have been attended to in Falmouth. But even those faults, rather than lower his opinion, actually imparted more of a personality and made him like her the more.

The mumps was a problem, but not a great one; he had spoken to the surgeon at length and, apart from probably making communication at Dublin a little more complex, it should not hinder operations greatly. *Scylla* was well manned and could easily stand the temporary loss of a few hands. She was also fully provisioned: water, the first concern for any captain, was good for at least eighty days, and he had all else he needed for long after that. He took a turn about the deck and caught the eye of King, the officer of the watch.

"A pleasant afternoon, Mr King," Banks said, wandering across.

"Indeed, sir," King did not salute as the captain was bareheaded. "We've been especially lucky this summer."

"Any further outbreaks?"

"The mumps, sir? Not that I am aware. Surgeon has taken some of the lads off duty for the time being, and four men who are suffering more than most have been moved to the sick bay. Other than that, just a couple more hands have complained, though they have no symptoms, and pass the test adequately enough."

"The test?"

King lowered his voice. "Surgeon examines them; if they have enlarged glands they are put to light duties or allowed hammocks. Should they appear well he issues them a cup of lemon juice. Any man who has the mumps cannot tolerate the stuff," King grinned. "It certainly sorts out the malingerers. Both the two drank it down without complaint, so the surgeon thinks they are swinging the lead."

Banks chuckled softly. "Mr Clarkson seems to be remarkably perceptive," he said. "I think I may as well pay him a visit."

The ship was sailing sweetly enough and the watch on deck were yarning in the shade beneath the boats on the main deck when their captain descended the quarterdeck steps. He acknowledged them good naturedly as their conversation suddenly stopped and attitudes of earnest attention were quickly assumed.

The sick bay was on the deck below and further forward, so was not blessed with much natural light and appeared almost dark after the sunshine of the upper decks. A row of filled hammocks were slung by the entrance; clearly these were for the men whom Mr Clarkson considered worthy of observation. He stepped quietly past, then knocked on the deal wood door of the dispensary.

To his surprise it was Mrs Clarkson who answered. Banks stopped himself in the act of entering and stood, for a moment uncertain, on the threshold.

"Please come in, sir," she said, standing to one side. "If it is my husband or Mr Manning you are a wanting they have been called to the stewards' pantry."

Banks eased himself past the woman and into the darkened room as she continued. "Apparently the cook is considering condemning a cask of pork and wanted them to take a look."

"Very well," he grunted. Mrs Clarkson was standing uncomfortably close, and there was insufficient space for him to move away. "I was just coming to inspect the patients, but can return if it would be more convenient."

"You're welcome at any time, sir," she said, and he noticed her eyes were especially bright in the low light. "It is your ship after all. There are a couple of the lads in the sick bay proper; would you care to see them?" she asked.

"Yes," Banks said, with slightly more enthusiasm than was necessary. "Yes I would, if you please."

He followed her through the inner doorway and was able to make out two young boys lounging on fixed bunks in the darkened room. They sat up on his arrival and one he recognised.

"Parfrey, isn't it?" he asked, approaching. The boy went to nod, then instantly stopped as if in sudden pain. Banks noticed that he was unusually fat about the neck and the other, who looked to be a volunteer third class, was very much the same. Banks held up his hand. "Do not try to speak if it pains you."

"It is fine, sir." Parfrey replied in a thick voice. "As long as no one makes us talk too much."

"Or larf," the other boy added.

"Or laugh," Parfrey confirmed seriously.

"Well, I promise not to do either," Banks said. "I imagine you are passing the time well enough. You have books to read, Parfrey? That is, if you wish to stand as a midshipman, and you..."

"Wickes, sir."

"Wickes. Yes, you know the Navy is always looking for young men with a desire to better themselves. Why, Mr Lewis, the master's mate, was a regular hand not so very long ago."

The lad looked back at him in the half light; it was clear that he had few thoughts beyond tomorrow, and Banks decided to leave well alone.

"Very good, with luck you should not be unwell for long and may return to your duties. I trust you will feel the better soon."

The boys thanked him a little uncertainly, and Banks glanced back to the woman.

"What treatment is being prescribed, Mrs Clarkson?" he asked, following her out of the sick bay and into the dispensary.

"Well, there ain't none, not really. Mr Clarkson's recommending a hot sea water gargle for the throat, and they may not eat fruit or too many vegetables."

"No fruit?" Banks asked.

"Encourages the saliva: makes 'em dribble," she grinned. "Besides, they find it too painful to eat."

The captain remembered King's words. "Yes, I had heard of the lemon juice."

"Would you care for a cup, sir?" The question was asked with an air of innocence that was clearly assumed.

"Me?" Banks's voice rose in surprise.

"You'd be amazed at the number who come here just for that." Mrs Clarkson laughed. "Word has got about that it is an indication, so men are all but queuing up for the stuff. And an awful lot of them are officers." Banks looked puzzled and she continued. "Most are frightened of catching mumps, you see. Even though they may have had a dose already, they've heard such stories of what it can do, an' they don't want no chance of catching it again, bless 'em."

"I see," Banks said crisply. He was also aware of the possible side effects, and could understand that in a predominantly male environment all manner of tattle-tale would be circulating.

"I just tell 'em not to be so soft, an' if they're still worried to come back later an' I'll check 'em out myself." Even in the poor light Banks could gauge the woman's expression, and he felt his face flush.

"Indeed. Well I am glad so see that everything is being looked after, Mrs Clarkson," he turned to go, knowing that her eyes were on him still.

Curse the woman; curse them all for that matter. He had never been at ease with the opposite sex, and especially the type who were in any way forward. The surgeon's wife was clearly of that ilk, and he made up his mind to give her the widest of berths in the future. "Please pass my compliments to Mr Clarkson," he said heading, rather too eagerly, for the small door.

"Very good, sir. Come and visit whenever you wish, you will always be welcome."

Banks cleared his throat; there was something in her tone, something that might even be bordering on insubordination. He glanced back; she was smiling at him quite blatantly; he could tell she had guessed at his awkwardness and was either enjoying his discomfort or openly offering a liaison. For a moment he wavered. Or had he misread the situation yet again? Was he just a clumsy lout, one completely devoid of social graces? Why did he have to think that every female must automatically be setting her hat at him, just because he was a post captain and a knight of the realm?

"Thank you, Mrs Clarkson," he said, a little stiffly perhaps. "You have been most helpful."

* * *

Crowley and the others had been allotted space on the orlop deck of *Hoche*. It was a dark and unwelcoming place, but it would be their home for the foreseeable future and Crowley, for one, was simply relieved to be there.

"The smell is rich enough to cook your boots," MacArthur complained, as they slung their ditty bags on the hooks that would later take the hammocks. "Sure it's even worse than the old *Charlotte*."

"You'll never find a British man-of-war scenting sweet," Doherty agreed. "But I'd have thought a Frenchman might have fared better."

"Aye, especially with the word that she is such a fine ship; yer man last night was almost cryin' 'cause he had to leave her."

"So maybe she has benefits other than her smell," Doyle said. "*Wexford* was a barkie sure enough. Sweet sailer and as faithful as a gun dog, yet she ponged from here to Tuesday." He paused for a moment, then continued, his eyes clearly somewhere else entirely. "She had a manner about her that was pure poetry. Never loved a ship so much in all my life, and neither shall I again, not ever."

"All ships are the same, no matter what they carry, no matter where they go," Crowley said firmly. "Anyone who tries to say they have personalities or souls, is simply talking so much rot." Of them all he was the only French speaker, even Walsh having barely a schoolboy's knowledge of the language. Consequently the last few weeks had been spent with Crowley involved in every conversation and decision, and now that the major problems were either solved or postponed he was starting to feel the strain. But they had finally embarked, and were to sail for Ireland in the next few days. They were heading an expedition that might settle the country's future. And if her bilges were a mite too fragrant, well he really could not care the less.

"Any sailor-men amongst you, lads?" A man wearing a black lacquered hat with the words *Éirinn go Brách* stencilled on it had emerged from the gloom. He was holding a small ledger and spoke in a light Irish accent. The men looked back at him with blank expressions.

"Never been to sea in my life," Crowley confirmed and the others agreed.

"You'll be with the land forces, then; let's have yer names." He marked off in his book as each spoke, then looked up.

"Uniforms'll be provided, though it might be jus' the hat an' maybe a jacket. There are arms a plenty, an' if you take my advice, I'd go for a pike."

"A pike, you say?"

"Aye, the British are using cavalry."

"Would not a pistol or a musket be of more use?" Doyle asked.

The man looked at him in mild contempt. "For the first time, maybe, but you'll find a pike the better weapon, and I'd guess you'll get the chance to use it more than once. You'll be shown how during the voyage, but there'll be precious little time for practice."

Crowley felt a chill run down his body; this was all becoming horribly real, and he knew that his faith, bolstered by Wolfe Tone and constant tales over the last few weeks, would be easily shaken.

"If you've no hand for a ship better stay below and leave it to the experts," the man continued. "It may not be the most comfortable of berths, but you will be fed whilst on board." He relaxed slightly. "I've had better scran, but it is plentiful, and you'll be needing all your strength where you're going."

"How long will it take?" MacArthur asked.

"The journey? Couldn't rightly say. We have the wind with us at the moment; if it stays that way we could be in sight of Ireland by the weekend. Otherwise it may be a fortnight or more, but you'll be informed." He looked at Doyle, whose red hair was tied back in a queue, his upper arms bare, revealing two massive tattoos. "You certain you ain't sailors?" he asked.

* * *

Surridge would have to face official retribution, of course. Few men could indulge in violence aboard a ship of war without incurring some form of punishment or discipline. And when two of any status came to blows it simply could not be ignored.

105

There was also the very real fact that he, being merely a quarter-gunner, had attacked a boatswain's mate; a far more respected rank and one that was also considerably senior. To strike a superior officer was a major offence, one which, if the captain chose, could be sent for judgement by court martial, and might even end in death at the end of a rope.

The captain interviewed both men and weighed the case with care. The facts were indisputable, witnesses abounded, and there was no argument on either side. One mitigating factor remained however: Surridge's medical condition. Black-hearted bastard he might be, but it was clear that the mumps had played an important part in precipitating the incident. For him to face court martial, and potentially a severe penalty, would be tantamount to punishing the man for being ill. Banks naturally hesitated before taking such a step and finally decided to deal with the matter himself.

Of course Surridge could have been flogged beyond the twelve lashes officially allowed. There were instances a plenty of quite vicious and unofficial punishments being doled out by a ship's captain, many of which were accepted as just by prisoner and crew alike. But this was a minor dispute between two men. Such an action might only inflame an already sensitive situation, and could even evoke sympathy amongst the hands. Instead he would be disrated, receive his dozen, and be denied spirit for a month. The loss of status and prestige, together with his prized daily grog, would compound into a very public humiliation, and might even encourage a change in Surridge's future attitude, although the captain was realistic enough to accept it was probably a vain hope.

But whatever the authorised outcome, all knew well enough that the lower deck would also organise their own resolution. The Articles of War might be the official rules by which all men were governed, but many more complex and unwritten laws existed that were every bit as important to the regular hands and enforced with just as much feeling.

The procedure was remarkably similar to that followed by gentlemen when a point of honour was to be settled. Johnston, as the injured party, had the right to choose the time, place and method of combat, leaving Surridge the alternative of a full and public apology, or compliance. The only other option was for him to refuse to take part. Such a denial must mark him indelibly, however; he would be shunned and excluded, forced to mess alone or with others so despised, and in the seaman's world at least effectively cease to exist.

But then no one anticipated Surridge backing down; the very reverse, in fact. During the short time he had been aboard *Scylla* the man had gained such a reputation for hostility and sheer bloody-mindedness that many were half expecting Johnston not to enforce his right. Both were set, however, and the time was arranged and fixed in under a week. Surridge might still be suffering from the effects of the mumps as well as his flogging, but for many of the same reasons that had influenced the captain, justice had to be swift and public.

And it would be a milling. It was a sport that most of the lower deck particularly appreciated, one that was uniquely suitable for their lack of space and privacy. Johnston had chosen the cable tier as being a suitable venue, far away from the eyes of authority, yet large enough to allow some to witness what occurred. And the time would be the first dog watch, when hands would be at rest and most officers dining. The night would also be close enough to allow for the inevitable woundings to be set to rights, as well as giving some degree of rest for the injured.

On the evening in question Johnston was the first to appear along with Dobson, his tie mate and unofficial second. His arrival was greeted by a low murmured cheer from the men already present, and he grinned cautiously in return. The bench was already in place and set beneath two hanging lanterns, with a length of light line attached to either end. Johnston removed his shirt and stretched his limbs, to the approval of the onlookers. He was judged to be well built, but also had the look of speed about him which would serve well. There was a good deal of money pledged on the fight; much of it had been placed on Johnston, as Surridge had few friends within the ship, and the men were clearly intending to will their man on, even before the business had started.

An ironic cheer greeted Surridge's arrival. He had Cox with him, a former shipmate from the *Egmont*, who appeared less than eager to fulfil his duties. Surridge pulled off his shirt; the man was constructed on similar lines to that of a bear, even down to the thick woolly hair that covered his deep and sculptured muscles. He glowered about, clearly recognising his unpopularity, and apparently drawing strength and spirit from the energy.

Both men were soon seated facing the other on the bench, with the line passed about their waists. Measurements were taken to ensure each was just in reach of the other's fist, and the seconds secured the opposing man with seamen's knots. For a moment no one spoke; they were ready, but uncertain how to actually begin. Crouch, a gun captain who had personal reasons for seeing Surridge put down, cleared his throat.

"Johnston is the aggrieved. He has already suffered one blow, so should strike first." The statement was received in general agreement, but still no one felt able to start them off. Crouch looked to Cox and Dobson, and received faint nods in return. "Very well then, gents: begin."

Johnston balled his fist and gauged Surridge's bullet head. The man was moving very slightly, it was an odd, rotating motion that would clearly accelerate as soon as the blow was signalled. The boatswain's mate gritted his teeth, wondering, not for the first time, if Surridge had more experience of this form of combat than he had admitted to. He began to move his own body to mirror that of Surridge, while all the time both men's eyes remained locked on the other's.

Eventually the first blow was struck: Johnston's fist landed square on Surridge's jaw, making an agreeable crack and bringing forth a murmur of approval from the crowd. It was of a strength and force that should have caused damage; even Surridge felt that a tooth or two might have been dislodged, and spat absent mindedly to one side. But it proved unproductive and Johnston had to disguise his feelings of disappointment. That had been his best shot: he had hoped for more and now must suffer another blow from a man who had already caused him a good deal of harm.

Surridge started to weave and dodge again. This time his movements were more exaggerated, but the look in his eye remained laden with evil. Johnston watched him warily, waiting for the first sign of attack.

He moved instinctively even before he had properly registered the action. Surridge's fist came straight for the centre of his head, but Johnston was fast enough to swerve and caught only the very edge, on the side of his chin. The pain was still intense, but there was nothing like the damage that might have been if it had found his nose, and Johnston felt his confidence increase. The men were cheering now, causing both seconds to call for quiet. Johnston pulled a sly sneer at Surridge, who looked pure hatred in return.

The process began again, this time with the pain in Johnston's jaw actually giving him encouragement. Surridge's eyes remained set, but there was possibly a falter as Johnston prepared himself and he was certain they actually closed just before the next blow was struck.

The eyes might have been shut, but Surridge had been ready and, as his head fell suddenly to the right, Johnston had the frustration of feeling his fist pass the expected contact point and flail uselessly in mid air. A collective moan swept through the small crowd, and Surridge gave a self-satisfied smirk. Now the advantage had been lost. Surridge could strike him again, and Johnston knew that an important point had been wasted, both physically and psychologically.

The man was preparing to attack, his fist clenched and level with the shoulder, while his head raised and lowered in a manner that was very nearly hypnotic. Johnston watched the moving image and braced himself to dodge or absorb the impending punishment. This time he missed it; the blow was half way thrown before the signal even registered, and Johnston was only able to pull back, lessening the impact by a mere fraction. It landed on his cheek; bone was trapped against hard knuckle, and Johnston caught a whiff of turpentine that told him Surridge had prepared himself with some care. The compressed flesh dissolved into bloody tissue and soon Johnston's chin and upper chest was warm and damp. The men about him gave a broad groan, and one or two added some choice swearing, but Surridge's low chuckle cut through all other sounds. Johnston looked to Dobson, who had a rag dipped in sea water ready. The wound stung from the cold cloth but the blood continued to flow. Johnston prepared again, telling himself that the damage was more spectacular than dangerous and he was certainly a long way from blacking out. He tightened his fist once more, and prepared to strike.

This time it was a clean hit, one that seemed to take even Johnston by surprise. Surridge was smitten fairly on the forehead, just above his left eye, and his face was soon a mask of red. The atmosphere in the cable tier grew more tense. All knew that a final blow could be expected at any moment, but no one could tell who would deliver it. Surridge, now clearly angry, was even more terrible with his ghastly visage, and emitted a low rumbling that sounded very much like a growl.

The men prepared again, with Surridge thoughtfully dipping the face of his fist into his own blood to make the next strike that much more deadly. They circled and dodged for upwards of thirty seconds with the crowd's total attention focused on them. When the blow was finally released it passed Johnston's left ear, and Surridge let out one single bellow of anger and hurt. Johnston composed himself; the blood was beginning to clot on his face, and he knew the big man was starting to tire. He went to make his move, and was just preparing to strike when Surridge unexpectedly delivered a sudden upper cut to Johnston's chin.

The crowd screamed loud enough to wake the entire ship; both seconds stood up in alarm, and almost came to blows themselves. Surridge gave an evil grin as Johnston realised that at least one of his upper teeth had been broken and casually spat out the remains.

Men continued to protest, and there were calls of differing opinion, but Johnston's head was now completely clear. Without waiting he launched one more thunderous attack on Surridge's face. The fist struck and Surridge let out a shriek of pain as his nose was crushed. His eyes were closed, and for a second Johnston wondered about a swift follow up with his left. It would have been easy, and he may well have right on his side. But things had to be finished in the accepted manner; that was the reason for the fight after all, and if he sank to the same level as his opponent the matter would never be settled.

Gradually Surridge recovered, opening his eyes and appearing surprised to see Johnston still seated in front of him. Sudden anger boiled, and he threw a mighty blow that the boatswain's mate dodged easily. He went to move again, clearly intending to throw another punch, but Johnston was in control now, and sent a crashing right hook to the side of the man's head. Surridge stayed still for almost three seconds while he absorbed the impact, then his body slumped, and he fell sideways off the bench. Cox stepped forward and released the knot, and the body crumpled to the deck amid cheers from the crowd and a deep sigh of relief from Johnston. It was finished.

CHAPTER SEVEN

The medical officers at Dublin were reasonably blasé about the mumps. Less than seventeen men had been affected, with no new cases reported in over a week. Shore leave was out of the question, although that was more due to the risk of desertion than concern for the illness aboard, and *Scylla* required nothing in stores or supplies apart from rosin and oil of cloves. Consequently she was permitted to remain in the outer harbour with the yellow fever flag flying, although even that was more to keep the hawkers at bay than for any real regard for the spread of infection.

Banks stepped from his gig and looked to the midshipman in the sternsheets. "Go back to the ship, Mr Barrow. I'll signal when I am due to return." Barrow touched his hat, the boat pushed off, and soon was starting the long pull back to the ship as her captain stood uncertainly on the stone quay. He glanced about and noticed a plain but business-like carriage approach and draw up. A smartly dressed civilian skipped nimbly from the doorway and began to walk briskly towards him.

"Sir Richard Banks?" The slim young man asked as soon as he was close enough, and extended his hand in greeting when they were still several feet apart.

"Michael St John, personal assistant to the Chief Secretary. I am to act as your escort to the Castle and bring you up to date on the way." St John was no more than thirty, Banks guessed, with dark intense eyes and a mop of unruly hair that was in need of a cut. He was also clearly impatient and added, "Will you join me, sir?" in a sharper tone that was very nearly a command. The captain opened his mouth to reply, but St John was already heading back for the carriage. Banks hurried to catch him up.

"If you have visited before you won't find a deal of difference in the capital," St John told him as he bounded along the stone flags. "Still over crowded and in want of a clean. It is the outer areas that have suffered the most, though the mob came as close as twelve miles from where we are bound."

"I had considered the rebellion all but quashed," the captain spluttered; even ten days at sea had robbed him of his ability to keep a straight line on solid ground, and the man's pace was far too fast.

"You are correct in essence," St John agreed, reaching the carriage. "General Lake had it right when he spoke of the flame being smothered but not extinguished. Mind, that is about the extent of his correctness," he added in a softer tone. For a moment the young man's piercing eyes flashed in Banks's direction. "There is much else to know, hence our meeting. But first, you have illness aboard your ship, I understand, captain?"

"The mumps," Banks admitted. "Nothing more, and not to any great extent."

St John gave a polite smile. "So I have heard; thankfully I am immune, as is my master." He clambered up first, then leaned out to hold the door for his guest. "Though I fear not all the cabinet are in such a happy position. There is no telling whom you shall see, so I had better be as thorough as possible. The Castle, driver."

The last words were directed out of the window, and the carriage moved off before the door was fully closed or Banks had properly seated himself. Clearly time was very important, and St John was not disposed to waste even a second.

* * *

Manning had already been called to attend one seaman the previous evening. The man claimed to have fallen down a hatchway, injuring his nose as well as catching a nasty clout to the side of his head. It was Surridge, recently punished for fighting and one of the first to exhibit the mumps. At the time the surgeon's mate had been suspicious, but he assumed the illness might have made Surridge more clumsy. Now that he was confronted by Johnston, exhibiting similar wounds and giving a story that was almost identical, he had further doubts.

"You shall have to lose it," he told him. His voice was unusually void of compassion as he peered into the man's mouth. "There's nothing else I can do."

Johnston agreed readily enough. His head still hurt from the effects of Surridge's fist, but that was nothing to the pain of the broken tooth.

"Upper left incisor," Manning told Betsy Clarkson, who always assisted him in the morning's surgery. She made a note in the log and reached for the small iron forceps that the surgeon's mate would need for a frontal extraction.

"Did you skin your knuckles when you fell?" Manning asked pointedly.

Johnston looked down and began to rub his bruised right hand. "Must 'ave. Like I said, I'm not really sure what happened."

"I am." Manning gave him a cold stare. "I had Surridge in here late yesterday evening, and now you present yourself. It is clear the recent flogging taught nothing; shall I report this to the captain, and see if he can prescribe a further dose, this time for you both?"

Johnston was silent, but shook his head very seriously.

"Well, I have neither the time nor the inclination to use my skills mending your petty squabbles, and do not expect to see either of you here for some while. Now open your mouth."

The tooth succumbed without incident, and Johnston was promptly despatched with a bloody piece of tow, instructions for hot salt water rinses, and a complete lack of sympathy. Manning wiped the tool on his apron and handed it back to Mrs Clarkson.

"Any more?" he asked.

"I don't believe so," the woman said vaguely. Manning looked at her; she had been somewhat distant all morning. Usually he was quite pleased to have the surgeon's wife assist: the seamen enjoyed her mildly forward manner, which seemed to put them at ease. They were even content for Betsy to be present during more intimate examinations; in fact, Manning occasionally wondered if some actually engineered their attendance at morning surgery when they knew she would be present. "But should you have the time, I would welcome some advice on a personal matter."

Manning raised an eyebrow. "If you require medical attention, you should really seek your husband."

"I would prefer not; for the moment at least. And I do not require examination, if that troubles you."

"Then I assume you have already reached a diagnosis?" Betsy Clarkson might be a trifle promiscuous, but she was certainly no fool.

Her eyes fell. "I am with child," she said.

"Why, that is wonderful news!" Manning relaxed; he had been fearing something truly awful. "You should tell William without delay; I heartily recommend it." She said nothing, although her face now bore a faint, ironic smile. "Should you be concerned at his reaction, let me say that I was not in favour of a family," he continued, mildly disconcerted that she was not sharing his emotion, "and yet on learning could not have been happier."

"When is your child due?" she asked.

"November," he said readily. "As far as we can tell."

"I am happy for you." It was an odd thing for her to say in the circumstances, and Manning's worry deepened.

"And I you," he said. "William will be delighted, I am certain."

"No!" her shout echoed around the small dispensary for a moment or two. Manning stayed silent, and eventually she continued with more control. "No, Mr Manning, he must not find out."

He looked at her doubtfully. "I am afraid that is somewhat inevitable," he said.

"No," she repeated. "No, it is not. There are ways; I know of them, and I want you to help me."

Manning winced as if struck by a pain. "I cannot do that," his voice was suddenly cold. "Any such action would be a crime. A crime on many levels."

"He will kill me," she said.

"I think not. It may take a while for him to come to terms maybe, but..."

"It is not his," she said.

Manning considered her again. "I see," he hesitated. "Then can I ask..?"

"Francis Marshall."

The name meant nothing to him.

"You will not know. He was a marine officer aboard this ship; he left just before my husband came back."

"But this Marshall person, he could not have been gone more than two weeks; if you are already certain of your condition it is highly unlikely to be his."

"We started a liaison long before that, and would meet even when William was on board," she said bitterly. "When he left for London, and the ship was in harbour and almost empty, it was much easier, 'though not so enjoyable, if the truth be known."

Manning closed his eyes for a moment. In the last few weeks he had come to know a little of Mrs Clarkson and the type of woman she was, but still would never have suspected such a thing. Certainly all were aware of her rather coquettish behaviour, and no one could ignore the age difference; her husband must be fifteen years or more the senior. He also accepted that affairs were by no means unusual, but to have another man's child was something else entirely. Manning guessed it was probably the most significant thing she could have done to destroy their marriage. And he also knew her husband: William Clarkson was his immediate superior. He liked and respected the man and would not wish a fate like this on him for all the world.

"Betsy," he said, using her Christian name for the first time, "Betsy, are you quite sure, I mean truly certain? Is there no way that the child might be William's?"

"It is definite that I am pregnant," she said at last. "And I should love it to be William's. Love it, as I do him, and that is more than you could ever know," her eyes were filling with tears, and Manning believed her. "But I fear it unlikely; I think it belongs to Francis, and would ask that you do something to help me. To help me and William, if that makes it any easier for you to comprehend. Otherwise I shall be forced to take a hand myself."

* * *

They could not have covered more than or four or five miles, and yet Banks felt as tired as if a day's journey had been completed. St John had filled the time with details of the uprising that had begun in May, and it was such a tale of bloodshed and confusion, mixed not a little with military blunder, sectarian conflict, slaughter, atrocities and plain bad luck, that Banks's head was now quite pained. Whatever the reports in the English press, it became clear that the Irish situation remained extremely delicate. In fact it was no nearer to being properly settled now than when the rebellion had been officially announced repressed and all the troubles at an end.

"Following the uprising, the French landed a powerful force in County Mayo. That was towards the end of August; it must be news in England by now." St John grew more confidential. "Heaven knows what the market will make of it; we can only be glad that your Admiral Nelson acquitted himself so well in Egypt. Those first accounts of his death did the Exchange no good whatsoever."

Banks considered him for a moment. This was a professional politician, he supposed. Whatever the situation his first thought would never be for the event itself, but rather what effect it might have elsewhere. The genuine relief Banks had felt when hearing that Nelson was not killed fighting Brueys had remarkably little to do with any money market. He cleared his throat and attempted to regain the subject. "I was informed of the landing, though no details were available."

"I expect London placed little value upon it; that is their way, though it pains me to admit so. But in truth it was nought but a small squadron of ships under a Commodore Savary; we knew they had sailed from Brest some months before, and frankly were wondering what had become of them."

"They left unobserved?" Banks asked.

"Observed, but not detained," St John confirmed. "I am afraid Admiral Bridport was hardly maintaining the watch as well as he might, though I understand the situation has now improved," he gave a sly smile. "And his London house is no longer considered a suitable place from which to command a fleet."

Banks was silent; the civilian continued.

"There were roughly a thousand men in all, commanded by a General Jean Humbert, something of a national hero by all accounts; he started as a sergeant in the National Guard. It was hardly enough to mount a proper invasion, but annoying, none the less. We suspect that the French were caught napping, and the original rebellion was due to be mounted some time later with more men to back them."

"A thousand might still make a difference," Banks reflected. In a country already torn by a failed uprising, the sudden appearance of an equipped and organised force of professional soldiers would have drawn any latent rebels like a magnet.

"And indeed they did. We estimate a further thousand United Irishmen joined them. Much had been done to remove what arms were available, but the French had brought provisions and weapons to spare. Before we were properly aware, there was a sizeable and well equipped army active in the north west. Within days they had captured two towns and were marching on Castlebar." He drew breath for only a second before continuing.

"General Lake was in command there. He had an army of six thousand, plus a good many artillery pieces, and the outcome could be reckoned inevitable." For a moment St John was silent again. It was as if in remembering the events he was still having problems believing what had really happened. "But Lake was taken off guard; I know it sounds preposterous, but he had assumed the French would attack from the Ballina road and made provisions for that eventuality alone. By the time he discovered they were coming across the marshlands, an area he had considered impassable, the British were decidedly on the wrong foot."

Banks was looking intently at the man and decided his earlier estimation of age was out. St John could be little more than twenty five, but certainly carried himself with unusual assurance, and had a sound appreciation of the situation.

"The French fought well, as did the United men. And bravely too, it has to be said. They made at least one bayonet charge that put the chill up our boys, and the next anyone knew the British were in all out retreat. Lake had several units of local militia under his command; I'm afraid some went over to the enemy: a hundred and forty of the Longford regiment betrayed themselves to the French in one body."

Banks closed his eyes. It sounded like hell on earth.

"Once an army runs it is all but impossible to halt," St John continued despondently. "The enemy chased them for no more than two miles, but Lake's troops did not stop until they reached the Shannon. They abandoned guns, equipment, ammunition, but more importantly, they left behind a successful and victorious army. Within days a further four or five thousand men had joined, and it took Lord Cornwallis and a force of nearly thirty thousand to finally stop them."

Dublin Castle was in plain sight now, and from Banks's first impression it was the very model of military excellence. The high stone walls and decorative castellations were imposing enough without the crisp sentries and two patrols of marching men that they encountered as their carriage approached.

"That was a few weeks ago, and the action was over in less than an hour," St John continued. "The French could see they were heavily outnumbered and did the sensible thing. Sadly, some of the Irish decided not to follow their example, and I am afraid all honour and sensibility was rather forgotten."

The carriage stopped but neither man showed any signs of leaving.

"The Irish lost over five hundred men to our twelve," St John said, his eyes focusing somewhere far outside. "It was carnage."

"What happened to the prisoners?" Banks asked.

"The French were brought back here by canal." He gave a short laugh. "We have since been told in no uncertain terms that our food is not to their liking."

"And the Irish?" Banks persisted. He was fearing the worst.

"I understand that those who are not already hanged soon will be." The civilian's face had lost all trace of humour.

But surely they are prisoners of war?"

"Some may say so," St John avoided Banks' eyes. "Amongst them was Wolfe Tone's younger brother."

"The name is familiar."

"I should think it is, though it often pleases him to be known as Adjutant-General Smith. In truth he is nought but a Dublin lawyer, but trouble; though I chance you might say the same about any of his profession. He was present on the Bantry Bay expedition; I believe you were involved in that?"

Banks nodded; St John was remarkably well informed.

"If he ever ventures into our clutches we will hang him for sure, but for the time being Cornwallis has made do with the sibling."

"He is executed?"

"At this very castle. Traitors must be dealt with, and there were traitors a plenty."

Banks remained impassive. He was a naval officer and had no right to judge the policies of the military. Still, it did not seem to be the act of men wishing to calm an already heated situation.

"So," St John said, his previous energy returning. "I trust you are now more *au fait* with the state of affairs." The man was clearly keen to go, but Banks stopped him.

"There is one more thing," he said, as the words were still forming in his mind. "Whatever started this?"

St John looked mildly surprised. "Started it? Why that is very hard to say. Though in essence I suppose it comes down to petty tyranny. Oppressive landlords whose chief interest is the pursuit of pleasure, and magistrates completely void of both integrity and courage. First they goad the peasantry into rebellion, then cry to the military for rescue. The British Army under Abercromby was at least organised and, though it might not have been thought of as such at the time, the old Scot had the right idea. Now Lake has entered the equation it is anyone's guess where it will end. Though I am certain it shall not be well."

"I understand Admiral Kingsmill is still at Cork," Banks said, as they finally clambered down from the carriage. "*Scylla* is attached to his squadron, I was surprised to be ordered to Dublin."

"The admiral may be at Cork, but he has only a worn out flagship. All other naval vessels are at sea." St John waited while the captain caught him up, then took up his customary pace. "As you will be, no doubt, within a few hours."

"I was not expecting to sail so soon." When Banks had left the ship the boatswain's crew were replacing some running rigging and the caulkers were having yet another try to seal the forecastle deck.

"I think this may be your last taste of land for a while, Sir Richard." They were approaching the main gate of the castle, and St John acknowledged the challenge and salute of the guard with an assured wave. "If, as we expect, the French are intending another campaign, your little ship is certain to be busy during the next few months." They passed through and into the darkness beyond. St John looked sidelong at Banks.

"And there will be action, sir, you need have no doubt of that. Action a plenty."

* * *

It was the coveted exercise hour, the time when those stationed on the orlop deck were allowed up and into the blessed daylight of the waist. Crowley may well have been better off joining the others as they strolled about the deck; in a ship as crowded as the *Hoche* space, fresh air, and a chance to stretch the legs were benefits not to be declined. But he was fascinated by the far off ships, and usually spent all of his time in the daylight staring through the same empty gun port.

The British had been following almost from the moment they had set sail. There was only one today: a heavy frigate that was just in sight off their starboard quarter. Whatever moves the French made, however hard they tried to shake them away, the same ship, or a small brig, and occasionally both, would be trailing them whenever he looked. Doggedly following their path, too far off to be caught, but close enough to let them know that they were under observation.

Crowley sat back on the deck, hands behind him, legs crossed at the ankles and his face enjoying the gentle rays from the afternoon sun. He could still just see the British ship, and not much was going to happen, but he would rather spend his time sitting there and watching than wandering about the place with men he was fast becoming painfully familiar with. The accompanying French frigates were maintaining poor order. Sometimes his ship, the *Hoche*, a seventy-four and the most powerful in their small fleet, was leading, on other days she was very much the tail ender, and no one seemed terribly bothered either way. But then this could partly be put down to the regular sail drills.

He had forgotten how little time the French spent out of harbour and had grown to accept the high standard of seamanship aboard British vessels. From the moment they had left France he was concerned; the hands, though in the main seamen, were woefully out of practice, and fumbled even the most simple of tasks. All those in his group besides Walsh were sufficiently competent to be rated able, and to find themselves in the care of such men was decidedly disconcerting. That was one of the reasons the British had caught them so soon; a simple passage like the Raz should have been negotiated in half the time; as it was, they had wavered and blundered about for so long the British would have been fools not to spot them.

But at least the captains of each ship apparently shared his dismay, and for all of the voyage to date several hours a day had been devoted to exercise. The constant training was starting to pay off, although Crowley knew that much more would be needed before any of their fleet could tack or wear like the British.

And that was just the seamanship. He had not witnessed either of the two gun drills held aboard the *Hoche*, but could tell from the shouts and disorder that filtered down to them that they had not gone well. He remembered watching the crew of *Pandora*. Admittedly she was a frigate, with only one main gun deck to serve, but still the coordination and timing was so fine that all the carriage guns moved as one, and her practice broadsides sounded off at least twice as fast as anything the French could manage.

No, the British bettered them on both counts, and *Hoche* and her companions were now firmly fixed in their sights. There were only a couple of them; but should more join, and they chose to force action, Crowley knew the French would not fare well.

* * *

Scylla sliced through the swell, her sails set stiff in the steady breeze. The wind, though not particularly strong, had been holding in their favour throughout and the faint chill that it brought made the late afternoon sun especially welcome. Since leaving Dublin two days before they had made a reasonable passage and spirits in the ship were high. On the foremast several of the hands were skylarking while Barrow and Rose had taken young Parfrey up the mizzen, traditionally the first mast for any man or boy to climb. Chilton looked up from his station on the quarterdeck; the trio were resting securely enough at the cross trees, and Barrow was pointing at the nearby mainmast, clearly instructing the kid. Parfrey was still slightly swollen from the mumps, but they had been so keen to go that, as officer of the watch, the lieutenant could hardly have refused.

He took two turns along the deck only to stop once more next to the binnacle. The run north against the wind to Dublin had been as frustrating as it was long, but since then they had been ordered back south and enjoyed sweet sailing. Now the energy was certainly returning to the ship; at any moment they expected to raise the Irish coast once more, and might even be anchoring in Cork that very evening. But somehow Chilton doubted they would be doing anything quite so placid. Nothing specific had been said, although the captain had impressed upon them all the importance of a good lookout. That could only mean that the French were probably at sea and likely to be in their vicinity; Chilton could not imagine *Scylla* staying meekly in harbour while that remained the case.

There had also been talk of a flying squadron joining them. For such a venture to be worthwhile it would have to be of sufficient force to deal with a major enemy. Then, with luck, they would meet, and there would be a fleet action.

A fleet action, and one that his ship would be involved in: for all his time in the Navy, Chilton had yet to experience combat on that scale and he felt his pulse race at the thought. The bell rang out three times; in half an hour the first dogwatch would come to an end and he could claim a few hours rest.

Ahead two men began to climb the weather shrouds, one at the fore and the other the main. Banks had ordered the lookouts doubled, with each man being relieved hourly, a bell apart. That meant that at any time there would be one who had been on duty for less than half an hour, and another to confirm or question anything he might see. It was about as much as they could do, and even then a ship, be it friend or enemy, could easily slip by beneath a cloud on the horizon.

"Sail ho, sail off the larboard bow!" Just as he was thinking, Chilton heard the cry. He made no move for a moment. For a sighting to be made this close to Cork was no surprise; the likelihood was strong that it was nothing more than a small coaster, or maybe even another warship. There were known to be several in the area, all scouting for the French. *Scylla* could have run into any one of them, or even another from England, despatched to join the hunt. "She's a brig, or a snow," the lookout continued, "beating up against the wind with all sail set."

The lieutenant glanced at the midshipman standing attentively nearby. "My compliments to the captain: tell him of the sighting."

The lad was off before Chilton had even finished, and he was considering another turn up and down the deck when Banks appeared.

"Where away?" he asked, as he buttoned up his shirt. His hair was awry and it was clear he had been sound asleep.

"Off the larboard bow, sir," Chilton said, pointing at the empty horizon.

"What do you see there?" Banks bellowed up to the masthead.

"Brig, sir," The answer came back almost immediately, and Chilton wondered how long the lookouts had been watching to be certain before announcing the sighting. "Close hauled on the starboard tack. And I'd say she were Navy, though it's still too far off to be sure. We're closing on her fast, though."

"Steer two points to larboard," the captain snapped, and Chilton called out the orders. *Scylla* took up speed as the wind moved further on to her quarter. Banks turned to the midshipman. "Masthead for you, lad. Take the glass and let me know what you see." The boy slung the leather bound brass telescope about his shoulder and made for the shrouds.

"Deck there, she's tacking." The officers on the quarterdeck waited while the lookout concentrated. Clearly the strange sighting had now seen and identified *Scylla,* and the fact that the she was turning towards them almost confirmed her nationality beyond doubt. "Yes, now on the larboard tack, and Miller here thinks 'e knows her."

"She's the *Sylph*, we was with 'er last commission," the second lookout called down.

"Commander Chambers White, sir," Chilton said. "Something of a rising star, in these parts." Banks looked at him and the lieutenant continued. "Captured several privateers in the last few years, and destroyed a French frigate when she had been run ashore."

"Indeed?" The captain said, staring forward where the sighting should appear at any moment. "Well, let us hope that he is bringing us good news."

* * *

"What fever, sir?"

The two vessels were less than half a cable apart. Banks had kept the brig to windward and ordered the fever flag hoisted once more.

"The mumps," Chilton bellowed in reply. The brig's crew gave a chorus of ribald laughter, which was answered by a couple of indignant shouts from the *Scylla*'s lower deck.

"Then I'll thank you to stay to leeward of me, sir!" Clearly

Sylph's captain found the situation just as amusing. For a moment Banks was annoyed, and decided that White was probably a young commander and clearly not insisting on correct discipline aboard his vessel. Then he remembered that it was hardly three years ago that he himself had been in a similar position, and collected the speaking trumpet in a slightly more tolerant frame of mind.

"Do you have news, for me, Captain?" Banks bellowed.

"Aye, sir, the French are out." The tone was more serious, as was the message. "We caught them off Brest and have been following for several days. My Lord Bridport will be aware b'now."

Banks pursed his lips. He disliked discussing news of this importance in front of the entire crew, but time, and the damned mumps, gave little option. "How many are they?"

"Nine frigates and a liner," White replied. "Some might be armed *en-flute*, but still a sizeable number."

The two ships were starting to drift apart; someone in the brig gave an order and she closed again, although they were clearly intending to keep a fair distance off.

"Who is following them?" Banks asked.

"Captain Countess in *Ethalion*, along with *Amelia*. *Anson* joined a day back; that is when we were despatched."

Banks knew George Countess: a sound man and, more importantly, ahead of him in the captain's list. And *Anson*, if he was not mistaken, was a heavy frigate, a *razee*, cut down from a sixty-four. It was a reasonable force, but not sufficient to deal with ten Frenchmen.

"Where is the enemy now?" There was a hesitation; it was clearly not a question easily answered: with British ships shadowing, the French were probably leading a merry dance. White had been out of touch for a day or more, and whatever he said would be more of an indication, a basis for the start of speculation.

"Last seen they were approximately fifty north, eleven west, and apparently heading for Ireland.

Banks nodded, it was the obvious conclusion. "And your orders, Captain White?"

"I am to head for Cork with the news, sir. Advise any ships met on the way, and then attempt to meet up with Sir John Warren."

"Warren?"

"He has been given a squadron, sir, liners and frigates, and should be in the vicinity."

That sounded a little more positive. Warren was another good man, and clearly had been equipped with a force powerful enough to deal with the French.

"Very good, Captain; I shall detain you no longer,"

"What are your intentions, sir?"

"I shall make to join Captain Countess, though will obviously be on the watch for Sir John as well; you may say that should you find him first."

"Very good, sir,"

Orders were shouted on board the brig, and the yards came round almost immediately. It was an example worth following, and *Scylla* was soon back on the wind and heading away. Hands aboard both ships waved and exchanged shouted messages, and it was just as the two were almost out of hailing distance that someone on *Sylph*'s lower deck delivered the *coup de grâce*:

"An if you can't fight the frogs, at least you can pox 'em!"

CHAPTER EIGHT

The weather stayed bright for the next few days, although the wind was not exactly in their favour and carried an edge that warned the true seamen amongst the crew of an impending storm. Once past Cape Clear *Scylla* had altered course and was keeping the coast of Ireland just in sight off her starboard beam to aid accurate navigation. Finding two small fleets in a wide expanse of ocean must be more a question of luck than judgement, although having some idea of the enemy's destination was a considerable help. There were bays and inlets a plenty on Ireland's western coast. Many would make an excellent landing point, and it made sense to keep such places under observation whilst they steadily headed northwards.

But so far they had found little other than fishing vessels and coastal traders. The few of any size they did encounter turned out to be neutral merchants: inspecting them wasted valuable time and proved fruitless, and Banks was just starting to wonder if Sir John Warren would actually meet the French and see action before *Scylla* made contact with either of them. The shout and clump of a musket from the marine sentry followed by tap at his cabin door brought him back to the present, and he called for the messenger to enter.

"There are two fishing boats in sight, sir." It was Parfrey, the volunteer. "And Mr King says he doesn't like the look of the weather."

"Very good, my compliments to Mr King and would he alter course to intercept. I shall be on deck presently." Fishermen remained a potential source of local knowledge even if he had learned very little from those he had already met. The lad touched his hat and was about to dash from the room when Banks called him back.

"Mr Parfrey, I assume you are now fully recovered?"

"Oh yes, sir; thank you, sir." The lad's chin and neck had certainly returned to normal, and his face actually looked quite ruddy with health.

"I am glad of it. There have been good reports from your divisional lieutenant which have also pleased me; continue with your studies and you shall have a bright future within this ship."

Parfrey left in a blur of smiles and thanks and Banks sat back in his chair. A lot had happened during the last few days and his mind was still something of a whirl. The interview at Dublin Castle had been inconclusive, although his talk with St John was almost worth the diversion on its own. As it was, with the Viceroy many miles away, he had spent a barely half hour with a deputy minister who added little to the briefing he had received in the carriage. The man could hardly have been less interested in a member of His Majesty's Navy, and closed the meeting promptly at one, presumably the time for his luncheon. It proved to be a meal to which Banks was not invited.

He thought about his brief visit to Ireland's capital city once more. The very castle itself seemed to stand as a metaphor for the military attitude to the Irish situation. On the outside strong, forbidding and considered, but beneath the stone façade there were just corridors of dusty, ill kept offices that had seemingly been added on a random basis without any thought for order or purpose.

The attitude of the staff was also at odds with a country currently striving to hold the safe ground between civil war and all out rebellion. On the way in he noticed two locksmiths who, according to his guide, were employed on pretty much a permanent basis. Apparently security was universally accepted as lax, with keys to the government offices frequently being lost or stolen.

Banks remembered St John's final words. Despite the official line that the rebellion was all but over, he expected further trouble; indeed, he appeared to sense it as a dog might game. But even one with such an agile mind and in an informed position was in the dark as to exactly where the fight may lie.

If it were at sea, against enemy shipping, then Banks had every confidence. *Scylla* was a fine ship, one that had already found a place in his affections, and her crew were loyal and ready for command. In straight combat with an identifiable enemy he had few doubts about how she would perform. But with the Irish situation as it was they were just as likely to be involved in a land based campaign, one where enemy might as easily pass as friend, and any action was bound to be horribly expensive in human lives. The idea did not appeal; but if the rumoured invasion force turned out to be real, and should they be given the chance to land in any one of a hundred likely places, there seemed little alternative.

His thoughts were broken for a second time by the rumble of feet upon the deck above. King was manoeuvring the ship, which meant the fishermen were close by, and he could waste no more time on idle speculation. He rose from his chair; previous interviews had brought little news, and he didn't expect this one to be any different. But the French may have been spotted; even now, as he made his way to the quarterdeck, they could be anchoring in some sheltered inlet, ready to disgorge their troops and start the whole murderous procedure off once more. He clambered up the short companionway and touched his hat as he approached the group of officers next to the binnacle. *Scylla* had backed her mizzen and was starting to wallow in the gentle swell. He glanced round; there were two small boats about half a cable to leeward, but what really drew his attention was the shadow off the larboard bow. The horizon was shielded by a dark fog and the very air felt heavy and torpid.

"Hail the fishermen, if you please, Mr King." Banks said, his eyes still fixed on the impending weather. "But I do not intend to waste any time; I fear there may be other matters to take our attention."

* * *

The ship's bell rang: he had half an hour left in the fresh air. The wind was also rising and Crowley wondered if this might be the last time he would be able to exercise on deck for some while. He eased himself up gently and stood, stretching each leg in turn and wriggling his toes to encourage the circulation. In an effort to shake off the pursuing British they had spent the last day and a half heading away from their destination. Crowley was hardly in a hurry to reach Ireland and certainly had no desire to start fighting; nevertheless he knew that, if the voyage lasted very much longer, most of the proud invasion force would be fit for nothing other that eating and sleeping. Those were the tasks that currently occupied their waking hours, and the routine would be hard to break. A movement from behind caught his attention, and he looked round to see a familiar face.

Wolfe Tone was often present during Crowley's exercise period. They sometimes exchanged nods, but that had always been the extent of their intercourse. Today however, he was clearly keen for conversation.

"I've noticed before you like to keep an eye on our friends." Tone was wearing a dark blue coat that was rather ostentatiously decorated with lace and ribbon, and he dug his hands deep into the pockets as he regarded the British ship.

Crowley snorted. "There is little else to do."

"They watch us, and we watch them," he said. "It is a strange arrangement, but one we can tolerate for as long as we must."

"Do you think they will give up?" Crowley knew the answer, but wanted to hear Tone's reply.

"No, we can play our little games; go this way and go that, but the British will stick with us for as long as it remains physically possible. We may be lucky: the captain says there is storm in the air. Or they may be lucky and run in with a force large enough to deal with us. But wherever fortune falls they will not go away of their own accord, of that you may be certain."

"I hears you have met with them before," Crowley chanced.

Tone kept his eyes fixed on the British frigate. "Aye, I have that, though we have yet to come to blows, more's the pity. But I certainly do not know them as well as you."

Crowley was surprised and not a little confused. "I was also on the Bantry Bay expedition, if that's what you mean."

"It wasn't that to which I referred." His eyes moved from the distant horizon and found Crowley's. "You served with the British Navy, or have I got that terribly wrong?"

Crowley felt the colour rise in his cheeks. "I did, for a spell, though you might say the same for many aboard this ship."

Tone was now looking at him with a fierce intensity. "The way I heard it, you have friends amongst the British, and were waiting to join another Navy ship before you came here." Crowley said nothing, but the stare did not relent in any way. "It's Crowley, isn't it? Michael Crowley?"

"It is," Crowley agreed cautiously. He had seen Tone on a platform; the man was fascinating to watch: he possessed a magnetism that was almost hypnotic. But close up that energy felt entirely different. Different and far more dangerous.

"Tell me, Michael. Are you truly dedicated to the cause?"

Crowley felt his body go numb. He already knew enough about Tone to class him as a true fanatic: one who recognised no limits or bounds. He also felt instinctively that he was the kind who would fight without consideration for himself. Like a lunatic he would punch, flail, or scratch, not caring if, in the process, he were also hurt. Even the look in his eye was enough to scare the stoutest heart, and Crowley realised, almost with a sense of epiphany, that this was a man to be feared. And yet he must answer the question.

"I, I am not sure..." The words came from him as if drawn by Tone's spell. "I believe in a free Ireland..."

"But you also have friends who are British?"

He nodded once more.

Tone seemed to relax. "It is good to have friends, Michael. Friendship is what the Brotherhood is all about. But it has to be the right friends, the ones who will not let you down. And I have never yet met a British man who could be trusted."

Crowley felt unable to reply. Not for years had he felt so intimidated, and yet Tone had not threatened, or even hinted at physical violence. Indeed, he was lightly built, and would have been simple to take down in a brawl.

"I wish you to state your faith, Michael. I would like everyone to do so who I am unsure of. Do you have an objection to that?"

"I see no reason why I should," Crowley said guardedly.

The other man rested his hand on his shoulder. "That is good, Michael. That is very good indeed."

Crowley tensed; Tone had misunderstood, and thought him willing to swear allegiance to the cause. His aversion to oaths was almost pathological and, however persuasive the man might be, he was not going to break a lifelong rule for a bunch of revolutionary crack-pots. He pulled away and had even opened his mouth to explain when a shout from the main masthead drew their attention.

A sighting had been made. The report was still being called down to the deck when a second came from the foremast. Soon it was clear that several ships were in view, a veritable fleet. This was news of the highest import and all thoughts of their previous conversation were wiped away as Tone and Crowley exchanged glances. "From the north, and a mighty number, that makes them unlikely to be Royal Navy," Crowley said quietly.

"Equally we can guess them not to be French," Tone agreed, his tone now light and neutral. "But whatever, it would appear that luck of some order has been dealt, and the situation is about to change." He looked across to the British frigate, still sailing off their larboard quarter, and presumably unaware of any mystery fleet. "And I would predict that before so very long we will either lose our loyal companions or form a far closer relationship with them in battle."

* * *

"What do you know of Betsy Clarkson?" Manning asked.

King considered for a moment, then pulled a face. "Nice apples," he said.

Manning snorted. "That was not the answer I expected, nor should it be heard coming from one who is betrothed in matrimony."

"Well, it was the first that came to mind," King protested. "And I wouldn't have said the same about many women."

"Even if they did have nice apples?" Manning's eyebrows were raised, and King found himself fumbling for an answer.

"Probably not," he blushed. "As you say, it is hardly in my nature. Yet Betsy rather encourages such comments."

"She might be a touch fly, I admit."

"And they are nice apples," King chanced.

"Oh indeed. But what else do you know of her?"

King could see that his friend was speaking in earnest, and gave the matter further thought. "Well, she is a deal younger than the surgeon," he said eventually. "And, as I have said, rather tends to play the floozy. Other than that, not much. Except that she makes a decorative addition to the gunroom table."

"Let us steer away from that or we will be back to apples," Manning said hurriedly. They were standing by the taffrail at the end of the second dogwatch. The evening was falling, but it was still just warm enough for idle conversation and, for once, there was no one near to eavesdrop. It had been three days since his talk with the surgeon's wife, and Manning had been hoping for just such an opportunity to speak with King, probably his closest friend. "Are you aware of her indulging in any particular friendships whilst on board?"

King thought some more. "Why, yes," he said, suddenly more serious. "There was that man Marshall. The marine: he left just before you joined us."

"Indeed, and did so in rather a hurry, as I collect."

"I think Mr Fraiser had something to do with that," King said softly.

"The sailing master?" Manning looked puzzled. "How so?"

This was becoming uncomfortable, and King looked about to make sure they were truly speaking in private. "It was while we were at anchor, I believe they were having a liaison. I heard sounds from the surgeon's cabin, and wondered about investigating."

"And did you?"

"No, I did not," his head fell. "I felt it better to leave be. But Adam Fraiser rolled up shortly afterwards, and did not share my thoughts."

"He confronted them?"

"Yes, and had Marshall all but thrown off the ship."

"Did he indeed?" The surgeon's mate was clearly impressed. "And was the captain involved?"

"I don't believe so."

"I see," Manning paused, and King was also quiet for a moment. He still felt mildly guilty about the incident, especially as Fraiser, heard through the thin deal walls of his cabin, had handled it with such competence.

"Tell me, does anyone else know of this?" Manning finally asked.

"Not that I am aware." In fact most of the other officers were amazed at the speed with which Marshall left, but then nearly all regarded him as merely a jollie and consequently not of any great importance. "Is Betsy in trouble?" King asked, looking up once more.

"Not that I may speak of," Manning replied. "Though you would help her best by keeping what we have said to yourself. And your eyes off her apples."

* * *

The mystery sighting revealed itself to be a powerful convoy. Upwards of a hundred merchants, according to the lookout, and well protected: three frigates could be clearly seen, and there were probably far more out of sight. That they would be British was beyond doubt. No other nation could summon that many ships and sail them blatantly across the oceans. The majority would be Indiamen, stuffed full of all manner of precious items that the country was effectively mining from the East. That one convoy alone must be worth several million in supplies, and there were others, equally valuable and also on the high seas. With such an amount of wealth constantly trickling into her reserves it was hardly surprising that Britain was able to wage a war against most of the rest of Europe.

Crowley turned back to the shadowing frigate, which was still maintaining watch, and stood a good nine miles off their quarter. It could not be so very long before they also spotted the convoy, and acted accordingly. Trapped as they were, the French would have to turn south, even further away from their destination – that or finally take the initiative and make towards the hounding British. With such a force it would be strange if even the French did not account for a few small ships, were the Royal Navy foolish enough to offer action.

The commodore was on the quarterdeck now, and Tone had gone to speak with him. Crowley could see the two men as they stood by the fife rail, their heads lowered in deep conversation. But as he watched Tone caught his eye, and he felt the man's stare upon him. Tone muttered a brief word, then beckoned down to where Crowley stood in the waist. Crowley looked to one side, hoping it might be someone else that Tone was calling, but he was quite alone, and clearly required. He walked slowly towards the quarterdeck ladder and clambered up.

This was the command deck, the area allotted to officers and gentlemen. In a British ship of war it would have been the smartest in the ship, with all lines correctly flaked and set, brass polished, and even the deck itself burnished to a high finish. It was no surprise to find the *Hoche* deficient in this respect; what should have been holy ground was as much of a shambles as any other part of the vessel, but then Crowley supposed the French had more important considerations, and were never a nation that believed in needless bull.

"This is my man Crowley," Tone said, as he approached. "We go back a long way, and he is something of an expert on the British Navy, isn't that right, Michael?"

Crowley blushed but had little option other than to nod meekly in reply, and was uncomfortably aware of Tone's galvanic presence as it descended upon him once more.

"So, what is it that the British will do?" Commodore Bompart asked. The man was in his early forties, and spoke reasonably good English. He looked at Crowley with soft, rather sad eyes, and the Irishman guessed that the mission did not inspire him.

"The convoy will give you no trouble, unless you attack it directly." That was just plain common sense. However much the Royal Navy escort must be straining at the leash at the sight of French warships, it would be a bold commander that denuded so many valuable merchants of protection. "But if you venture too close, you may well be taken," Crowley continued; there was little argument in that either. With three frigates in sight, there must be at least another six or seven within signalling distance; and such a force, combined with those already following, could wipe out the French without great difficulty.

Bompart was apparently satisfied with Crowley's comments, but Tone, it seemed, wanted more.

"And what of our friends to the east? Will they not join with the others, and maybe attack?"

Crowley pursed his lips. "It is possible, but only once they are certain of their existence and strength. In ten, maybe twenty minutes they will have sight of the Indiamen, and it will only take a while longer before it is obvious just how large a fleet they are."

"So you are saying we should move now, before the British become aware?"

He shrugged: he supposed he was.

Tone regarded the commodore. "I see it as the only hope," he said in a voice that held both power and decision. "Steer for the frigates; despatch our own in advance, if you think they can be trusted. But send the British scurrying for shelter; and do it now, while we still have a chance of ever seeing our destination."

Bompart said nothing for a moment; he was clearly not a man who took action quickly, and Tone was becoming visibly frustrated while he waited.

"It is what I suggested from the start," he said, pressing his hands still deeper into his pockets. "With them on our shoulder it is merely a question of time before we are brought to action; even a simple sailor-man like Michael can see that."

Crowley ducked his head slightly as the attention was momentarily brought back to him.

"And that is not the object of the exercise, Jean." Tone said, resuming his thread. "You may regard the British as something you must fight, I see them as an obstacle, and one to be avoided. If we can rid ourselves of these few small scouts we might resume our journey, and carry out the task that was originally given to us."

"But if we steer for them, they will run," the commodore's voice was very nearly a whine.

"Maybe so, but we would have made the effort," Tone was starting to sound exasperated. He paused, and Bompart looked to him, thinking – hoping – he might have finished. But there was further shot in the locker.

"You must see to it that we reach Ireland; that is your responsibility," he said. "Mine starts when we touch Irish soil. But if you fail to get us there, if I am once more thwarted by the incompetence and faint heartedness of French seamen, I will make every effort to see that whoever is responsible comes to notice." Bompart swallowed, clearly Tone was not speaking lightly; indeed, he had connections a plenty in the Directory, and was known to be a close friend of General Bonaparte. Then Tone smiled suddenly, and his shoulders relaxed.

"All I am asking is that you attempt to see off those ships," he said, his voice now softer and almost friendly. "Despatch a few frigates to send them on their way, then alter course. Take us to Ireland. Let us do our job, Jean, it isn't much to ask. And remember: it is an invasion force that you command, not a battle fleet."

* * *

Fraiser had listened to Manning with quiet attention and was silent for a very long time afterwards. But when he did speak it was with his usual quiet assurance. And what he said was so complete and made such sense that the surgeon's mate needed no further advice. He thanked the elderly sailing master, leaving him to the contemplation he had originally disturbed, and went to talk with Mrs Clarkson.

He knew she would be in the dispensary. The morning surgery did not start for another half an hour, but she was usually there early to make certain all was ready, and Manning was reasonably sure they would not be disturbed. She looked up from the ledger when he came in and gave her usual free-hearted beam. Manning acknowledged her coldly in return, and the look faded.

"Betsy, I'd like to speak with you," he said.

She closed the book, instantly aware of the subject. Manning pulled up the stool used by the patients and sat close by so that their words would not be overheard.

"I've given this some thought, and hope to have reached a conclusion."

"I also, Robert – I can call you Robert can't I? There are a number of ways we can..."

He held up his hand and she stopped as if so trained. "Thank you, Betsy. I don't want to ignore what you wish to say, but please let me speak first." She nodded. "Are you well?"

"Yes, thank you."

"There is no morning sickness?"

"None whatsoever. I have been very lucky."

"What of William: has he noticed any change?"

Her eyes fell for a moment. "Not that I am aware. Nothing has been said, at least."

"And the pregnancy; you are still quite certain?"

"Quite."

He drew a deep breath and studied her for a moment. Indeed, she did appear amazingly bonnie. Her face, always so full of health, was now positively blooming, and there was a brightness in her eyes that even the dull light of the dispensary could not hide.

"And you are absolutely certain the baby is Marshall's?"

She held his stare for a moment. "I have no reason to think otherwise."

Manning considered this; it was, he supposed, an encouraging answer. "And what if Marshall had the mumps?" he asked.

Her look froze for a second, then broke and she very nearly laughed aloud. "The mumps?"

"Yes, I understand he was exhibiting many of the symptoms."

Manning was looking at his hands now, being suddenly unable to meet her eyes. Shortly he would betray both Clarkson and his Hippocratic oath, but he knew all that must be discounted. What really mattered was that Betsy accepted the slender lifeline he offered.

"It was before I joined, but there was talk in the gunroom the other evening," he carried on relentlessly. "Some even suppose it was he who brought the illness to the ship."

"No, no it could not have been." She sounded vaguely flustered. "His face was quite normal and... and surely I would have known?"

"You might not have," Manning said with an apparent honesty that amazed even himself. "The mumps can effect people in different ways. There is, however, one symptom that is all too common in older men."

This was a difficult moment. She was no fool and even had a good deal of medical knowledge. It would also be reasonable for her to have read up on the condition, considering the recent outbreak.

"Well, I know it carries the chance of infertility..."

He glanced up briefly and noted that Betsy Clarkson was blushing.

"But I didn't notice any difference," she ended lamely.

"You may not have," his attention was once more on his hands and he began to fiddle absent-mindedly with his own wedding ring. "Especially if precautions were being taken, which I assume...?"

She agreed, and still he avoided her eyes, although Betsy's face was now very definitely aglow.

"So tell me, is it truly beyond doubt that this child is not your husband's?"

There was no answer for a while, her thoughts were clearly set somewhere far away and it was with an effort that she finally returned to the real world and his question.

"William's?" she hesitated. "I, I suppose it possible. It just seemed so obvious it must belong to Francis."

"Well I think we have established such a possibility to be unlikely." That was a lie, as he guessed both of them understood well enough. But would she have the sense, or the gall – it mattered not which – to accept it? Manning felt the heat rise under his collar, and told himself what he was did was for the best. The best for everyone. "If you think the child could be William's, you should tell him immediately. To delay further would appear strange."

"Yes I see that," Betsy spoke slowly, and he wondered if she really did.

"And as soon as possible, Betsy."

She looked at him, but he did not meet her stare. "You don't mean now?" she asked.

"I see no reason why not. There may be a few sprains and knocks from the topmen, but no ongoing patients that I cannot cope with. Go seek him out: he will be delighted."

Manning knew this was the time when she would either reject the story or start to willingly believe it. "You are certain?" she asked, her voice heavy and intense. "About Francis, I mean?"

"You know I cannot be positive."

"No," she said, considering. "No, of course not."

Once more they both considered this, and it was with effort that Manning finally spoke.

"Betsy, I feel it better that the child is William's." There could be no argument with that, and he found the words easily. "I would also predict that he will make an extremely fine father."

"I love him so much," she said, pushing her head forward in a way that was half imploring, half desperate. "And I should never do anything so foolish again, you have to believe that."

"It is not I who must believe anything," Manning replied almost sadly as he raised his head and finally looked straight at her. "The truth can be dangerous. It must be handled with caution. And sometimes is better used sparingly." Then their eyes met, there was a moment of mutual understanding, and Manning knew that he had won. "Now go tell William," he said.

* * *

It took them a considerable time, but all the French ships

had finally tacked and were now heading for the nearest British frigate. She had also turned, as if in her own length, and after adding royals, dug her stem into the waves and made off. Her speed reduced as soon as two other ships came into sight, and Bompart's fleet was even allowed to gain slightly. But at no time was the distance sufficient to bring the two squadrons to fighting range, and it was clear that it never would. Crowley was watching from the forecastle, his usual vantage point being useless with the British almost directly ahead. A number of officers had also gathered there, and he was not unduly surprised when Tone joined them. But it was Crowley that he singled out and drew into conversation.

"You're friends are running, as we would have predicted."

Crowley did not turn. "They are not my friends," he said softly.

"That's right." Tone agreed. "Your friends are safe in Portsmouth, and likely to remain so for as long as their ship stays in the dock."

This time he did look at the man. "How did you know?"

Tone gave a short laugh. "You may put that down to one of the advantages of the brotherhood," he said. "But enough; the British are finally on the run, that is all that need concern us for the moment."

"As you said, it was predictable."

"It was, but at last we are heading in the right direction." he lowered his voice. "Had matters been left to the commodore we would be half way to America by now."

The ship dipped, and a larger than average wave broke over her bow. The officers stood back and there was a smattering of laughter. The dark sea was crested white and the wind grew more ominous by the second.

"I should say we were back to trusting luck," Tone

continued, his voice still low. "If the weather grows worse, and we continue to chase, it is likely that damage will be caused. There are ten of us to be lost and only three of them, so we can afford to leave several of our own behind in order that they be caught. And if nothing happens the chase may even continue until our goal is in sight." He stopped to brush some spray from his coat, before looking up and into Crowley's eyes. "We are already that much nearer to our home soil, Michael. And Ireland itself is that much closer to becoming a free country."

CHAPTER NINE

It turned out to be a first rate autumnal gale. The wind whistled through *Scylla*'s taut lines, her canvas cracked and spars groaned as the ship beat her way into the very heart of the tempest. Banks was on deck, as he had been since the brief but useless interview with the fishermen. That had been some seven hours ago; now the evening was fast descending, and he knew it would be a sleepless night for them all.

Fraiser was at the binnacle making notes from the traverse board. It was likely the storm would last a good few days, with little chance of noonday sights. Nevertheless it remained his responsibility to plot the ship's position, and Banks was glad to have someone to hand with the competence and experience the sailing master possessed. Dead reckoning, using an estimation of the direction and speed of current and wind, was more an act of intuition than science, and Banks was not gifted in either discipline. But he could sail a ship through the strongest of gales, and was quite content to give the current task all of his attention and leave other capable men to their own speciality.

"Take a further reef in the topsails, if you please, Mr Chilton."

The lieutenant touched the brim of his sou'wester and bellowed for topmen. Banks had hoped to ride the weather out with a single reef, but the spars were starting to complain, and it would be foolish to suffer any unnecessary damage aloft, especially when speed and manoeuvrability were likely to be needed over the next few days. The men flowed up the shrouds and soon passed along the topsail yards. Then, with their weight resting mainly on their bellies, they began grabbing at the sodden canvas, pulling it upwards and towards them, and finally tying the excess back. It was another job that the captain would rather avoid, and he turned his attention away just as a shout came from the main masthead.

"Object in sight off the larboard bow." Banks could see the man pointing, but the horizon was completely dark. "It's a boat, a fisherman, or something similar," the look out continued. "'bout three cables off."

Banks walked forward to the break of the quarterdeck and peered into the gloom. Sure enough there was a shape just visible, although it was apparently drifting, without masts or canvas. He looked up to the yards; the last of the topmen were clear and most were already heading back to the deck.

"Heave to, Mr Chilton!"

The sighting was almost in the eye of the wind; it would be futile to do anything other than hold their place, and allow the storm to bring the vessel to them. The afterguard hauled the yards round and *Scylla*'s hull was swept to larboard. Banks crossed to the opposite side of the deck where the boat could be seen more clearly. It could hardly have been more than thirty feet in length, and had struck both masts. It was also well laden; two heavy crates were obvious amidships, and there were several bales, casks and sacks under a cover that was flapping wildly in the wind. Two men were visible in the sternsheets, but a second tarpaulin just forward of them might well have been sheltering more.

"Boat hooks, there!" Lewis, the master's mate, had joined him and was assessing the situation. "You, Crouch, ready when they come past; we don't want to do this twice."

A party of men were now hanging from *Scylla*'s fore and main chains, boat hooks extended, while further hands were ready with lengths of line. The boat was approaching quickly, and should actually collide with the frigate's hull. As soon as it did there would be about two or three seconds in which to secure the craft before the current and wind rushed it past. Banks watched as the small vessel drew closer. The men at her stern were in heavy oilskins and neither made any attempt to move forward to receive a line at their bow.

"Ready lads," Lewis was holding his hand up, gauging the moment to the second. The boat passed out of Banks's field of vision, and the master's mate cried out in the darkness. Those at the falls threw their lines while the seamen with boat hooks leaned down, almost out of sight. There was a brief moment of confusion, then someone gave a solid cheer and Lewis looked back at his captain.

"We have them, sir."

"Very good, have the passengers brought on board as fast as you can; the boat you may abandon." He had no intention of risking men's lives and slowing their passage further by attempting to take a heavily laden vessel in tow.

Lewis was bareheaded, but touched his forehead, and bent to bellow at the working party. Banks retreated to the binnacle. Hauling passengers aboard in the teeth of a gale was yet another task that was better left to someone else.

* * *

The storm had also reached the *Hoche* and she was making heavy weather of it. Even from his cramped hammock Crowley had the feel of the ship, and knew things were not right. He moved, nudging Doyle with his shoulder and hardly hearing his friend curse in his sleep. They had been below for at least eight hours; the storm had blown up in that time and Crowley sensed that it would stay with them a good while longer. He had no way of knowing what conditions were like on deck, but the ship had been badly managed from the start, and he didn't expect the recent change in the weather to have improved things. He swung his legs out and jumped down from his hammock. This time both Doyle and Doherty swore, but he had no ears for either. Making his way along the crowded orlop he could hear the pumps in action and knew that the ship's timbers must be straining painfully. A party of men were seated by the main hatchway that led to the deck above. There was a strong smell of wine in the air, and one was talking in an especially loud and high-pitched voice. Crowley supposed that fear was likely to effect people in different ways, and pushed his way through.

At the top of the steps a soldier was sitting with his back braced against a wooden post, clearly attempting to maintain some form of equilibrium in a vertiginous world. He noticed Crowley with surprise, shouted out a challenge and made as if to rise. The Irishman could not be bothered with the language, and roughly pushed him back down onto the deck. The private struggled up and caught hold of his arm. Suddenly all of the tensions and doubts of the last few weeks welled up inside, and Crowley glared pure venom at the man. "Leave me alone, you bloody frog," he hissed. His glance alone was enough to turn milk, and the soldier drew back. Crowley roughly shook the man's grip from his sleeve and continued.

There was no guard posted at the next hatchway and soon Crowley was on deck. He was lacking both coat and hat, and the spray stung his skin, but strangely the Irishman did not feel in the least cold. He looked about. Men were sheltering under the gangways, and there were four hanging grimly to the wheel. The *Hoche* was showing topsails without reefs: it was far too much canvas for such conditions, and the spars and shrouds were under great strain. He approached the quarterdeck steps and climbed half way up. Apart from the men at the wheel only one other was near to the binnacle. He was crouched down, seeking what shelter he could from the lee of the mizzen mast, and so soundly wrapped in oilskins as to be unrecognisable. Crowley waved his hand, but the man ignored him. Swearing softly he made his way up and lurched across the deck in a series of short but carefully timed bursts.

"You must take in the sail," he yelled, his face inches from the man's covered face. "Take in the sail" he repeated. "*Descendez la voile!*"

There was no sign of recognition in the eyes; disgusted, Crowley moved on and was about to start back for the waist when another oilskin encased body emerged from the officer's companionway. Crowley waved, and he drew closer.

"Too much sail!" Crowley shouted, and this time the man responded. Staring up at the tophamper he brought a metal call to his lips and blew a long blast. Soon men were appearing from the waist and forecastle and stood waiting for instructions. The ship gave a sudden lurch, and there was an ominous crack from higher up on the mainmast. There was very little time, and without further thought Crowley made for the windward gangway.

He had reached the weather mainmast shrouds, swung himself out, and was starting the climb to the maintop before he even realised others were following. The shrouds were iron tight, but each ratline hung loose beneath his bare feet. It was several months before that Crowley had last climbed aloft and probably years since he had done so during a storm. His muscles ached and he knew that he was not in practice. Still, as he reached the futtock shrouds, his instincts kept him safe. He swiftly transferred himself to the topmast shrouds and was making reasonable progress when the mast gave another loud crack. Then the sail in front of him grew slack, and a line whipped passed his head. For a moment he considered descending to the maintop. He glanced down, but there were men behind: he must continue.

A shout came from the quarterdeck; the ship was heaving

to, but Crowley knew they had to make the yard and get that sail in. Then he was at the crosstrees, and the topsail yard was immediately within reach. Reaching up he pulled himself onto the wooden beam, his feet finding purchase on the footrope. Another man was following, and there were several after that.

The ship was still lurching violently in the storm, with every movement amplified by the height of the yard. He made his way along, resting after every third or fourth foot. His belly protested at the unexpected exertion, but soon he was in position, and there appeared to be enough with him to handle the sail. Leaning forward he grabbed at the canvas. It was wet and heavy, and several of his nails broke as he brought it up. But he made progress, and there were others next to him being as successful. For a moment he drew breath, the call had been close, but it looked like they had acted in the nick of time. And it was then that it happened.

The ship had turned slightly, but a freak gust of wind caught them at just the wrong angle. The main topsail suddenly snatched itself from the grip of the topmen and billowed out to leeward. Crowley felt himself tugged sideways, and grabbed at the yard for support. Another loud crack, and more lines parted. Then the entire topmast began to fall.

He had known he was going even before the spar started to tilt. Beneath him was the torrid sea, and next to that an unforgiving deck. The water might at least cushion his fall, but once down he could expect no rescue, and would be drowned for certain. The mast slipped further, and he felt himself slide down the smooth wood of the topsail yard. The man to his left let out one desperate cry before disappearing into the gloom and Crowley knew that their time was all but spent. A line passed him by and instinctively he made a grab for it, winding the rope about his forearm. It felt like standing rigging and snaked down from the foremast: probably the topgallant mast stay. Without thinking he released his grip on the spar and felt it fall away from beneath him. His weight was now entirely on the stay, and he dropped and swung violently towards the foremast. The wind caught him: for a moment he was floating in the rain filled air, then he felt himself pushed against the foremast shrouds. Crowley snatched at them; he was on the leeward side and they were dangerously slack, but still offered support. Releasing the line, he clambered onto the shrouds, his feet gratefully resting on the ratlines. To his right the main topmast was now hanging at a crazy angle, but he had found safety at least, and slowly began to climb down to the deck.

"Well that was quite a sight, Michael." It was Doyle, last seen snug and warm in his hammock ten, maybe fifteen minutes before. "Few of us can say they climbed the main, only to come down the fore." There were further men on deck now, and the broken topmast was being lowered in a tangle of line and canvas. Whistles screamed and there were shouts and calls, but Crowley took no notice. He reached the deadeyes and swung himself inboard, landing with a stagger on the heaving deck. His friend caught him, and they both laughed for a second, then Doyle's eyes grew serious.

"What is it with you?" he said. "You're shivering fit to raise the devil."

Crowley went to speak but somehow the words would not come.

"Go aloft in just a shirt, Michael? Man, you're lucky not to catch your death."

* * *

As soon as she heard there were women amongst the rescued Betsy Clarkson claimed them as her own.

"You poor dears, let me take you below, and get you warm." The older of the two women readily took her arm and both were guided through the dark decks, past the interested gaze of the watch below, and into the sick bay where Betsy closed the door, adjusted the lantern, and began to bustle with a small spirit stove.

"There," she said when it was finally alight. "Let's have those dreadful wet clothes off and get you properly dry. We will have no men hereabouts, apart from maybe my husband and Mr Manning," she said, considering for a moment. "But they're both surgeons so don't count."

The women, one considerably older than the other, peeled off their sodden dresses and undergarments and gratefully rubbed themselves dry with the coarse woollen towels that Betsy provided.

"I can't do much for you until this wretched storm abates," she said, heaving up a bundle of clothing from a nearby locker. "But you may have the surgeon's watchcoats for now, and these will keep you decent."

"Pray do not trouble yourself," the older one announced as she regarded the seamen's duck trousers and cotton tops that Mrs Clarkson began laying out with disdain. "I have plenty of dry clothing in our boat."

"Oh I am certain something more suitable can be found by and by," Betsy reassured her. "Mrs Porter, the boatswain's wife, is about your size," she said. Then, regarding the younger woman, "And I about yours."

She was indeed very similar to Betsy Clarkson, both in age and height, though her damp hair looked far darker, almost black, in fact. She smiled readily, slipped a vastly oversized watchcoat over her bare shoulders, and picked up the seamen's clothes with obvious interest.

"I shall not mind wearing these for a spell, mama," she said, holding them at arms' length and smiling appreciatively. "Quite like the night suits uncle brought back from his last trip to the East."

The older woman sniffed, and draped a watchcoat about her

as if fearful of allowing the rough fabric to touch any part of her skin. "Well, you won't find me wearing trousers; get my things from the boat, young lady."

Betsy looked concerned. "I'm afraid I do not have them, and rather think your boat has been abandoned."

"Abandoned?" The woman was clearly astounded. "But it held all we have in the world. All that we could rescue from those murderous thieves, that is."

"I will check to be sure, but we are in rather a severe storm at present."

As if in support *Scylla* gave a particularly heavy lurch to one side. Clearly she was back on the wind, and not faring too well. The women sensed this and looked about in alarm; the ship started to heel almost immediately, and a trickle of water ran down one of the bulkheads.

"You needn't worry over that," Betsy chuckled. "The old girl always weeps a bit in bad weather."

"Well, I must say this is preposterous," the woman snarled. "We have been plucked from the sea, separated from all our possessions, and now find ourselves on a leaking boat. I demand to speak with the captain forthwith." She stopped, realising her current state of undress, and added, "That is, just as soon as you have found me something more suitable to wear."

* * *

"That boat contained nearly everything that I value," the man told him crossly. He was holding a steaming cup and wearing one of Banks's own dressing gowns. His damp hair was clogged with old powder and hung in clumps that swung about with each movement, taking much of the sting from his apparent anger. "Damned near everything I owned; all else is left behind. I trust you have good reason for your action, captain?"

Banks said nothing for a moment. To have been rescued at sea in such conditions would usually bring forth a very different reaction. It was quite clear the man was either mad or considered himself highly important, and in either case he was not used to being treated with anything other than fawning respect.

"It would have been impossible to secure your boat, sir," the captain said finally. "But I trust that you and your passengers are safe, and would prefer to be aboard this ship than left in the ocean?"

"Damn your impertinence, sir; I have every right to expect assistance from one of his Britannic Majesty's ships. It is why you let my possessions go that riles me."

"I regret no more could be done in the circumstances, but at least your family are safe, as well as their servants."

"Servants? They are naught but a couple of fishermen from the village and can go to hell for all I care: nothing more than pigs, the both of them. If they knew more about their duties and treated their betters with a deal more respect we wouldn't be in this mess." His gaze had wandered from Banks and was roving about the cabin. "As if the damned rebels aren't bad enough, I have to put up with a couple of palaverers in my own employ."

The ship's motion was increasing. Banks knew his place was on deck, rather than speaking with an ungrateful old man, and stood up from his chair.

"Well, I am glad to have been of service, and look forward to escorting you back to dry land in due course."

"Dry land? I wish to go to Galway, sir. There we have friends and family who will aid us. You will take us now, and as fast as you are able."

Banks stopped on his way to the door and gave one short sharp laugh. "I regret, that will not be possible."

The man regarded him over the brim of his cup. "I do not

wish to pull rank on you, sir, but I happen to be a magistrate; I also have some very influential friends who would be more than happy to ruin the career of a simple Navy captain. Now put this boat about and we will make no more of it."

"I repeat, that will not be possible; you will excuse me, I am needed on deck."

The man spilt his drink as he stood, and actually took a step towards Banks. "You, sir, are an imbecile. You will do as I ask without delay."

Banks spun round, his face suddenly revealing the anger that had been growing steadily. "I will not, and if you continue to make unreasonable requests I shall have little choice but to strike you below. Now forgive me, sir, while I attend to the business of my ship."

* * *

In the galley they were having more luck. The two fishermen were being entertained by Barrow, Rose and Parfrey, who had sought them out through curiosity rather than any direct order. The men, who had been given dry clothes by the purser, had already eaten one full plate of lobscouse each, and were just starting on their second helping of plum duff. The junior officers accepted their appetites as being perfectly normal in any circumstances, and were gradually prising the story from them as they ate.

"We struck the masts as soon as the storm began," the older man, who appeared to be the father, was explaining. "Old man Monroe had laden us down so far it weren't possible to attend to the boat. It seemed like riding it out was the best option, but we failed to allow for the current that took us straight out to sea."

"How long had you been travelling?" Barrow asked.

"Four days," the son replied. He was a well built lad, slightly older than Parfrey, and had his father's dark red hair. "Four days and four nights, and it weren't the nicest of experiences, I can tell you."

"Why were you carrying so much?" Parfrey had been one of those assisting the passengers aboard, and knew how low in the water and heavily laden the small boat had been.

"It was Monroe," the older man told him, as if that was all the explanation necessary.

"He wanted to get everything aboard," the second expanded. "With no ideas of how a boat will swim."

"Well he's lost it all now," the father said with more than a hint of satisfaction. "Be a lucky man what finds that little lot washed up on the beach."

"What were you carrying?"

"The crown jewels," the father replied. "Or you would think so to hear how the old goat went on. Not a care for his wife or daughter, just had to keep the bloody paintings dry and not break any of the china."

"A strange cargo," Rose commented.

"Aye, an' there was silver as well. Not plate mind, the real stuff. My, he's going to be one unhappy man when he finds out."

"Look, I don't understand." Barrow said. "How did you come to be in the middle of the Atlantic with half a shop full of household goods aboard?"

The father eyed him with an amused twinkle in his eye. "Well, it wouldn't have done to leave it now, would it? Our Mr Monroe is not the most popular of men in the village; it was either take it and run, or just run. If he had stayed another day the old codger would have ended up hanging from a tree, or stuck so full of pike holes he'd have never enjoyed another glass of port in his life."

"You mean the rebels would have killed him?" Rose asked,

aghast.

"Them or the French, it wouldn't have mattered which. We would never have agreed to take him, but he was offern' more than I shall earn the rest of my life, and a man's got to make a living."

"I don't see how the frogs come into this," Barrow said, then his eyes widened as the awful truth dawned. The father looked at him as if he was especially stupid.

"Why, haven't you heard?" he asked. "The French have landed."

Chapter Ten

Before long they were free of the storm and *Scylla* was once again moving with a spirit of purpose. As soon as he could, Banks had increased sail, adding royals and jibs to topsails, driver and forecourse. The wind was on their beam and fitful, but they were making a credible speed with a white cream of spray showing occasionally at her bow as the ship pressed through the still heaving waves. Once Fraiser had set course for the coast of Donegal a council of war had been called and the officers met in the great cabin, aware that something of importance had been learned and ready to hear the full story.

"The French have landed, but it does not appear to be the fleet we are looking for." As Banks spoke he observed his officers carefully, noting the subtle reactions each gave to the news. Many captains would have saved such a tasty piece of information to build up the speech and, in turn, their own importance, but Banks had no time for such tricks.

"A small ship has been spotted near Arranmore Island," he continued. "Last seen it was anchored in the sound, and is carrying troops and supplies. It is also rumoured that a certain James Napper Tandy is aboard. For those who are not aware, Tandy was one of the founders of the United Irishmen."

There were nods and grunts from the assembled officers and someone gave a low whistle; Tandy was well known to them all and would be an ideal candidate to kindle another revolutionary fire in Ireland.

"You will be aware that my informant is Mr Monroe, a local magistrate. He took to his heels as soon as the news emerged, so cannot be relied upon for more, but I think the story credible enough for further investigation. Of course we cannot tell from whence Tandy came, or if his force is the spearhead for a far greater body of men, possibly even the fleet for which we are currently searching. And chances are strong that he knows nothing about the recent French defeats. However, I consider it vital that we close with his ship, before he has the chance to become properly established. From what I gather the country is still ripe for revolution, and he is likely to find loyal sympathisers near at hand."

More nods, and Caulfield added a hushed "Yes." If Tandy intended to recruit men from the local population it would take time. The faster *Scylla* and her marines could intervene, the smaller the enemy they would fight.

"Mr Fraiser tells me the invasion point is approximately a hundred miles from our current position. Tandy has several days start on us; by the time we arrive he may well have set up a bridgehead or, of course, the military might have dealt with him. But in any event we will be making that our primary objective."

There was a unanimous nodding of heads, and Banks felt mildly relieved. Diverting to the northwest coast of Ireland was hardly disobeying instructions; by now the French invasion fleet may even be anchored there. But *Scylla* would have little chance of keeping their watch over the Atlantic while making detailed investigations of Arranmore Island. He turned to Westwood.

"We will be landing your men, Captain; they are ready, I am certain."

"Indeed, sir." The marine beamed back, clearly eager to get to grips with an enemy that was likely to outnumber his own small force several times over.

"Very good." His attention switched to the first lieutenant. "Mr Caulfield, we will also need a party of seamen; suitable hands must be found, and told off, and all boats checked."

"Do you envisage a night landing, sir?" Caulfield asked. It would be the safest way with a small body of men when the surrounding area was thought to be hostile. *Scylla* might even attempt to stay out of sight, and send her boats in for the greatest element of surprise.

"Initially I think a small force to reconnoitre, but a lot will depend on the hour we arrive," Banks told him. "I certainly do not intend to waste time. The last I heard Lord Cornwallis and the majority of the Army were a good distance to the south. It is quite possible that they are unaware of Tandy's ship, and taking no action at all. As I see it, our mission will be to deliver a force powerful enough to keep them at bay, then take *Scylla* to raise the alarm." That made sense, even if the ship would end up sailing with a skeleton crew, and with every likelihood of meeting a powerful enemy.

"So, gentlemen, if there are no further questions, I suggest we adjourn and make what preparations we can." Banks looked once more at the assembled company, and found he was more than satisfied. *Scylla* might not be a line-of-battle ship, and doubtless there were officers and men who could be considered more experienced elsewhere. But he felt he had forged a reasonable weapon to use against the enemy, wherever and whenever they finally met.

* * *

"Mr Fraiser said to tell you all that he will resume the taking of noon sights today, and regular navigation classes are to be reinstated at two bells, afternoon watch."

The announcement, which had been practised several times on the journey down, brought forth a series of moans from the occupants of the midshipmen's berth, while Parfrey just looked relieved after successfully delivering his message. Most of the lads were still in their hammocks, but Barrow, who had risen, sat at the mess table sipping Scotch coffee, and Rose was by the washstand scraping a dry razor over his completely hairless chin. "How's the weather topside?" The latter asked.

"Storm's passed, and there's a touch of sun, though Mr Fraiser says it will go soon, more'n like." Parfrey was in no rush to return to the deck. "Boatswain's having a look at the forestays, there's a party caulking the forecastle again, an' the passengers are up on the quarterdeck an' gettin' in everyone's way. Oh yes, and there is something else," he added with an air of drama.

"Well, come on, spill." Barrow looked up and even Rose paused in his shaving. Parfrey's eyes grew large, and his voice more confidential. "One of the passengers is dressed like a man."

At first there was no reaction, then Barrow's bored voice sounded from just above his cup. "And is it a man?" he asked.

"No," Parfrey told them, disappointed and mildly confused. "No, it's a young lady. But she's got a seaman's rig on. Duck trousers, shirt – only thing missin' is an 'at."

"That don't sound right," Barrow shook his head. "Women dressed as men: passengers dressed as hands. Where will it end?"

"Are you sure they are seamen's clothes?" Rose asked.

"Certain." Parfrey was emphatic.

Barrow sighed. "Well I'm afraid that won't do at all. You'd better go straight back and tell her to take them off immediately."

"Very good," Parfrey said, and left.

* * *

Mr Dudley, the purser, and marine lieutenant Adshead had

given up their cabins in the gunroom to the Monroe family. Dudley had lost more than his accommodation; the fat and spoilt gunroom tabby had transferred her allegiances to Sarah, the magistrate's daughter. She provided a far more accommodating lap than the bony old purser, and the two had been almost inseparable from the start.

On the first evening following the storm both of the older Monroes had been invited to dine with the captain in his quarters on the deck above, and Sarah was sitting quite contentedly stroking the cat at the gunroom table when King came in from the second dog watch.

"Have you eaten?" King asked, as he handed his watchcoat to a steward and took a seat opposite her.

"Yes, and very well, thank you," the girl smiled.

King stared for a moment at the plate of stewed beef that had been placed before him before helping himself to a biscuit from the pewter bowl. "I expect there would have been better fare with the captain," he said, still looking at his food.

"I have spent four days and nights in a small boat with my parents," the girl said deliberately. "Doubtless they will find much to discuss with Sir Richard, though I am just a little tired of their company at present, and really found that beef to be quite pleasant."

"Do you live at home?" King was absent-mindedly tapping his biscuit as he stirred the stew with his spoon. She shook her head.

"No, with my brother and his wife in Sussex. I had come back for a visit just before the troubles erupted in May, and it was considered prudent for me to stay, rather than risk travelling home alone."

King glanced at her surreptitiously between mouthfuls. She was young, certainly no more than twenty-five, with a pleasant, clear complexion, attractive eyes and a compelling, lively personality. It seemed strange that one so blessed should be lodging with a sibling – usually the role of a widow or an old maid. "Is Ireland not to your taste?" he asked.

"Oh no, Ireland is very much to my taste." She leant back in her chair and began to stroke the cat's head. "It is indeed the most beautiful of countries. But I am afraid I cannot condone the way it is ruled and, in particular, my father's method in that respect."

"I see," King had heard a little of the overbearing manner in which land owners and law enforcers were rumoured to assert their powers. "That must make things rather difficult."

"It has been the hardest six months I can remember," she said. "Each one of us has been frightened for our lives on a number of occasions, though I must confess the uprising was suppressed for a long time, and had to be expected. The final adventure was that dreadful boat trip; we were so grateful that you pulled us from the sea as you did. And that is all of us, Mr King; my parents included, though I predict that you may not hear as much from their own mouths."

"They do come across a mite resentful," he gave a wry grin. "But then I suppose it must be difficult, leaving most of your possessions behind,"

"Yes, and then the small amount that we had taken was lost as well."

"Indeed."

"It was father's own fault," her voice was surprisingly cold. "Dungloe, where we live, could have been an absolute heaven. But for forty years he has bullied and intimidated his way about the place, making it hell for all, and himself the most unpopular person in the county. I was somewhat aware when growing up; the only friends I could make were the sons or daughters of other landowners, and the townspeople's resentment was unmistakeable. My brother left first and it was only when I became twenty-one, and stayed with him in England, that I was able to take a more dispassionate view. As soon as I did I had no wish to ever go back, and had been putting off visiting my parents for years."

"England is hardly a fair country," King said. "There is injustice and iniquity a plenty."

"But more in Ireland." Her eyes were a deep brown, and it was a little sad to see them quite so serious. "Much more, in fact; I could not stand to live there a moment longer, and will not return while the system remains."

"Well, I'd chance that the events of this year will see it altered."

"Absolutely: there will be revolution, that is certain. And it will happen with or without the help of the French."

"Revolution?" King's eyebrows rose in alarm.

"Oh, only in the strictest sense." She smiled suddenly. "Change is a better word, I suppose. But you are right, the old order must go. There is talk in London of Ireland being adopted into the Union, a true United Kingdom: all the British Isles under one common rule. I think it would be for the best, though there are those who do not, and are willing to fight to prevent it." She sighed. "And more yet willing to fight for other reasons. It seems that whatever the aim, it cannot be achieved without killing. Yet, as I have said, Ireland is such a beautiful place."

King was sorry to hear one as young and naturally vivacious speak in such a way. The woman was clearly no fool, and totally sincere in what she said, although he found it hard to accept that his countrymen could have behaved so very badly in a country so close to their own shores.

"And you will return to Sussex, when this is over?"

"I fully intend to, though I gather that the time might be a while in coming. We are heading back for Arranmore are we not?"

"We are."

"What do you think we shall find there?"

King shook his head. "That is difficult to say. The ship you saw may well be the first of many; an invasion force perhaps. If others, possibly the fleet that we have been sent to find, have been successful in joining them, they will probably be established by now. Lord Cornwallis is many miles to the south, but eventually he will hear of it, and must bring the invaders to battle. In which case..." he hesitated.

"In which case it would not be a healthy spot to land a family of civilians. Especially those who are already deeply unpopular with the local population."

"That is so."

She gave a dry smile. "I cannot help but think it unhealthy for us, even if the French have not been reinforced. With the rising in May, many of the townsfolk started to regard father with open hostility. It was as if they suddenly realised the power they held. Two of his barns have been burnt down this summer, one just the week before last, when it was full. There have been many other instances of sabotage and hardly a tree is left that has not been robbed of its branches for pike shafts. As soon as news of the French landing came, he ran; that will not have gone unnoticed: father will be marked, but then I would have given very little for his chances of seeing Christmas should he have chosen to stay."

"Is he aware?" King wondered just how far a man might fool himself.

"Oh yes, he knows and is frightened, though you might not guess so from his manner. We were heading for my aunt in Galway; she is married to a farmer there, but father did not intend to remain for long. He wants to quit the country entirely, and frankly I think it would be best for him if he did."

"Probably best for Ireland as well."

They both laughed, and King finished up the last of his stew. "Will you take coffee?" he asked. "The gunroom has a store and it is hardly used."

"Thank you no, I will retire shortly, but may take a turn on deck first, if I can persuade this foolish cat to move." The animal made a complaining noise as Sarah raised her briefly in the air, before settling once more against the girl's breast. "I am sorry if I have depressed you with my talk," she said rising from her chair. "I know I am one to get carried away: my brother is always telling me of it. Not a suitable manner for a lady, he says."

"Not suitable?"

She stopped on the way to the gunroom door. "Yes, you should hear him on the subject," she said. "Women are purely for decorative purposes apparently, and not expected to carry thoughts, let alone give any clue as to what they may be."

King considered this as she left the room. There were two women in his life; his fiancée, Juliana and Manning's wife, Kate. Both were very ready to hold opinions, and extremely keen and able to voice them. He supposed he must just be especially fortunate.

* * *

Chilton and Fraiser had been given the red cutter and a crew of eight. There were no marines; a detachment could have been taken but both felt the extra men would only have got in the way. Besides, if they were to run into the French it would need more than half a dozen bootnecks to fight their way free.

Scylla had reached the coast off Arranmore Island at twilight – the ideal time – and was lying hove to several miles off shore. On arrival she would have been hardly visible to even the sharpest lookout and should now be totally concealed. The moon was due to rise in three hours; they had that time to send the small boat in and inspect the area. A fleet at anchor would be obvious, and if the French had been and gone after recently landing an army, that should also be relatively easy to spot. In both cases Chilton would simply turn about and head back for *Scylla*, if necessary waiting for the moon to make her easier to find. Then Banks would be left with the decision of whether to stay and keep watch over the enemy, or make haste, either to find Warren's squadron, or head south and raise the alarm. The other worrying option was if the army had already departed; they could be many miles away by now, possibly even bearing down on an unsuspecting Cornwallis. The only means to establish that would be to land, although such an operation could not be staged tonight. He had already decided that a proper landing party must be readied, to be well supported by the ship, and with their full contingent of marines.

But before any of that could happen Fraiser had to concentrate on getting the small boat around the numerous islands and inlets, while Chilton made notes of the military and naval forces *Scylla* would have to overcome. It would not be an easy task, and the chances of being captured by the French were extremely high, but then all in the small boat had volunteered for the duty. An undertaking such as this was what attracted the officers to volunteer for the Navy in the first place, whereas most of the men would have originally been pressed into service. But then all were already an integral part of *Scylla* and her crew, and positively relished the excitement of a clandestine mission. Besides, on that particular evening there were none of them with anything better to do.

* * *

Banks was waiting for them on the quarterdeck. The sea was quite still and only a gentle breeze hummed through her lines as *Scylla* drifted aimlessly in the quiet night. At every bell or so the officer of the watch would bring her back to the wind and regain the position she had been holding when the boat departed, although it was more a gesture of goodwill than anything else. The sky was still clear and as soon as the moon rose it should be a simple task for both vessels to spot the other and rendezvous.

Quite what he would do with the news they brought was a problem Banks had yet to solve. To send word of a landing might be regarded as completely futile, and would mean taking the only available warship away from the enemy. They may even sail while he was gone, and go wherever they wished untracked. But to stay and attempt to blockade what probably constituted a vastly superior force was also a dangerous course. For all his pride and love for her, *Scylla* remained a thirty-eight gun frigate. She might account for one, maybe two ships of a similar size, but could do nothing to stop a determined enemy of ten or more. The captain was also bitterly aware that whatever decision he came to would later be judged with all the luxury of hindsight. Few would allow for the dilemma he now faced, or give credit for taking the initiative that had already put him off Arranmore Island in the first place.

The bell rang again and King, who had the watch, ordered the helm over. The ship's sails filled and *Scylla* was just starting to pick up speed when a figure appeared at the top of the quarterdeck steps. It was the young Monroe girl. She was wearing a dress, presumably borrowed from one of the other women, and carrying the gunroom's cat. Banks stiffened. He ought to have remembered; she had appeared on deck at roughly this time yesterday evening: clearly either the girl, or the cat, or both were creatures of habit. He had managed to avoid them both then, and supposed he would have to do so now, although it was damned inconvenient, as he really wished to be present when Chilton and Fraiser returned.

Damned inconvenient: what was he thinking of? Was he the captain of the ship, or some little strumpet he had fished from the sea? He might find the opposite sex difficult to deal with, but that need not mean it was he who should necessarily leave. Why, he might have her struck below, if the thought appealed. Confine her to the gunroom, or even have her placed in irons. He found he was smiling quietly to himself, knowing that he could no more have given such an order than personally carry it out, and when the girl broke off from a brief conversation with King and approached, the expression unaccountably remained.

"It is a clear night for observations, Sir Richard," she said, stroking the cat and peering out towards the invisible shore.

Banks nodded politely. "I am hopeful they will return before long." He considered checking his watch, but that might convey anxiety; besides, he was well aware of the time. Once again the damnable signs of awkwardness were starting to appear, and Banks began to think of ways to end the conversation.

"I used to sail about here with the fishing fleet. That was when Mr O'Malley's father was in charge, and I was but a child. It is really very beautiful in the daytime."

"If you have knowledge of the waters, ma'am, it might have been prudent to mention it before."

She smiled, ignoring the stiffness in his tone. "No, that was many, many years ago; I have not been welcome for some time. We live very different lives hereabouts; there is little socialising between Irish and English."

"So I have been led to believe." This really was impossible, he must think of an excuse to leave before he made an utter fool of himself.

"Where is your home, Sir Richard?"

The question took him by surprise, and it was with an effort that he formed an answer.

"I – we, my family have a London house," he said at last. "And another in the country."

"Whereabouts?"

" Lombard Street."

"And that in the country?"

"Berkshire." He knew his answers were clipped, stilted and unhelpful; surely she would take pity and let him be?

"I have never been there, nor indeed to London. My brother has a house in Hailsham; I believe rope is made for the Navy there?"

"So I understand." He opened his mouth, searching for something more to say, but the words would not come; eventually he was forced to foolishly repeat the phrase. His skin tightened, and he hoped the evening light would be hiding his blush.

"Would you mind holding Sophie, captain?" He almost visibly jumped; the girl was offering up the damned cat for him to take. "If you would be so kind; I must attend to something."

He took the creature in his hands, being careful not to crush the tender body. The thing was warm and vibrating, and quickly made itself comfortable against the broadcloth of his uniform whilst the girl fumbled at a pocket in her dress. Banks instinctively made a soft reassuring sound; he supposed he must have held a cat before, but could not remember an exact instance, and knew that he was doing so now rather clumsily. The cat, on the other hand, seemed perfectly at ease, and was soon purring softly against his chest. It was an oddly soothing sensation.

Then the girl sneezed; it was quite loud and most unladylike. Thankfully her handkerchief was ready, and they both laughed, although Banks noted that the cat had stopped purring and dug its claws into his jacket.

"I am so sorry," she said, after blowing her nose. "I don't know what came over me."

"That's quite all right, ma'am." It would be time to hand the cat back, although the woman was apparently in no hurry to take it.

"Please, Sir Richard. You must call me Sarah," she said, replacing her handkerchief. "That is, if it does not offend any protocol?"

"Indeed not," he was a little easier now. "And I am Richard."

She acknowledged him as if they had just been introduced, although Banks felt as if he had known her far longer. The cat was purring again, and he found himself stroking the head in a tentative manner that was clearly appreciated.

"Would you take the cat back?" he asked.

"No," she replied, and her eyes flashed wickedly. "I think you should hold her; she likes you."

"Oh, I prefer dogs," he said, scratching the thing under its chin. "And then mainly for hunting."

"There is no reason why you should not like both." He noticed that she was smiling at him, almost laughing in fact, and it was with a great effort that he did not join her. "And the cat," she said, "has a name: she is Sophie."

* * *

On board the *Hoche* they had been busy. The main topmast had a crack midway along its length that was not possible to fish or, as the French would have it, to *jumelle* with any degree of certainty. They carried very few spare spars and the only one in any way suitable was shorter and, in Crowley's estimation at least, far too light for the task. Nevertheless it had been set in place; the battleship's main now boasted a reefed topsail, and could even set a small mizzen royal if called upon. Their speed was significantly slower, however, forcing the frigates to be called back to protect them, although the damage had also proved helpful in a strange and unexpected quarter.

Bompart now showed no further desire to keep up the pretence, and as soon as they were under way again, steered to the northwest, a direct course that would take them to Ireland with the least possible trouble. The shadowing British duly followed, but one had also lost a topmast, and the French were actually extending their lead when further dark clouds appeared as evening was about to fall.

"Aye, we're on for another," Doyle said as they took the night time air. "Let's hope it is a little more kindly this time."

Crowley could only agree. In helping to rig the replacement topmast the Irish had already revealed themselves as competent sailors, something that was almost as rare in the French fleet as spare spars. Consequently they were no longer required to stay cramped on the orlop deck, and could roam the ship pretty much as they wished. The downside to this freedom was regular sail drill and other work aloft alongside their French colleagues, most of whom lacked both their skill and experience. And all were very well aware that the Irish would be kept extremely busy if the storm proved anything other than a minor squall.

Walsh sauntered over. Although no seaman, he had benefited from his friends' improved status and was self-consciously wearing a French military coat that was slightly too large for his scrawny body.

"Well look at what the cat dragged in," MacArthur said as he approached. "Found yourself a decent piece of cloth did you, Liam? Why don't you have it cut into a coat?"

"The cold was starting to get to me, so they've given me this a touch early." Walsh informed them, pulling the garment into place and smoothing the fabric about him. "They'll be handing out the uniforms to one an' all tomorrow morning. And there'll be cutlass and pike drill straight after."

"No muskets?" MacArthur asked.

"No," he said a little stiffly. "I find we are not to be trusted with muskets."

"How's that then?" Doherty and Doyle said almost in unison.

"It would seem there's been trouble in the past allowing untrained men firearms. They get their charges stuck halfway down, then bash the barrels on the ground and bend them to buggery."

"Give us a decent drill, and it shouldn't be a problem," MacArthur said, somewhat aggrieved.

"I'm only tellin' you like it is," Walsh replied. "Pikes and cutlasses, first thing in the forenoon watch."

"That's if the storm doesn't break first?" Doyle said sagely.

"Storm? Is there another due?"

"I'd say so," Crowley this time. "So why don't we all go and kit oursel's out now? That way we might not catch our deaths afore we get there."

"I think we're going to have a swearin' first." Walsh said in a quieter tone. "That will be at first light, afore breakfast."

"Swearing?" Crowley was mildly alarmed.

"It's for anyone who has not taken the oath of brotherhood. Takes no longer than a couple of minutes, an' they'll be more likely to trust you with a warm coat afterwards."

"I don't hold with swearing," Crowley said defiantly. "I'm not taking no oaths, not for no country, nor no cause. I never have, an' I'm never going to."

Walsh regarded him with a look that was remarkably close to contempt. "I think you'll find you will," he said.

* * *

"Object in sight off the starboard beam."

Banks jerked himself back to the real world with a start. He and the girl had been talking by the taffrail for what must be almost an hour, and had quite forgotten about Fraiser and Chilton out in potentially enemy territory.

"What do you see there?" he asked, moving forward along the quarterdeck.

"Looks like our cutter, sir," the lookout replied. "They're under sail and makin' for us. I thinks I can see Mr Fraiser and Mr Chilton: yes, sure of it."

Banks had reached as far as the binnacle before he realised he was still holding the cat. "Here, take this," he said hastily passing it to Rose, the midshipman of the watch.

"Boat ahoy!" They must be travelling at speed, if they were already being hailed. The answer came back: there were officers aboard, and Banks made his way to the entry port to meet them.

Before long the boat was bumping against the frigate's hull, with Chilton and Fraiser standing in the sternsheets. The lieutenant was up first. As officially the senior officer it was consequently his privilege, even if it were doubtful as to who held the greater importance to the ship.

"What did you find?" Banks asked rather briskly as he helped him aboard.

"No sign of the French, sir." Chilton replied. "A complete lack of shipping in fact, apart from a few fishermen; very little evidence of life at all. Certainly no bivouac fires, or even excessive smoke from the cottages. We went as far as the village, but all was as silent as the grave."

Fraiser was up next, clutching a rolled up sheet of paper. "I've taken soundings, and would be happy to conn the ship into the bay, sir. There looks to be plenty of deep water, and a stable bottom."

Banks paused for a second. No enemy to fight and none apparently landed; it was the one option he had hardly considered. "Very good," he said hurriedly, moving to one side to allow the rest of the men to clamber on board. "You've all done very well, I am sure you can use a hot drink." He looked towards the duty midshipman who was still holding that darned cat. "See that the boat crew have something warm, Mr Rose."

The lad touched his hat a little awkwardly, then passed the animal into the waiting arms of Sarah, who had joined them.

Banks found himself smiling, both at the woman and the memory of their conversation. "It seems your visitors have fled," he said.

"Yes, I heard. It is good news."

He supposed it was, although he would have to continue to hunt them until they were found and brought to battle. "I should gather it will mean that you will wish us home," she continued.

That was another thought that had not occurred, and Banks gave this one as much consideration. Yes, in theory there would be nothing to keep the family in *Scylla*; they could return and see what was left of their home. Any trouble they might encounter with the local population would be a problem for the local militia, and certainly not his concern. In fact, he would probably never meet with any of them ever again. And then it came to him, quite suddenly, that it really wasn't very good news at all.

CHAPTER ELEVEN

"In the awful presence of God I, Patrick Chapman Doyle,"

"Do voluntarily declare that I will persevere in endeavouring to form..." Walsh prompted.

"Do voluntarily declare that I will persevere in endeavouring to form,"

"A brotherhood of affection amongst Irishmen of every religious persuasion..."

Doyle's voice droned on, repeating Walsh's words that all in the waist had already heard at least a dozen times that morning. The sun was hardly up, they had yet to eat breakfast, and most of the assembled men were fidgeting restlessly with little other than the next meal on their minds. But Crowley's thoughts were far more centred. He knew his long held aversion to formal swearing was both odd, and had been allowed to become far too important. He had no stated faith, rarely prayed, certainly did not consider himself a Christian. And he could cuss and curse with the best of them. But he still maintained a childlike belief in God, and felt physically unable to reconcile himself with any holy allegiance, especially one which he considered nothing more than a wild ideal cooked up by a fanatic.

The only time he could remember making a statement that entailed even a degree of commitment was at his first communion. That had been well over ten years ago when he was hardly at an age to make a reasoned choice. But this was a different story; the oath they were standing in line to swear was fundamental and far reaching. In a few carefully chosen sentences it totally revoked any loyalty he might have to his British friends, and allied him to a cause that he was not completely in favour of. More than that; despite any soft words to the contrary, Crowley knew he would be under a holy pledge to fight for that cause to the death. And it was a death that seemed increasingly likely in the current circumstances.

Doyle had finished now. He handed his groat to Walsh – another part of the proceedings that Crowley was unhappy about – and shuffled off to join the men waiting for breakfast. Tone was there, watching quietly from under the larboard gangway with one of the French military officers by his side. It would soon be over; Crowley had engineered himself the last place and was well aware that only MacArthur stood ahead of him, as Doherty began to say his piece. He looked about, eager for some distraction or emergency that might provide deliverance at the final moment, while wondering vaguely if the introduction of a false middle name, or even a subtle changing of the words would go unnoticed. But it was futile. He was too well known to his friends, and the lines had already been spoken so many times that the rote would have been ingrained on every man present. Doherty was coming to a close now, and in only a matter of minutes it would be his turn.

"Or give evidence against, any member or members of this or similar societies..."

The old fool was obediently repeating the phrases in a solid monotone that was tiresome to listen to. He reached the end, and felt in his pocket for the money, then there would only be MacArthur. Crowley waited, trying to resign himself to what was to come, when MacArthur failed to step forward.

There was a brief moment of confusion before Walsh lost his expression of bored compliance, and glared over in their direction.

"You're next," he grumbled, as keen to see his breakfast as

any man present, but MacArthur simply shook his head.

"I will not swear," he said, in a soft voice that might just as easily have been declining a second portion of plum duff. "I'll serve, and I'll fight, but I have a conscience and a faith. More than that, I have read my Bible and know that what you do is wrong."

Tone immediately drew away from the Frenchman; this was a private problem, and only of concern to the Irish.

"Your oaths are not for me," MacArthur clarified. "I have already made all the commitment necessary by being here."

"This is to bind us together," Walsh said. "To unite us all in one common brotherhood."

"And you need an oath for that? We are Irish: it ought to be enough." There was a smattering of laughter, and Walsh looked uncomfortably to Tone. "We are here, in another nation's warship," MacArthur continued, speaking up and to the crowd. "Sailing to fight against the English who have taken our land. There is no way out for us, no quick retreat; it isn't as if we can get out and walk."

Now the laughter was fuller and more general, and several small conversations had struck up, clearly in support of MacArthur.

"You speak of bonding together men of different faiths; well, my faith tells me that swearing and oaths are forbidden. In the book of Matthew, our Lord said 'swear not at all'. His word is good enough for me, and if you mistrust us so much, it is a wonder we have been brought so far."

There was silence now, and the atmosphere had grown tense. All looked to Tone, who actually appeared momentarily at a loss. Despite the call for toleration of religion, he was known to have a poor view of Papists, and was even suspected by some of having no faith at all. Then Tone moved forward and gave a grin that Crowley found frighteningly casual.

"If I may speak for a moment as a lawyer," he said, stepping into the centre of the deck. "And I can assure you that my opinion here will not cost a penny..." There was polite, but expectant, laughter: every man present was waiting to hear what he had to say.

"What you are taking now is not an oath at all, but an affirmation." MacArthur looked at him doubtfully and Tone continued, addressing the entire company as much as any one man. "It may have been called an oath, and God is certainly mentioned, but that is just for simple folk. Clever men, like MacArthur here, know the difference, though it is strange that he has not listened to the words carefully to have realised; Lord knows we have all heard them often enough."

Now the humour was more on his side, and he rode the wave with ease.

"Any one of you can take this vow, knowing in full it will not contradict your beliefs, religious or otherwise. Indeed, when I drew up the pledge, that was very much on my mind. And I would like to state yet again that the union of affection does not seek to discriminate, or disconcert any man or his faith." He turned back to MacArthur. "So now that you know; now that I have explained, will you affirm?" he asked.

"I will indeed," MacArthur said. "I should have no problem with that at all, now why would I?"

Tone nodded at Walsh who began to read once more. Crowley breathed a deep sigh of relief, conscious and eternally grateful for the last minute reprieve. An affirmation was totally different from a holy oath and, as far as he was concerned, did not contain any obligation that a man might worry about breaking. MacArthur was repeating the words obediently enough, having no trouble with any of the commitments or obligations they contained. And neither, Crowley decided, would he.

* * *

"No bottom, no bottom with this line."

Fraiser had been right, the sound had an excellent depth and would provide a first rate anchorage. They were considerably past Arranmore Island, and could shelter in its lee, whilst being close enough to both it and the mainland for a landing. The current also ran helpfully against them: *Scylla* was barely creeping forward under topsails alone, and could be halted at any moment.

"By the mark, fifteen."

That was more like it. The ship nosed forward a little further as the leadsman began to spin the line for another cast.

"By the deep, twelve."

Now it was starting to shallow; there seemed little point in delaying.

"Anchor, if you please, Mr Caulfield."

The first lieutenant gave the order: sheets were released, the stopper let go, and *Scylla*'s bower dropped into the placid waters of the sound.

"We shall remain at a single anchor," the captain announced. Mooring the ship at two might be more secure, but it was a relatively safe spot, and Banks still suspected that they might need to move off in a hurry. Fraiser was starting to take bearings while Caulfield backed the mizzen to increase the pull on the cable. Banks walked forward to the break of the quarterdeck and looked down at the assembled marines in the waist.

"Captain, you may begin to disembark your men."

Westwood gave a smart salute, while Adshead bellowed orders in a sharp and unpleasant nasal voice which Sergeant Rice quietly translated into commands the men could understand. The marines would provide the military might to secure a suitable landing point, then it would be a question of going ashore and seeing what was about. Banks singled out a midshipman.

"Pass the word for Mr Monroe; tell him we will be leaving presently."

The lad was off, and soon came back with Monroe, who was looking as cantankerous as ever. The magistrate carried with him the faint scent of brandy, and Banks guessed that he was not relishing the prospect of returning to his home soil. Both women were staying in the ship at the captain's orders. Sarah had done so without the least objection, and was now playing cards with young Parfrey in the gunroom. Mrs Monroe was not to be seen, and Banks found he cared little what had become of her.

The marines were now in both the pinnace and the launch, and it was quite a sizeable force. Banks watched as they set off for the nearest suitable landing stage and made the boats fast. He regarded the elderly man.

"If you are ready, Mr Monroe, we shall make our way."

The man grunted something unintelligible, but Barrow, who was in charge of the cutter, soon had him seated. Banks followed, and in no time they were heading for the shore.

A group of civilians had wandered down from the nearby village and were watching with interest. Westwood had his troops lined up along the small quay, and one man in particular was clearly waiting to meet with them as soon as they landed. Banks clambered from the boat, and strode on, ignoring the complaints from Monroe, who it appeared had managed to get his feet wet.

"Are there any members of the militia hereabouts?" Banks asked Westwood as he drew closer.

"Not that I can tell, sir." The marine's manner was crisp and businesslike. "If there are they have singularly failed to make themselves known, but that is not unusual with hobby soldiers."

"Very well."

The civilian cleared his throat. "If you'll excuse me, captain?" Banks turned to him; he was a small man with thinning red hair that was turning grey, and a hooked nose.

"There is no military in the immediate vicinity," he said in an accent that held a good measure of English, "that is British, Irish, or French for that matter; but a militia garrison is stationed nearby and in good communication; they might be raised at a few hours' notice."

"And you are, sir?"

"He's Foster, the postmaster," Monroe answered, as he stumbled up to them. His voice was thick and he was clearly having difficultly speaking and keeping upright simultaneously. "Calls himself an Englishman, yet sides with the Irish every time."

Foster regarded Monroe with interest. "I hadn't expected to see you hereabouts, Mr Monroe," he said softly. "Thought you had deserted us for good."

"I've come to see what is left of my property, if it is any of your business,"– the words were slurred and over loud – "though I expect it will be a wasted journey, once you and your paddy friends have finished with it."

"I have not been near Dungloe these last few weeks, Mr Monroe." Foster spoke with obvious control and Banks found himself warming to the man. "Indeed, there was far too much excitement hereabouts to venture further."

"We have heard of a French landing," Banks said. "Perhaps you could enlighten us?"

Foster regarded him seriously. "There is little to tell, sir."

"What of the ship?" Monroe demanded "The one with Napper Tandy aboard?"

"It sailed the following morning," Foster replied coldly. "As you would have discovered if your departure had been a little less hurried."

"Have you any idea where they were headed?" Banks asked.

"Not specifically, but they set off northwards."

"And did you make contact with them at all?"

"Aye, what plans did the two of you cook up?" Monroe added.

"I spoke with Napper Tandy himself, as well as his ship's captain, a fellow called Blanckman, and a General Rae." Foster switched his attention from the magistrate and focused entirely on Banks. "They had made a fast passage – from Dunkirk, or so I believe – but still were sadly ill informed, and knew nothing of the French defeat at Killala. It seemed that Tandy was convinced, but the other two not so. Fortunately I was able to produce British newspapers that had arrived only that day. With those as evidence I could persuade them their mission was futile."

"Very good," Banks told him. "And did they give any indication of their future plans?"Foster smiled. "That is exactly what the last Navy captain wanted to know."

"We are not the first?"

"*Cygnet* called here a few days after Tandy left; with luck they will be close on his tail."

Banks drew a sigh of relief. *Cygnet* was a hired cutter based at Belfast and would be in communication with that squadron. If she had already collected the information it freed him to continue to look for both the French and Warren's ships.

"Did Tandy attempt to raise the local population?"

The postmaster gave a short chuckle. "He tried for a spell, and those that were with him were certainly keen to continue. But we are tired of the French politics about here, and they made little progress."

"I see." That was also good. He regarded the man; English by the sound of him, and yet clearly comfortable and respected in the town, and still carrying out a responsible position of authority, whereas Monroe had needed to flee in fear of his life. Perhaps if there had been more Fosters and less Monroes they might not be in such a situation.

"Very well, Mr Foster; I can only thank you and, if there is nothing we can do to assist, we shall also be on our way."

"I'm glad to see that you at least will be in a different state to friend Napper Tandy, captain."

"How is that, sir?"

"He had need to be carried to his ship. Drunk as a lord, he was," Foster caught the eye of Monroe and his expression deepened. "Or should I say, drunk as a judge?"

* * *

The promised storm lasted all of three days but was less severe than the one that had taken their topmast. It also delivered a rare piece of good luck, something the French fleet had barely encountered on their mission so far. At dawn on the first peaceful morning, Crowley, Doyle and MacArthur were aloft inspecting the jury rig when the French lookout reported a clear horizon, and realisation slowly dawned on them all that the British had actually gone.

MacArthur shook his head and continued to scan the empty horizon, unable to believe what his eyes told him, while below the news was received with excited chattering by the rest of the men. But Crowley was silent; his attention remained totally set on the topmast fixings and he showed no visible sign of any emotion. The shadowing force might have left, and they were certainly free to continue for Ireland without hindrance, but strangely the good news came as no great surprise to him.

For most of his life Crowley had harboured the feeling that his path was somehow destined. No matter what the difficulty, he always seemed to be saved at the last moment. When the frigate he had been travelling in was taken on the last expedition it had looked like disaster, yet that was how he first met with King, and the others from *Pandora*. During both Camperdown and St Vincent he had remained safe while so many fell beside him. And in small matters, like his release from the press, and escaping the British when entering Brest; even with the recent incident of the falling topmast: he always managed to survive pretty much unharmed. In fact, good fortune had been such a close companion he was beginning to accept it with quiet grace. Were he a religious man he might even consider the possibility of a guardian angel, but Crowley was always quick to deny such superstitious nonsense and would never have lowered himself sufficiently to admit so much as a latent belief in any higher being.

Still the thought stayed with him, and actually gave a degree of reassurance in the present circumstances. It may even have helped him draw near to a decision that had been slowly forming for some time. In fact he was considering the matter at that moment, quietly contemplating the possible options while his two friends celebrated the current news with rather more volume.

"It would have been the second day," Doyle said, still staring out and grinning wildly. "We saw that frigate lose her rig."

"Aye," MacArthur agreed. "Belike the others stayed to assist, and we've outrun them all!"

It was certainly a viable theory, but Crowley did not feel the need to speculate further.

"That means we have them at our stern," Doyle clearly lacked any of Crowley's reticence. "And there is nothing between us and *Hibernia*."

"Nothing between us and Ireland," MacArthur said a little more more firmly; he for one wanted no confusion as to their destination.

"The British are gone!" Doyle said, almost to himself. "We'll be landing before we knows it!"

Crowley supposed they would. Certainly without the shadowing frigates the chances of meeting up with a superior force were very much smaller. And with so many ships stuffed to the brim with soldiers, they would be delivering an army that must surely set the whole of Ireland ablaze. But Crowley could gather no great enthusiasm for the news; he was forming plans of his own, and ironically the incident of the affirmation had been the final spur.

It had not been anything as binding as an oath; that was a step he would never have taken. But even the declaration he had made, a statement given without any true commitment and backed by nothing more than the breath in his lungs, even that had been too much. He had publicly allied himself to a cause that he was steadily losing any regard for, and he knew that his involvement must come to an end without delay.

The whole escapade had been a mistake from the start, he could see that now. There was no blame to be placed: he was quite sure that, if faced with any of the individual steps once more, he would take them just as readily. The fact remained, however, that this was not where he wanted to be, and he felt he owed it to himself, and his previous good fortune, to get away as soon as a chance presented.

It must be during the landing. He had a rudimentary knowledge of the country, and would be a poor sort of seaman if he weren't able to slip off during the confusion that was bound to accompany so many ships disembarking troops. Once free, once he had set a good few miles between himself and the invaders, he should find little difficulty in blending into the surrounding area. If he didn't immediately find a home or employment, he was resourceful enough to live off the land, and it would only be a matter of time before peace, or stability of some variety, was restored. Then, if he chose, he could find his way back to England. England and even the new ship *Vernon*, and his friends, if he so wished. Or, he was philosophical enough to realise, he may find a life worthwhile where he was, and decide to stay; maybe that was his true destiny, and his association with the British had merely been just another rung on the ladder.

But of one thing he was absolutely certain; there was no place for him in an invasion army, and he was determined to see himself free of it at the first opportunity.

* * *

They had wasted enough time; Napper Tandy was said to be heading north: the Belfast squadron could be trusted to deal with him. That meant Banks could turn westwards and continue in his search for the French without further delay. The wind was light and in the northwest, and *Scylla* was close-hauled under topsails, royals, staysails and jibs as she butted her way through the Atlantic swell. Once again there was the scent of storm in the air, which combined with a feeling of expectation that filled the entire ship to make the atmosphere almost brittle with tension.

It was ten o'clock in the morning. King had passed the watch to Chilton some two hours ago and had just come back on deck after his breakfast nap when they heard the call. It came from the mainmast lookout, and was quickly confirmed and repeated by the man at the fore. Chilton sent Rose to advise the captain and rolled his eyes at King as they waited by the binnacle.

A small squadron: it could mean so many things. French warships, crammed full with soldiers and about to bear down on the nearby coast, or Warren's fleet, desperately groping about in search of them. Or it might just be part of a homebound India convoy, or even a bunch of deep sea fishermen, and the lookouts were being a touch too spirited.

Banks appeared, bringing with him his customary air of calm and competence. "Where away, Mr Chilton?" he asked, checking the deck log to refresh himself on the ship's movements.

"Off our starboard bow, sir." Chilton replied. "West-nor-west. They have the wind."

"Very good." He glanced across at the midshipman. "Oblige me by joining the maintop lookout with the deck glass, Mr Rose."

The lad touched his hat and was off for the starboard shrouds with one of *Scylla*'s Dollonds slung over his shoulder. Banks turned back to Chilton. "How many ships?"

"Five, sir. Five sighted."

"And heading eastwards?"

"Yes, sir."

Banks thought for a spell, then opened his mouth to say more when he was interrupted by a call from the maintop.

"I can see topsails, and what looks like a further two, maybe three behind."

"Colours?" Chilton asked.

"No, sir. No colours. They're the right size for John Company, but the sails are far too white. An' one looks to be a little larger an' jury rigged."

"Yes, she's lost a topmast." Rose's voice rang out clear as a bell; he had done well to make the maintop in the time and was not in the least out of breath.

"Are you certain, Mr Rose?" Banks asked.

"Yes sir," the lad replied. "Her main topmast is lower than

her fore. She's showing a heavily reefed topsail, and I'd say she were definitely bigger than the rest."

"A line-of-battle ship?" Banks asked.

There was a moment's delay; then Rose's voice again, but this time a little less certain. "I cannot tell, sir."

"Very good, Mr Rose; keep her in view."

It would be incredibly difficult to be sure with the sighting still hull down and only her spars to judge by. And always better to be positive, rather than make a guess that was subsequently proved wrong. The mystery ships were sailing on what was near enough a converging course; they would know for certain in no time. The tension steadily mounted while they waited, and then dissolved entirely as Sarah came up on deck.

It was unusual for any of the passengers to appear quite that early, and even then they customarily used the quarterdeck steps, rather than the companionway next to the captain's quarters. Chilton almost jumped at the sight and King was so surprised that he thrust his hands into his pockets, only to remove them again when he realised he had committed such a heinous crime. Banks touched his hat to her but made no further comment, although it was obvious to all that she had been alerted by the sighting, and had probably been taking morning coffee, or even a late breakfast in the great cabin when the word was received.

With the French landing having failed, and no sign of further dissent in the area, there was little need for the Monroes to stay in *Scylla,* and everyone had expected them to be set ashore with no further ado. The magistrate was clearly an unpopular man in the town and feared for both his life and property, but the militia stationed nearby should have been sufficient to protect a local official, and his welfare was not exactly the concern of the Royal Navy. Consequently it came as a surprise, a shock almost, when only the two fishermen disembarked, and *Scylla* sailed out of the sound and passed Arranmore Island with the family still aboard.

Of course there was gossip and speculation on every level. Their evening conversations could never have gone unnoticed and even small instances like the gunroom cat being found in the great cabin had fuelled the scuttlebutt tremendously. In a wooden warship rumours could spread as easily as fire, and few were in any doubt that Sir Richard Banks had finally found himself a piece of soft. But even if they grinned and whispered there were none who blamed him. Sarah Monroe was certainly a prey worth the hunting; besides, the captain had been far more equable since they had met.

"Eight ships in sight now, sir." Rose's voice cut through, and all looked up to the masthead. "The jury rigged ship seems like a liner, an' I'm pretty sure the first two are frigates. Their forecourses have a deep roach to them, an' they are sitting right for a warship. Though I suppose they still could be Indiamen," he added lamely.

Rose was not to be blamed. From a distance there was little to tell between a ship of the Honourable East India Company and a heavy frigate. Hull length and mast heights would be almost identical, and some merchants even took to disguising themselves with fake gunports and Royal Naval embellishments to make identification even more difficult. But a collection of John Company ships in convoy with a single ship-of-the-line was an unlikely combination. Warren's squadron contained three line-of-battle ships, which would have been obvious by now, and it seemed increasingly likely that they were facing the French invasion force.

The ship's bell rang: the forenoon watch was three quarters of the way through; it would be less than an hour before the hands took their midday grog, followed by the main meal of the day.

"Nine ships in sight now, sir." Rose's voice rang out again. "The last are single-deckers as well, I'd say eight frigates and a liner. There might be something beyond, and possibly a schooner or a brig, I cannot say."

The French for certain. Banks looked about and caught King's eye, as Caulfield appeared at the quarterdeck steps. "Gentlemen, we will keep them in sight for this watch. Take in the royals and allow them to gain on us; I intend to turn and take up their course when they are within six miles." The assembled lieutenants absorbed his words with serious expressions. Their need to find Warren's ships had grown considerably, although now they were effectively tied to the French. If necessary Banks would have to shadow their progress all the way to Ireland, unless of course he chose to abandon them in favour of raising the alarm on shore.

"Send the hands to dinner as usual, but we shall clear for action immediately afterwards." That made sense: if everyone kept their heads little could happen in the next few hours, and it would mean the men would have a hot meal inside them, albeit one that might have to last them a considerable time. Banks moved away and was about to take a pace or two about the deck when he saw Sarah waiting patiently beside the taffrail. He knew that his movements were being watched by most on the quarterdeck, and wandered across almost self consciously, in a gait that was something between a saunter and a casual stroll, finally arriving by her side as if by pure chance.

"We may be in action shortly," he said, his words clipped and muted to prevent anyone overhearing what the vast majority already knew. "I would see you and your family safe, before that occurs."

"Thank you, Richard. I will ensure that my parents do not get in the way."

"And you will remain safe yourself," he said, his tone unusually soft.

"I shall, and you also," she went to raise her hand to him, but stopped just in time, and brushed down her dress instead. He smiled, noticing the movement, before hurriedly wiping his face clear of any expression as he realised his mistake. Then they both very nearly dissolved into giggles and she had to turn back and consider the ship's wake to hide her expression. This really was extremely difficult; he was behaving like a love struck youth and she was little better. But somehow, with Sarah, such foolishness seemed not to matter at all. They had spent so long in quiet conversations that he felt he could tell her anything, and she had already said much that showed her trust in him.

"Make for the orlop deck once you hear us beat to quarters," he said when they could speak again. "Mrs Clarkson will find you a place that is comfortable enough. Until then you had better go below – to the gunroom, he added hastily." It would be unthinkable for a female passenger to be alone in the great cabin. There had been enough risk with her taking coffee with him, and what the rest of the officers would be making of their present conversation was only too predictable.

But Banks cared little for that as well. In fact, he had never felt quite so untroubled in his life, even with a hostile fleet bearing down.

"Of course," she said, "I shall be perfectly safe; worry not." She added a private look. "You truly think the ship will be in action?"

"I would say it were almost certain."

"Then I will leave now, and maybe we can speak again later?"

"I hope so."

She stopped and looked back at him, her expression now serious. "Oh, there will be time, my love, I know it. But you must be careful; it is indeed wonderful that we have met, and I would hate to lose you quite so quickly."

* * *

Crowley heard the call and his spirits dropped. A frigate; a bloody British frigate, and just when they were almost in sight of Ireland. But it was only a small ship, one that they might simply brush aside; indeed, it would be strange if it even offered combat at all. However he was experienced enough to know that where there was one there were likely to be many. The whole of the western approaches was probably cluttered with warships out hunting for them, and now that the Royal Navy had their scent, it must only be a matter of time before they were caught.

But even then the situation seemed easily solved. Were Crowley in charge he would split the fleet and send two of their fastest sailors to see the swine off. They still had the windward gauge; even French seamen could benefit from that. The British ship might not be destroyed, but at least it should be distracted long enough to enable the rest to slip by. Then a suitable landing spot could be found, and the process of disembarking the troops begun. Admittedly it would be a lengthy and hazardous business, and one that the British might well interrupt, but really all Crowley wished for was a chance to get away, and he could not have cared less about anything else.

He wanted out, wanted to be gone. And as for the hateful little ship that was in his way, the one that quite probably stood between him and freedom, well he didn't think he could curse it soundly enough.

CHAPTER TWELVE

The wind was still in the north west and blowing stronger by the minute. Another storm was due and all aboard *Scylla* were well aware of her perilous position. The enemy lay to windward and less than six miles off; it would take little more than an important piece of tophamper to carry away and the British frigate would be swamped by a vastly superior force. They were heading northeast, on a course that should take them past the northern coast of Ireland, and at any moment the loom of land was expected.

"What do you see there?" Caulfield called up. It was a redundant question. All were painfully aware of the enemy's proximity, and if there were even the hint of land, or another sail, the lookouts would have certainly reported it.

"Enemy fleet is maintaining position," Miller, the hand at the masthead, dolefully reported. "No other sighting."

Caulfield looked about, conscious of the public display of his anxiety. There were few who blamed him, however, and hardly any who did not wish to ask the same question sixty seconds later.

A gunroom steward came up on deck and began to pass out steaming mugs. King, who was officially officer of the watch, collected two and handed one to the first lieutenant. Caulfield shook his head, but King pressed the mug on him.

"Take it," he said. "You might not get the chance later, and it will warm you."

Caulfield sipped at the drink. It was coffee, strong, sweet, and very welcome. He had drained half the cup before realising quite how hot the liquid was, and had to suppress a shudder as it found its way into his stomach.

"Wind's rising," he said. Both men had been watching the sails. The canvas on the upper masts was stretched tight and would have to be taken in shortly. They had allowed their lead to dwindle in order to identify the French ships, and now were desperately trying to claw back some sea room. The ship's bell rang. The afternoon watch had two hours to run; they would certainly reach the coast within daylight; then the fancy manoeuvres would begin.

No one in *Scylla* had the vaguest idea where the French were intending to land; they would have to continue to shadow the enemy fleet, anticipate their movements, whilst being careful not to become trapped between them, the wind, and the shore. It would be a difficult trick to pull off; any mistake on their part might easily cause the loss of the ship, or the French to escape. And there was also the problem of signalling the enemy's position. Warren's fleet could not be so very far away; it was the duty of frigates to bring opposing forces to battle, and yet to do so would mean abandoning the French to go in search of support.

King sipped at his coffee. The captain had made his decision and ordered them to keep in contact with the enemy at all costs. To do otherwise, and fail to raise Warren, would be a disaster. But then there was little a single fifth rate could do to stop ten ships, and Sir John might find the French easier to destroy were he to encounter them at anchor and disembarking their troops. Not for the first time King was glad that the responsibility lay with someone other than him.

Banks had gone below after they had cleared for action. His quarters, the great cabin, had ceased to exist, and was now merely an extension to *Scylla*'s gun deck, but King supposed the captain had found a place to rest. Possibly the gunroom, and probably he had company in the form of Miss Monroe. Well, so be it; if conversing with a pretty girl gave him the relaxation he needed to see them safely through the next few hours it was hardly his concern. And he was absolutely positive that Sir Richard would be a perfect gentleman; there would be little privacy for anything else.

"I suggest we take in the royals," Caulfield said finally. "Mr Barrow, send word to the captain that I am shortening sail. We have increased our lead by two miles or more, but the wind is still rising."

Barrow touched his hat and disappeared below in search of Banks, while Caulfield nodded to Johnston, who ordered the topmen aloft. In many ships the first lieutenant would have waited for permission from the captain, especially considering their current position. But Banks had sailed with most of his senior officers a good while, and there was a strong element of trust that was appreciated by all parties.

"Sail ho, sail on the larboard bow!" It was the cry that all had been waiting for, and it took several seconds for the news to sink in. Caulfield looked at King, then collected the speaking trumpet.

"What do you see there?"

The pause was to be expected. Royals were still being taken in, and the lookout must have called the sighting at the very first opportunity.

"Topsails, sir; nothing more." Caulfield opened his mouth to call for a messenger, but Barrow was already searching for the captain; he glanced about for another when Banks himself appeared. He was wearing oilskins, a sensible precaution in the circumstances, and one which told the officers that he had intended to come on deck before the sighting.

"Sailing with the wind on her quarter," the lookout

continued. "She'll sight the French at any moment, if she hasn't already."

"Mr King," Banks said. "You will oblige me be taking a closer look."

"Yes, sir." King touched his hat then thoughtfully stuffed it into the binnacle locker as he retrieved a glass. Barrow was back on deck, but this was a job for a more experienced eye, and King had no qualms at being sent to the masthead.

He clambered up the main shrouds, conscious of the curious eyes that were following him. Though still in his twenties, he was aware that much of his skill at working aloft had been lost. Any of the topmen and some of the general hands could have made the journey in a faster time. But then, they weren't a lieutenant, he told himself a little pompously. They didn't have to cope with the responsibilities the position carried. He heaved back up the futtock shrouds, and was panting slightly as he started up the topmast. And they were fit.

Once at the main crosstrees he secured himself with a line and unhitched the Dollond from over his shoulder. He might go higher; Cooke, the lookout, was several feet above him and clinging onto the topgallant mast while he peered into the wind. But King had to handle several feet of brass telescope and was still very much out of breath; he felt the stability of his present perch to be preferable.

"I'd say it were a frigate, sir." Cooke told him. King looked up. "Tell by the set of 'er masts, an' she just got the feel about 'er," the lookout continued. "Didn't like to commit m'self, though."

King raised the glass, and soon found the sail that Cooke had reported. Gradually his breathing fell back to normal, and the image grew sharper. Yes, there was what looked like a commissioning pennant, and as he caught the flash of a weathered forecourse his mind was made up.

"British frigate, sir," he bellowed, more than happy to commit himself. "She's seen the enemy and is altering course."

The yards came round and the ship was now pointing more directly at *Scylla*. King could hear Banks ordering a change of course and the private signal prepared. The newcomer was to windward so it would be up to them to act first, but the captain had clearly accepted King's judgement.

"She's settled on our reciprocal course." The ship was certainly sailing fast; he could now see most of the hull, but then *Scylla* had also turned. King took a quick scan about the horizon before concentrating on the frigate once more. She grew closer with every second, and he could hear that they had sight of her on deck. There was no doubt that she was a fifth rate, similar to themselves. Then he noticed a black mass of bunting running up her fore.

"She's making a signal," King called as it broke out, but Barrow had already reported it, and was replying with *Scylla*'s number.

"I think there's another beyond, sir." The lieutenant looked up to see Cooke, perched above his head, pointing towards the oncoming ship. He focussed his glass but could see nothing, then caught a brief flicker of canvas: a topsail or possibly a royal, he could not be certain. And there, just to the right, what might be another. He strained through the spotted lens, willing the image in. Yes, it was, for sure.

"Two ships sighted beyond, and on the same bearing," he called down. There was also a commissioning pennant, he was almost certain, but would wait a moment longer before reporting it. The only thing that really mattered was a squadron of British ships were coming down on them. They were still to leeward of the French, and might only amount to half their force, but *Scylla* was no longer alone. And, if the mystery squadron was Sir John Warren's, there would be a battle, of that there could be no doubt.

* * *

When clearing for action part of *Scylla*'s orlop deck was allocated to the medical department. The bulkheads to the midshipmen's berth and other accommodations were struck down, and an area made clear for two operating tables. Space was also left for the wounded waiting for attention. These would be placed in line on a deck that had been covered with two layers of canvas. Each man was taken in order, with scant regard for the degree of injury, and little for their rank or standing. Patients who had been attended to were moved further forward, while any who died were neatly stacked to one side for later disposal. The gunroom on the deck above and even the officers' cabins would also be liable for requisition if the numbers grew too high.

Clarkson and Manning had supervised the moving of drugs and equipment from the sick bay and were now laying out their tools, while the loblolly boys, assisted by Mrs Clarkson; Mrs Porter, the boatswain's wife; and Miss Monroe finished preparing the area.

"You shouldn't be lifting, my dear," Clarkson told his wife. She stopped in the act of moving a bench and obediently stood back to allow the surgeon to slide the wooden form against a bulkhead.

"I had no idea you were with child," Sarah told her.

"Oh yes," Betsy replied, sounding every bit the seasoned mother. "It is only the first few months, but you know what men are like."

Sarah said nothing. In fact she knew rather less than Betsy, but did have a far greater understanding.

Two of the loblolly boys began dragging midshipmen's sea chests to form the operating tables, which Sarah and Betsy immediately covered with canvas, and four heavy lanthorns were hung from the deckhead: it would be poor light, but close examination was rarely necessary. Most of the surgeon's work involved the removal of splinters and amputation of limbs, and even if Manning prided himself on his fine needlework, there was rarely time for anything but the most basic stitching when it came to closing wounds.

"We'll need an empty barrel," Mrs Porter said. "Speak to the cooper will you, Taylor?" The man knuckled his forehead and Betsy glanced at Sarah.

"That will be for the legs and wings," she explained. "The bits the surgeons remove that are no longer required."

Sarah swallowed. She had volunteered to help the medics, thinking it would be more pleasant than sitting the battle out with her parents in the cable tier, but now she was beginning to have doubts.

Betsy sensed the other woman's uncertainty and instinctively took her hand. "I am sure you will find it easy enough when we are busy," she told her. "To be frank, much of our job is instinct. Tell the men they shall be well again, even if you know it to be otherwise, and comfort them as much as you can."

"Yes, thank you. I think I shall be fine when there is more to do."

"The waiting is more'n likely the worst part," Mrs Porter agreed, joining them. "Tell me, do either of you have a pen and paper?"

"No, I..."

"Then I shall see they are available." The boatswain's wife bustled off determinedly while Sarah looked again to Betsy for an explanation.

"Some near death may need to tell us things," she told her. "Maybe instructions or messages; it would be better to write them down." Her eyes grew a little distant as a thought occurred. "And there could be those who think we are someone else: their mother or their wife, or perhaps just a lover."

Just a lover? It was an odd phrase, but Betsy was still speaking.

"When a man is near death his mind may play strange tricks. Though I am sure you will say whatever is needed."

"Yes, thank you. I think I understand."

"Bibles are kept next to the drug cabinet, should any ask. If all fails it might help to read a passage or two. Maybe a psalm?"

Sarah nodded; it all made sense, and she was reasonably sure she could cope, especially with those as experienced as Mrs Clarkson and Mrs Porter close at hand to guide her. "Betsy, have you been in action many times?" she asked finally.

"Lord no," the surgeon's wife replied. "This is my first."

* * *

The British had certainly found them, but this was not the biggest problem the French fleet faced. The storm that had been building steadily throughout the day had reached it zenith by evening; it was the third they had encountered in a short time, and most of the seamen knew this was likely to prove the most dangerous.

The wind bore down relentlessly, while waves broke over the heavily laden hulls, soaking any part that the rain might have missed and terrifying the human cargo packed tightly below. Many of these, whether French soldiers or Irish patriots, were desperately sea-sick, and any that were not appeared drunk. And all the while the savage Irish coast was in their lee, waiting to welcome them with beckoning breakers and razor sharp ridges of rock that would be glad to rip the bottom off any ship, or strip the soul from the body of a man.

To avoid this danger Bompart was desperately clawing back as much sea room as possible, but his efforts were causing great strain on his ships. The fleet itself had separated, and all were paying scant attention to their fellows as they fought their own private battles for survival.

The scene that Crowley and the others had witnessed on the *Hoche*'s orlop had brought forth images of hell powerful enough to convert the most determined sinner, and despite the atrocious conditions on deck, had sent them up to the open air of the waist. Now they huddled together, taking what shelter they could under the gangways, while above them the tophamper creaked and groaned in a manner that chilled the seamen's hearts.

"If it lasts the night out I'll count my blessings and never go to sea again," Doyle told them with total sincerity as they watched the jury main topmast working in the storm. They were carrying fully reefed topsails, but even that scant amount of canvas was dangerous in the present conditions.

"He must be clear of the coast b'now," MacArthur grumbled, although none felt inclined to look, and all were well aware of the dangers of a lee shore.

"We have to take in that sail," Crowley said, his eyes still fixed on what served as a main topsail. "It isn't going to hold, and if we lose the mast we'll be in a worse fix than ever."

He even rose, and was starting for the quarterdeck steps, but as he did a terrible groaning came from above. The men watched, fascinated, as the jury topmast bent and split before their eyes. Then the topsail itself billowed and cracked, while the bulk of the mast began to fall.

"It's going, it's bloody going!" They stood, transfixed, not knowing where to run as the tangle of rigging started to collapse above them. A block fell, landing between Doyle and Doherty, and there were shouts and cries from all about.

"Under the gangway!" Crowley shouted. The ship's boats and what few spare spars they carried appeared to give some shelter, but the gangway planking would offer better protection from falling tophamper. The men ran back as the mast fell to leeward, snapping lines and ripping shrouds as it went. Then there was a further shout. The fore and mizzen topgallant masts were going also, their fragile housings being far too weak for the topmast's tremendous leverage. The *Hoche* fell off the wind and began to roll in the hollow swell while wreckage tumbled down, dragging the ship round like one large sea anchor.

"Axes, men!" Crowley was first up and bounding across the heeling deck. There were several ready use hatchets stored on beckets by the mainmast: prime tools for hand to hand fighting, although they would now be used for a very different style of combat. Crowley reached the first taut line and smacked his axe down against the bulwark. The rope separated and disappeared instantly, only to be replaced by another, which Doyle attended to. The jury topmast was smashing against the side of the ship, seemingly determined to burst a hole in the hull with its death throws as the seamen continued to hack at the lines that held it. Then, with a sound that was audible even above the noise of the storm, the maze of wood, canvas and line fell away and was left to float alone.

The ship righted, then began a regular roll as she gave herself entirely to the whim of the current. Crowley looked back to the quarterdeck, where the officers, ridiculous in their full length oilskins and oversized hats, were desperately calling for hands. He had no idea quite how close the shore might lie, but knew well enough that the ship must inevitably be pushed towards it. They would have to rig another jury mast, or find some other method of raising a balanced suit of canvas if they wanted to beat away from its impending embrace. A sudden gust of wind took them, laying the hull over for a few desperate seconds, before the ship reluctantly reverted to her steady roll. It would mean working aloft, a dangerous exercise in the present conditions, that or face the certainty of the ship beaching on a lee shore. Crowley glanced about at the others, all equally aware of their predicament, while a wicked thought occurred. They had all been so keen to see Ireland again; now it was apparent that they might be there in a way none of them had imagined.

* * *

With the bulkheads down, the galley stove cold, and the ship stripped of nearly all comforts, those in *Scylla* rode out the storm with grim determination. On the berth deck the watch below had slung their hammocks in the normal way, but with their canvas screens removed it was a bleak and draughty place, and they missed the fire to dry their sodden clothing. The midshipmen and volunteers had lost their quarters to the medical team, and were bunking in various storerooms and passageways. Dudley, the purser, and marine lieutenant Adshead, who had earlier been moved from their cabins in the gunroom to make way for the Monroes, now found the stewards' pantry they had been sharing to also be the home of Barrow, Rose and Parfrey. The only area that retained some degree of normality was the gunroom itself, and even that had been disrupted. The captain had taken over King's cabin, forcing the two lieutenants to share Chilton's quarters, while the dining area was now a general mess for other junior officers. But with the ship in the very teeth of a storm, a powerful enemy fleet and a lee shore known to be close at hand, cramped conditions and lack of privacy were hardly important considerations.

Fraiser sat at the gunroom table, his chart of the western approaches laid out in front of him. The bread bin and a shielded sconce held the paper flat while he worked a set of parallel rulers across the page. Lewis, a master's mate, was seated to his right and followed the older man's calculations in silence. Dead reckoning was a skill he had yet to perfect. He knew that with care and attention a feel for the work could be acquired, and having a tutor such as the sailing master to learn from was a definite asset. Fraiser finally looked up and treated the younger man to one of his rare smiles.

"Well, it is impossible to gauge the strength of the current, but I would say we were safe enough for the time being."

Lewis looked again at his master's workings, a small triangle of neat black crosses showed their estimated position, with the nearest stretch of coast being the Rosses, which still lay a good few leagues to leeward. He nodded without saying a word. Besides the current Fraiser had allowed for a strong but fluctuating wind, as well as the leeway that any ship was bound to make in such conditions. They might as easily be anywhere within a five or even ten mile radius and, with no evening sighting, Fraiser could hardly have been blamed if they saw breakers at any moment. But there was something in the older man's calculations that rang true; it was almost as if he had cast a spell and willed *Scylla* to that particular spot, although Lewis would naturally never speak such blasphemous nonsense out loud. But witchcraft or not, Lewis was as confident of Fraiser's estimation as the captain would soon be. More than that, he felt he had learnt a little of the ancient art himself, and in a few years might even be able to emulate the master in his work.

* * *

By midnight the storm had eased, and once the clouds permitted, the moon gave a fair amount of light. But that was all that could be said in favour of the night. It took two hours of hard work to clear away the wreckage and repair the damage done aloft before the last suitable spar, a fore topgallant mast, could be released from its fixings. It now lay on the skid beams ready for raising into position. The ship was still rolling heavily; it would take skill as well as brute force to bring the spar upright and manoeuvre it against the lower mainmast. A single gust of wind when it had been lifted but not secured, or a rogue wave nudging the ship unexpectedly, and the mast would be lost over the side like its predecessor.

A lantern had been fixed to the mast cap, along with four lines that led up through the lubber's hole of the maintop. These would first raise the spar upright and then, after being passed about the maintop and refastened, used to keep the mast from tipping in either direction as it was raised. Two stout halliards ran from beneath the heel to provide the upward pressure. They passed up and over the lower mast cap, and lead back through a succession of blocks to two teams of eight men stationed on either gangway. The spar was far lighter than the original main topmast and even the jury mast that had replaced it, and should prove easier to lift, but would remain just as vulnerable during the short journey up the lower mainmast. The boatswain, or *maître d'équipage*, stood at the break of the quarterdeck, an ideal position to supervise the entire process.

On the quarterdeck Bompart and Maistral were standing as mute observers. Neither Commodore nor Captain were particularly skilled in such intricate seamanship, and appeared quite content to give those that were a free rein. They had, however, insisted that the work be carried out immediately. Dawn might not be far away and such a delicate procedure was very much more dangerous during the dark hours, but morning was likely to reveal a British fleet close at hand, and no time could be wasted. Crowley and the other Irishmen were amid the larboard gangway team and stood fingering the line expectantly as they waited for the call to begin.

It came in the form of a shrill note blown from the boatswain's silver call. On hearing the sound the four men at the cap falls began to haul on their lines. The lantern described a wide arc as the spar was slowly raised upright. At the maintop it was gingerly guided through the lubber's hole and held in position while the lines were removed and reattached. All waited while the work was done, and held their breath when the ship heaved unexpectedly to larboard. But in time the new fixings were ready, and one of the maintop team called down to the boatswain.

The first part was over, now all that was needed was to guide the spar up the lower mast. Both gangway teams took up the slack; the boatswain blew on his call once more and began to count as the men on the gangways heaved the spar skywards.

"Un, Deux, Trois... Tribord!" The unexpected shout stopped everyone instantly. The mast was leaning too far over; the boatswain on the quarterdeck held one arm in the air and pointed in an accusing fashion at the masthead. All waited while the men with the guiding lines made subtle adjustments until, apparently satisfied, the boatswain sounded his call again. The spar rose further, and was now more than half way through its journey. Crowley could see that it was far too light and short to do the job properly. It might, however, be suitable for mounting a small square sail, and would provide a suitable anchorage for stays. Then the call was heard for the last time: the mast was now as high as it would go.

Men on the maintop started to set the lower housing, while those who had been guiding secured their lines to keep the upper mast stable long enough for proper shrouds to be mounted. Once fully rigged, a replacement yard could be set up. It would be an arduous and time consuming task that may well stretch on beyond the dawn, and *Hoche* was by no means out of peril. But the main danger at least had passed; it seemed that some of their former luck was returning and they could hope to meet the next storm, or the British for that matter, on slightly better terms.

* * *

The storm's cessation was no less welcome to those in *Scylla*. There were no major repairs to carry out, but all bad weather is disruptive. The men were tired, and the knowledge that an enemy force was near did not sit easy with any of them. By three bells in the morning watch there was finally light enough to see the true position. The French lay in two loosely formed parallel lines off the starboard bow; there appeared to be one ship less; although, as this was the first time they had been viewed from a close vantage point, that might be an illusion. The north-northwesterly wind had fallen and the fleet was making slow progress towards the southwest: it was the only course they could steer with any hope of escape. The flagship had clearly sustained serious damage aloft and was now under a jury rig that would prevent her coming closer to the wind. Meanwhile *Foudroyant* and *Melampus,* in clear sight off *Scylla*'s starboard beam, effectively blocked any move the French might make in that direction, and the remainder of Sir John Warren's ships could just be made out to the east, where they were closing fast on the enemy's stern. If the wind held, the British might be within long range in an hour or so, and it would be only a short while longer before they brought their broadside guns to bear.

Banks closed his glass with a purposeful air, but continued to study the enemy fleet. It did not do to anticipate one's commodore, but Banks guessed that Sir John would order a general chase. The first two French frigates were slightly ahead, while the rest seemed to be holding back to protect their flagship, much in the way a swarm of bees might defend their queen, and it would seem probable that they would remain in that defensive position should the British choose to launch an all out attack. That was the instinctive reaction after all, and would probably be the choice of most commanders; although, in this instance, Banks felt they would be making a very big mistake.

Most if not all of the French frigates would be carrying troops, and even without those packed inside the flagship, their number must be substantial. The French *raison d'être* lay not in fighting the British but delivering an invasion army; a force of any size landing in Ireland would be better than none at all.

It might not even need the full weight of the fleet's cargo to kindle a revolutionary fire large enough to deem the whole project a success. If Banks were the French commander he would order all the accompanying frigates to make off, using their superior speed, and then do what he could to delay Warren's ships from following. With luck the frigates would get as far as the Irish mainland, and may well be able to disembark their men and supplies before the British found them. It would be the sensible course, and would ensure the project was not a total failure, albeit at the sacrifice of one seventy-four.

He glanced back to starboard where *Foudroyant* was beating as close to the wind as she would lie. The old liner was roughly eight miles from the nearest Frenchman and making heavy weather of it, forcing *Scylla* to hold back in order to keep pace. Beyond, and perhaps a mile further to leeward, was *Canada,* Warren's flagship. It would be later still before she came to grips with the enemy; in fact the best that could be said of her position was that it gave the British commander a grandstand view of the action. *Scylla* was far better placed and had speed in hand to act, but, as a mere frigate, could do little to stop the French unsupported. The bulk of at least one two-decker would be needed, unless *Scylla* was used as nothing more than a sacrifice: a sprat to catch a mackerel.

And it was then, as he stood on his quarterdeck and considered the situation, that Banks first became aware of a curious and disquieting feeling of impending doom. Instinctively he knew that Warren was not going to release the ships to pursue as best they could. This would be a more considered action, one where personal judgement would not be required. And *Scylla*, perfectly positioned as she was, seemed the ideal candidate to carry out a major part in the proceedings, and would inevitably come out the worst.

He looked about, as if desperate to share the terrible thought that now seemed so blatantly obvious. Sir John had every reason to not be confident of catching the entire fleet from astern. In fact it was highly likely that the leading French ships would slip clean away. In which case it could only be a matter of time before *Scylla* was ordered in to stop them and, despite her size, she must necessarily go alone.

Single-handed they would have to run amok amongst the enemy, causing as much damage as possible in the hope of slowing the leading ships down. It might not take long, twenty minutes, maybe half an hour, just sufficient to allow the rest of the British fleet to catch up. But in that time his ship would probably be pounded into a wreck, and he could even be forced to strike.

Banks actually closed his eyes as he considered the proposition. One ship to stop many; it was an appalling thought, albeit peculiarly similar to the role he had loftily decided would be right for the French flagship. Then he cursed himself for the fool he was, and grudgingly recognised the difference between theory and practice.

"The French are manoeuvring," Caulfield said softly. The first lieutenant had been standing next to him for all of the watch but had said nothing as the dawn revealed the two opposing fleets. King and Fraiser were also nearby, and equally silent: there had been no comments or trite remarks from any of them. All had been in action together before. Each understood that sober and considered judgement was particularly important at this stage, and would be all but impossible amidst an atmosphere filled with excited chatter and unnecessary speculation. Banks was reasonably sure that Caulfield had only spoken now because his captain was apparently focusing on the British liner, and he was quietly thankful that he had such a team supporting him. But despite their quiet concern, had any of his fellow officers realised the invidious position that *Scylla* now found herself? He thought not, and rather envied them their ignorance.

He turned back to the enemy squadron. Caulfield was right: there were signals flying back and forth, while some of the far column of frigates were increasing sail and altering course. Maybe he had been wrong, maybe the French commander had ordered them off and was going to fight a rearguard action. Or perhaps they were intending to form one single line of battle.

Banks thought not; that was battleship tactics, and all but one of the French ships were frigates. But a line of battle was also easier to stop, especially when there was at least one ship in an ideal position to throw herself in front of the enemy's van. He glanced across at *Foudroyant*, still determinedly stubbing the waves and making scant forward progress. She might be able to join in the action later, but was too slow for any dramatic opening moves. Too slow to take the first or second ship, engage them in battle and hang on determinedly like a single dog might to a raging bull. Too slow to bring the bulk of a battleship just where it was needed most. Too slow by half, he told himself bitterly; that job would fall to a frigate. Frigates were faster and far more expendable.

"Signal from the flagship," the midshipman's voice cut into his thoughts. "Our number..."

Banks waited while the expected order was received, and the men about him began to take in what he had foreseen some while ago. He supposed it was a reasonable enough solution. After all, were the leading frigates allowed to escape it would hardly be a complete victory. They might even get clean away, and actually land some troops in the manner he had predicted; should that be permitted, the action against the other ships, however victorious, might still be seen as a defeat.

But if he were successful, if he and his ship delayed the enemy long enough to see their total destruction, that must be an end to the matter. The French would have been stopped and there could be no further chance of invasion. Nine French taken for the loss of one: yes he could understand the wisdom in that.

It would in fact be a very good result indeed, one sure to win the public's approval and probably a further honour for Sir John. And even if *Scylla*, his own precious *Scylla*, even if she were the ship to be lost, and his people, the officers and men he knew so well, were those about to be killed, even then he could not argue with the plan nor the logic it contained. It was suicide of course, but still made perfect sense.

CHAPTER THIRTEEN

Crowley thought he had never been so tired. Despite the easing of the storm, rigging the jury topmast had taken both energy and concentration; now he felt as if the life had been sucked from him. To make matters worse, he wondered if it had been really worth all the effort. The ship might be more easily controlled and the lee shore could certainly be avoided, but as dawn broke it became increasingly clear that the accursed Royal Navy was not to leave them be. From their position on *Hoche*'s leeward gangway he and MacArthur could clearly make out the untidy straggle of ships that currently dogged their tail. More were approaching on their larboard quarter, and there was a frigate, a rather ponderous liner and something substantial beyond, off their larboard bow. The French ships still outnumbered them, even allowing for the *Résolue* that had sprung a leak and fallen behind during the night, but he could see at least two British warships that were every bit as large as the *Hoche*, and Crowley had no illusions as to the relative merits of each nation's navy.

From the quarterdeck came a babble of orders, and men began to haul the yards round as the ship changed course.

"We're turning a point or so to the west," MacArthur commented.

Crowley nodded. It must take them about as near to the wind as the old girl could manage with her butchered rig, but he doubted if the alteration was worth the making. The nearest land was hardly a danger now, and their speed, such as it was, would be reduced still further. Commodore Bompart was on the quarterdeck, along with Captain Maistral and Wolfe Tone. They seemed to be having some sort of argument: at one point the Irish devil even stomped away for a moment or two and stood with his hands behind his back glaring at the oncoming British. But he returned soon enough, and shortly afterwards there were more orders, and a second batch of signals made to the other ships of the squadron. The French had already formed a somewhat irregular line-of-battle, and Crowley wondered vaguely what miracles the all wise commanders had conjured up to see them clear of this mess.

"The enemy are also busy," MacArthur pointed towards the two-decker furthest off their larboard bow. She could be seen more clearly now, and was obviously the British flagship. She had maintained an almost continuous stream of signals since first light; this time Crowley thought he actually saw the result. A line of bunting broke out from her foremast, and shortly after the frigate closest to their van began to make further sail, drawing ahead of the liner immediately behind her. They watched in silence as she picked up speed, and memories of the fleet action off Cape St Vincent came back to Crowley. The frigate, either ordered or not, was attempting a similar feat to that Nelson had carried off the previous year. By breaking away from her support, she was effectively taking on the entire invasion fleet, or at least the very head of it. Their action would seriously affect the French: some might try to steer to leeward, but that would simply drive them nearer the two battleships; others might plough on, but confusion and delay was pretty much guaranteed. It would come at a price, of course: even if just a few of the French engaged, the jaunty little ship would be a total loss within minutes.

The sound of heavy cannon came to them, and both looked round to see the British liner off their stern had opened fire.

"And so it begins," MacArthur said quietly and Crowley

could do nothing but agree. They were certainly the first of many guns to be fired that day. However long his journey had been, however far he had travelled, this was the point when matters must finally be addressed. He now knew for certain that there would never be a full scale invasion, and the likelihood of the mighty army even setting foot on Ireland was very small. Equally slight were the chances of the French escaping. In fact a British victory, and capture, seemed the very best any of them could hope for, and even that would not come before many hours of fighting and countless other cannon had been fired.

So what of his guardian angel now? Crowley might have considered himself as one who was in some way charmed, but even in the pell-mell existence he had led, there had been few occasions when the odds had been stacked quite so high against him. Now, and for probably the first time, he was starting to doubt his chances. Doubt he would see the current situation through to a happy end, doubt that he himself would survive long enough to turn the misery that was to come into a happy anecdote, one that could be told to laughing shipmates by the warmth of a late night alehouse fire. His thoughts naturally moved on to his British friends, somewhere miles away and still awaiting their liner, and he felt profoundly sorry.

He would not see them again, of that Crowley was quite certain. If capture was the very best he could expect, he would certainly be missing that particular ship. Of course they might meet again in the maelstrom of a continent at war: stranger things had happened, and he must not blight his luck by wishing it away. But Crowley inwardly knew that this was the end of his good fortune, and the sadness stayed with him. Then the sound of gun fire came to them again. A broadside this time, and as neat a ripple as he had ever heard. The British were clearly well trained and knew precisely what they were about.

"So it begins," Crowley repeated softly, and to himself, "and so it must end."

* * *

In the short time that he had been with her Banks knew that *Scylla* had never sailed quite so sweet. The addition of royals had given her a kick of more than a knot, and even sailing as close to the wind as she would lie there was still a respectable cloud of spray streaming from her bow. The men had been sent to quarters after a cold and dry breakfast, but now their spirits seemed surprisingly high as the ship edged ever closer to the enemy's van. Banks watched them and felt mildly ashamed; they might wish for battle, for the chance to fire their guns and shoot their muskets, and put all of the hard learned lessons of war into action, but they were heading for a very different style of combat from the one they had been weaned upon. Few of those present had ever fought in a fleet action; there were many who had never actually heard a gun fired in anger. But such was the way of the all powerful Royal Navy; and, if the next hour or so butchered the majority and disillusioned the rest, the end result would still be positive.

It would be known as the Battle of Tory Island, Banks supposed; the nearest land mass often being a point of reference for a naval action. History would see it as a British victory, despite the fact that the French had the windward gauge and were numerically dominant in both ships and guns. Some might recall *Scylla*, the sacrificial lamb that was sent to head off the enemy line, the insignificant stumbling block that caused a herd of charging bulls to trip and so be halted. And of those who did remember, nearly all would consider her action heroic. Some might even raise a glass or say a prayer for those few brave men in one small ship who had done so much for their country's freedom. But they would be wrong.

Banks supposed that there had been times in his life when he had been mildly brave. Nothing stood out, even if the capacity, he hoped, remained. But heroes should not be ordered to their valour; this was a case where to reach the giddy heights of a Nelson, a Duncan or a Howe all he would have to was simply obey orders. Obey orders and see them through to the end, however dreadful that might be.

And he must remember that it was no harder on him than any other under command. When Nelson directed *Captain* out of the line to take on the might of a Spanish fleet, he had effectively placed every man aboard in peril of his life, and there had been no room for them to voice their opinions on the matter. Those that returned were treated like victors, those that did not became revered in their deaths, but little choice was given as to if they actually wanted to go.

Banks sighed; it wasn't so much that he resented his part in the action. Indeed, it could be said that his entire naval career had been directed towards this one particular point. And given the choice he might willingly have chosen to take his precious ship on such an important task. But he could not ignore the faint feeling of resentment that came from having been so directed. Somehow being ordered to be brave was completely different from gallantry achieved through one's own volition.

"They've opened fire!"

Caulfield's words made him start, so deep in his thoughts had he been, and Banks looked up to see the remains of broadside smoke as it dissipated in the wind. It had been the nearest frigate, and was long range for what would probably be eighteen pounders. How typical of the French to waste the first broadside, the one that had been loaded with care and patience, on an optimistic whim. A stray ball might conceivably have reached *Scylla*, but it would have been all but spent and little damage could be expected. More foolish still when that same target was about to become so much closer. The shots duly rained down on an empty sea just before the sound of their discharge reached the British. Banks turned to address the quarterdeck in general. "That'll be one less for us to face later," he said, and the officers laughed politely.

"Shall I cast the log, sir?" Barrow asked. Banks looked at him, then realised that in truth this must be a favourable pace for a close hauled ship. He reckoned that little harm would be caused by measuring their speed, and it would certainly keep a few of the hands occupied while they closed the range. And if any survived, and the record was retained, it might speak well for the ship.

* * *

Despite his demotion, Surridge was a talented gunner and had been given command of a twenty-four pounder on the forecastle battery. It was a carronade; of all the guns in the ship they threw the heaviest shot, and nearly as far as his old and beloved thirty-two carriage pieces. Carronades also had the advantage of requiring a smaller crew, so Surridge could have greater control over her loading and tending. In a relatively short time, he had become truly enamoured with the weapon.

The nearest French ship, a frigate, had already unloaded her guns, and he was more than ready to return the compliment. He longed to see his own piece fling a ball of hot iron their way, and his hands all but itched at the firing line. But the time would come, and to vent his frustration he hurled an insult at Cox, one of the loaders. They were tie mates and each represented the closest thing to a friend either possessed. Cox took the abuse in good heart and replied in kind, adding a less than subtle discharge of wind that caused the other servers to laugh, comment or cuss appropriately. In less than ten minutes they would be in action, fighting what would be the darkest battle in their lives, and there was little harm in preparing for action.

* * *

King had charge of the gundeck and was standing with Rose in the waist just forward of the mainmast. From their position they could see little of the French line, other than a shadowy image of the nearest frigate that appeared and disappeared through the starboard gunports. They had heard the first enemy discharge and even now could smell the smoke as it rolled down upon them, but both knew it would be a while longer before the captain ordered any reply. In the meanwhile the gun crews sat or squatted on the deck beside their primed pieces. Each of the starboard battery was run out and roughly laid in favour of the nearest French ship. The salt boxes were filled with charges enough for two more rounds, and ready-use shot of every type was to hand. Some of the men prayed; a couple, King was almost certain, were playing an illicit game of crown and anchor; and there were numerous muted conversations interspersed with the occasional inappropriate shriek of excited laughter. King had been in action many times, far more than most lieutenants of his age, and knew there was nothing unusual in any of this. The waiting was always difficult and if men took relief where they could – in intellectual talk, meditation or coarse humour, or even more phusically through the pissdales and gunports – he would do little to stop them.

The sound of light thunder rolled out, followed by a commotion beginning at the stern, and soon there was excited whispering and someone actually cheered. Rose looked to him, his face unnaturally pale.

"What goes there?" King shouted to the nearest gun crew.

"It's the *Robust*, sir," a hand at number seven gun told him. "They're leadin' the attack on the frog's rear. She's just loosened off her first broadside."

King and Rose walked across the deck and peered through the gunports. Yes, there was the British seventy-four. She was almost alongside the sternmost ship, and was currently covered in smoke from her own guns. He watched as the air cleared. Only a few pencils of returning fire came from the French ship, a frigate far smaller than the British battle-wagon. It was nigh on point-blank range; a broadside from a two-decker would have caused tremendous damage to the fabric of the lighter ship, as well as knocking much of the fight from her crew. But the frigate would be filled with armed men, and could well swamp even a liner should *Robust* be foolish enough to draw too close. As he watched another broadside rolled out. That was good timing, and must doubtless dishearten the French still further. Then there was the sound of another broadside, and he realised the ship behind *Robust* must also be in range.

His glance moved towards the nearest enemy to them. They had made good time. *Scylla* was closing at an obtuse angle; apparently Banks had chosen to turn slightly to larboard in order to increase speed and allow their broadside guns into action that much sooner. As he watched the French ship disappeared behind a wall of smoke and fire as she released her load, and King found he could watch quite dispassionately as the shots came towards him. There were a series of splashes about half a cable from their side, and one ball skipped twice before vanishing below the surface, thirty feet from where he stood. It was still long range, and at the speed they were going King felt it would not be that ship they closed with, but the next one ahead. There was another beyond that, so Banks was probably intending to penetrate the line there, and may well turn into the wind, stopping the enemy in its tracks and allowing both batteries to come into play. It would be a bold move, one that must cause the ultimate confusion amongst the French, and he hoped that *Robust* and the others would be on hand quick enough to rescue them. He leaned further out of the port and attempted to look back to where *Foudroyant* and *Canada* must be. He could see no sign; they were probably shielded by *Scylla*'s hull, or were too far behind to make a difference. Either way he knew that help would not come from that quarter; it was *Robust* and the others astern of her who could save them, no one else.

* * *

Ahead, the British frigate was still heading for destruction. Crowley watched it go, wondering at such reckless behaviour, although inwardly he acknowledged the gambit. Without doubt the ship would cause chaos amidst the leading French, and was likely to hold the entire line back, making them a present for the squadron coming up on their stern to enjoy at leisure.

Thinking of the second group of ships, he naturally turned to them, and was surprised to see they had crept uncomfortably close. The leader was a seventy-four. It had already engaged *Embuscade,* the tail-ender, and then moved on to *Coquille* immediately behind his ship. As he watched, another thundering broadside rolled out from the British liner's great guns, leaving the frigate visibly shaken. Smoke could be seen coming from her forecastle, then the foremast began to topple. Crowley knew she was already as good as dead, and there were plenty more British following their leader to finish her off.

The seventy-four was clearly of the same opinion and soon the battered frigate was left behind. The Irishman swallowed; the huge enemy ship would be heading for them next. It would be far more of an even fight; *Hoche* was, after all, a solid two-decker, and mounted a weight of guns more than sufficient to tackle any British liner. And the frigates must have caused some damage in return for the drubbing they had received. But he had no illusions about the French ability in action. They might man their cannon with all the zeal of revolutionaries, and fight with every bit as much bravery and determination, but the British were the better trained. Hardly any of their ships spent as much time in harbour and while at sea they exercised almost continuously. It was not unheard of for two British broadsides to be despatched in the time it took for the French to send one, effectively doubling their fire power. And British built ships, though not always blessed with the finest of lines, were well equipped and usually handled with such professionalism that most other navies seemed amateur in comparison.

"A vos armes!" The captain had also clearly noticed the threat and was ordering the men to their guns. Crowley moved across to the quarterdeck carronade that had been allocated exclusively to the Irishmen. It was not the only piece so served: the French had been sensible in using the men they had to hand, and recognised that friends and fellow countrymen work best together. Crowley had handled a carriage gun before, as had Doyle and MacArthur, and the two exercises that they had been permitted demonstrated there was nothing terribly different about the procedure with a carronade. Walsh was actually made gun captain, mainly because he had the better eyes, although in true revolutionary fashion all were keen to share any responsibility. The British seventy-four clearly intended taking them from the leeward side and was making no attempt to stand off; it would be close range and, when the two line-of-battle ships met, pretty brutal. So be it, but the British captain would be a fool to come too close. *Hoche* was carrying a good many soldiers, most of whom were almost mad with frustration at being crammed aboard a ship for such a while and would be only too pleased to vent their anger in a boarding action. The deck beneath them vibrated as the flagship fired her first shots of the battle. They would be the stern chasers, although it would not be long before the entire broadside came into use.

"Reckon we'll be boarding afore we knows it," Doyle said, eyeing the enemy ship as she crept ever closer. The British liner was now off their larboard quarter, and certainly it would take little for Commodore Bompart to order *Hoche* out of line to engage her. It was clearly a day for impetuous action, and that might even be on the enemy captain's mind. For the French flagship to turn, abandoning the protection of her fellows, would be a bold manoeuvre, however; even if the *Hoche* were able to come alongside and board the British, there were several undamaged enemy ships just astern ready to re-take the prize and capture them into the bargain.

"No," MacArthur said firmly. "It will be a tight battle, but your man will keep his distance."

"*Êtes-vous prêts là-bas?*" It was the voice of Wolfe Tone. Crowley felt his heart fall. The man was prancing up and down the quarterdeck dressed like a marionette in that absurdly decorated blue coat and pantaloons. For a moment their eyes met, and Crowley knew he would come and speak with them.

"And you, my lads, all ready for the fray?"

"Aye, Theo," Walsh said calmly. "We're ready as anything, and fit to fight until night fall."

Tone laughed and patted Walsh on the shoulder, then ruffled Crowley's hair in the way a father might a favoured son. Crowley closed his eyes and waited for him to leave them be.

"It's a wonderful day to be Irish," Tone continued relentlessly. "We'll whip this little lot into a heap, and be landing our troops by the afternoon." He looked over the bulwark, clearly not seeing the British ship-of-the-line that was about to attack them. "Tonight we shall be sleeping on Irish soil, and in the morning we can start to re-take our country, think of that!" He slapped Crowley on the shoulder for good measure, and beamed at the rest of the gun crew as if he had just delivered a heaven backed promise against death or disfigurement.

"Aye, think of that, why don't you?" MacArthur said softly as the man finally moved on. "An' all the little leprechauns will gather together to whistle us on our way."

"Ask me, the cove's been reading too many of his speeches." Doyle said a little louder.

"Aye," Doherty agreed. "It's all well to look on the bright side, but would be nice to be on speakin' terms with reality."

Crowley looked at them side on and listened in silence as they continued to grumble. It was the first hint of any dissatisfaction he had noticed from the others. He knew himself to be the victim of circumstances: had he not met up with them that night in the ale house he might never have thought of returning to Ireland. At that moment he should have been just one more sailor waiting for his ship and trying to avoid the press. But the others: they were revolutionaries. They wanted to be here: no amount of misfortune or bad luck would have prevented them. And yet they were clearly fed up.

He supposed it was not to be surprised at. Spending weeks in a cramped ship, risking all to come this far, and then the only sight of their mother country was a grey smudge behind an enemy battleship. It, or one of the others, would soon see them dead or prisoners, and in the latter case they would be lucky to hold on to their lives for very much longer. No, their reaction was not to be surprised at, and Crowley found himself feeling mildly reassured. But, at the same time, deeply disappointed.

* * *

They were now well within long range of the enemy's great guns and had already withstood two French broadsides, *Scylla*'s timbers being sound enough to see off the partially spent shot. Banks had brought them up, almost in line with the leading frigate, and was considering the time to turn. By steering as close to the wind as he could, he reckoned the distance would be covered relatively quickly. If they could survive without desperate damage aloft, he intended placing *Scylla* at the optimum angle, with the larboard broadside raking the leading ship's stern, and the starboard the bow of the second in line.

It should take no more than ten to twelve minutes; in that time he would receive at least two, probably four, or, if he was especially unlucky and the French in good practice, maybe six broadsides. So far the French had been mainly aiming at their hull, but as soon as the range shortened, he expected *Scylla*'s masts to become the target. Were they to sustain critical damage aloft, or even the loss of a single minor spar or piece of rigging, the time for reaching the enemy line would be correspondingly extended; that or become both irrelevant and measureless.

Banks turned to his first lieutenant. "I think we may make for the enemy, Mr Caulfield."

Caulfield touched his hat with due formality, then was surprised to see the captain's outstretched hand, and shook it with genuine affection. The two had been through much together; this might prove to be just one more action, but both shared an inner feeling that neither they, nor anyone else on board *Scylla*, would emerge from it unchanged in some way.

"Larboard your helm, take her two points to starboard," Caulfield ordered.

"Two points to starboard, sir."

The ship crept further towards the wind and presented her starboard bow to the enemy line. The yards creaked round, and soon they were heading on a collision course. A broadside was due from both of the nearest ships; all on the quarterdeck waited expectantly. The French might be holding back, waiting for *Scylla* to become a better target, or just plain slow, it was impossible to say which. But the ship was now on course, and Banks looked up thoughtfully to the sails and weathervane.

"Do you think she will take another point?" he asked the quartermaster.

"It's a fickle wind, sir," the man said after considering for a moment. "But I could bring her a little closer if you wish. That's if you don't mind me easing back for a spell when I 'as to."

"I should not mind at all," Banks said evenly.

Scylla leant further into the breeze, and now was visibly gathering up the sea room between her and the enemy line. The details of the French ships were becoming clearer by the second, but they remained silent, and the broadsides did not come.

Then there was a cry from a midshipman on the forecastle and, as if signalled, the first flash of fire appeared on the leading ship. It was quickly followed by more as both ships discharged their guns in *Scylla*'s direction. The shots were erratically aimed, with some crashing into the British ship's vulnerable bow and hull while others smashed through her tophamper. Lines parted, the fore topgallant billowed out, and there was a scream from the break of the forecastle where three men had been struck down with one ball. But a good few missed the ship entirely, falling ineffectually into the ocean, and *Scylla* was allowed to maintain her course and way.

"Splice the fore backstay there and get that t'gallant sheeted back!" The boatswain's voice came up from the waist, but the men were already moving and the work was soon addressed. On the quarterdeck Banks and Caulfield exchanged glances. They could expect several minutes of peace now before either enemy fired again, and already it seemed unlikely that they would be able to fire more than one additional full broadside before *Scylla* penetrated their line. Lieutenant Adshead and Sergeant Rice were forming their marines along both bulwarks, each line sheltered by the hammock-filled netting. The densely packed canvas offered a far better defence than any wood that could splinter and shatter. The gun crews were waiting to fire their pieces, topmen and afterguard stood ready at their stations, and all was crisp with anticipation.

"Secure the men, if you please, Mr Caulfield." Banks's voice rang out quite clearly in the expectant silence, and the men were responding before the first lieutenant even began to bellow. All knew the drill as well as the reason behind it, and took what shelter they could. Those in the waist ducked down behind the reinforced knees that formed the ship's frame, or stood in the lee of the lower masts. Even the marines were permitted to lower their shakos and present as small a target as possible, while any in the tops drew back and tucked themselves behind the bundled mounds of the studding sails. And all remained quiet as they waited for what was to come; only the officers stood bold, trusting in luck and whatever else they held dear to protect them as the ship drew steadily nearer to the line of enemy warships.

This time the French made far better practice. The first broadside came from the second in line and was quickly followed by the leading ship, and both were well laid and far more even. The shots had begun to strike *Scylla* even before the last had been fired, and a cloud of dust and splinters flew up, hanging over the ship as she was battered by the flying iron. A carronade on the starboard bow was struck soundly on the muzzle, causing the entire gun to fall to one side and crush two of its servers. The bower anchor was knocked unceremoniously into the ocean, and several foremast shrouds parted. The red cutter, that had been filled with water so as to act as a reservoir in case of fire, dissolved into her constituent parts, drenching the men sheltered below. A marine was struck by a splinter that carried away a good part of the flesh of one leg. The entire crew of a quarterdeck carronade, who were crouched together behind a bulwark, crumpled to the ground as two shots crashed through the seemingly impregnable oak defence, and all about there were cries and screeches as chaos threatened to reign.

Damage was also taken to the hull; *Scylla* vibrated and seemed to stagger as the heavy round shot dug deep into her vitals. And these were important hits: ship killing blows that might be difficult to find and all but impossible to plug. The carpenter and his mates were stationed below, ready with wood, lead and leather, but the best they could offer was a postponement of the problem; *Scylla* had been hurt, and hurt deeply; such punishment could not be withstood indefinitely.

But through it all there was some semblance of order. Calls sounded and instructions, even if screamed, were at least obeyed, and men moved instinctively to save their injured mates. Some were pulled back from further danger and dragged to the nearest hatchway, others had wounds attended to on the deck, bandages and tourniquets being deposited throughout the ship for just such a purpose. Men calmed excited nerves or the first signs of shock with a reassuring nod or friendly slap to the back. Meanwhile others did what they could in minor ways to secure the ship: round shot knocked from a garland was gathered up, or water thrown on a burst salt box. And soon, before anyone had truly noticed, there were no more shots.

From the quarterdeck Banks could see as much as he needed to. The masts and sails were apparently unaffected, although shots that had struck them low in the hull were still an unknown danger. But even if *Scylla* had been especially unlucky and sustained some terrible damage below the waterline, he felt she would now stay afloat long enough to complete her task. Relieved, he went to speak to Caulfield and was surprised to see him bending over a crumpled figure on the deck.

Young Parfrey had been injured and was bent double, his hands held tightly to his face. Banks moved across and laid his arm across the lad's shoulder: the woollen cloth was warm and wet. The volunteer raised his head to look at his captain; his cheek had been neatly split, either by a wooden splinter or some other piece of flying debris, and was bleeding profusely.

"Get below, lad," Banks said, forcing himself to look the boy in the eyes. "Let the surgeon attend to you."

Parfrey mumbled something incoherent but Caulfield was

already summoning a hand.

"Take Mr Parfrey to the surgeon," he said. The man went to knuckle his forehead but quickly realised this was not the time for formality, and gently took hold of the boy's arm. Banks watched them go, relieved in part that the lad had not been killed and would now be relatively safe. He had seen flesh wounds every bit as bad heal up sound enough, even if some of Parfrey's youthful looks might suffer.

The French were that much closer now, almost within range of *Scylla*'s forward guns. The British cannon were double shotted; the gunners would be retaining their first broadside for the time when they were hard up against the enemy, and the place where they should cause the most damage. Banks could see King standing in the waist waiting for the order to open fire, and next to him Rose, the midshipman that he could remember so well as a young and innocent volunteer in *Pandora*. Lewis, a master's mate, was on the forecastle, another face from his previous ship, and Fraiser, the ever reliable sailing master, stood next to the binnacle. They were all men he knew well and trusted; in addition there were many others whom he had grown to like and respect even so early into the commission. He still considered Warren a fool to treat his frigates like so many liners; a general chase would have used their sailing qualities to far better effect, and *Scylla* would not have been placed in such an exposed position. But if he had to take his ship into danger, he could think of no better men to face the peril alongside.

CHAPTER FORTEEN

The crew on the quarterdeck carronade were working like a machine. As soon as the British seventy-four came alongside they had been released from the strictures of broadsides, and each gun was discharged as soon as the weapon became ready. There was neither the time nor energy to measure their work against any other crew, but the Irish served cannon must have been one of the faster and more efficient of the killing devices in use that day. The British were also keeping up a substantial rate of fire, and both ships began to show signs of damage. Crowley, who was working the rammer, had time to glance back while Walsh primed the piece, and saw the second British ship closing on them from astern. The gun was fired and all became temporarily obscured by smoke, but when the air was clear once more, and a fresh charge and round had been tamped home, he looked again. The seventy-four alongside was spilling her wind to maintain position, while the frigate immediately behind had put her helm over to avoid a collision. It was the sort of confusion that would do no harm to the French effort, and Crowley was just starting to feel his spirits rise when a shot came through the bulwark, scattering splinters in every direction and sending him gasping into the scuppers.

He pulled himself up and snatched angrily at the rammer that had fallen on the deck beside him. His breath was coming in short shallow draughts; he must allow himself time to recover: men had been known to die from the wind of a passing ball, but the tumble had both shaken him up and strangely ignited his wrath. The gun was still and silent as he clambered to his feet and glared about.

Doherty was dead. Crowley took in the fact without emotion. There could be no doubt; the poor devil must have taken the shot full on. And Walsh had been badly wounded: his left arm hung limp and lifeless and his trousers were soaked in blood. He looked to MacArthur and Doyle; both were as dazed as he was, and no man moved for several seconds.

"What are you doing there?" It was the voice of Wolfe Tone. Still dressed in that absurd rig, he stepped nonchalantly over Doherty's body as he approached them. "A silent gun is an insult to the cause," he said in that same patronising voice, and Crowley found himself reacting without thought. With a straight right that came as a surprise to both parties, his swung his fist at the lighter man. Tone caught sight of the move at the last moment, but was fast enough to both dodge the blow and catch the outstretched arm of his assailant.

"Hey, there, Michael; be still, be still." Both men were panting but the fire was dangerously bright in Crowley's eyes. "Fine, I was a little hasty, and spoke out of turn. But we'll look after your man, and tend to Liam, so we will."

Crowley felt his anger dissipate, and knew that tears were very close, but Tone continued. "Hey there, you; deal with this and take this gentleman to the surgeon: *Allez chercher le chirurgien!*"

Two young soldiers came and collected what was left of Doherty. They looked no older than fifteen, yet picked up the body expertly enough. Crowley knew that on a British ship his friend would have been despatched straight over the side, but the French, it seemed, were a little more sensitive. Walsh followed them on foot as they made their way towards the hatch while Tone returned to the remaining three.

"So," he said, looking especially at Crowley. "We have wasted enough time, and will still be one man down, even if I joins you. But what say we get this gun back to its proper job, and we to ours?"

"It is loaded," Doyle told him warily. "Just need to prime and fire."

Tone glanced at him for a second, then bent down and collected the priming horn that had fallen to the deck and gave his attention to the gunlock. Easing the hammer back, he poured enough of the fine meal powder into the touch-hole and snapped the frizzen shut. There was little need to lay the gun; the seventy-four was in plain view and at point blank range. Tone stood to one side and tugged at the firing line, watching as the cannon recoiled, and the shot smacked visibly into the hull of the British ship.

"Well, ain't that a satisfying experience?" he said, turning and grinning at the rest of the gun crew. "Why don't we tries it again?"

* * *

The wind had shifted marginally in their favour and *Scylla* made the last few hundred yards to the French line in something of a rush. In the waist King was walking backwards and forwards behind his gun teams, his eyes constantly roaming about those under his command. It was important that order was maintained; the natural reaction for any man going into battle was to fire at the first opportunity. But if any of *Scylla*'s great guns were let off early much of the impact from the initial broadsides would be lost. And there could be no denying the psychological power of her opening attack. The position they were claiming should place the British frigate at the stem of one enemy vessel and the stern of another. Both areas were fragile in any warship, and allowed shot not only to penetrate, but travel the entire length of the hull. King was determined to time each barrage so that the maximum effect could be gleaned. Were the broadsides despatched too soon, the blows would strike the side of the hull, and might even be deflected; he must avoid that, and the only way to do so was through control.

"Hold it, hold it..." he said, pacing back and forth, while Rose peered through a starboard gunport and Barrow to larboard. "Anyone even thinks of firing and I'll see them at a grating tomorrow, and their back bones shortly afterwards." It was a measure of King's desperation that he had descended to threats and outright bullying. But the men knew him well enough, and understood the reason for his concern.

"Starboard ship is turnin' to leeward," Rose shouted.

That was to be expected, and meant that at least one of the enemy had given up trying to turn them away. The move might lessen the impact of *Scylla*'s broadside somewhat, but it would take time to shift the hull, and King was still hoping to achieve a partial rake. But the news contained greater significance, which he was quick to appreciate. Having an enemy ship wear out of the column meant that most of their task was already achieved; the French had been stopped, and without a shot being fired.

They would be arriving a full cable behind the leading frigate, and slightly more than half in front of the second. The two ships were more or less in line, so he would have to order close on simultaneous discharges. Then both batteries would continue to fire for as long as the enemy remained in range. *Scylla* was well manned, but her gun crews would be stretched considerably. Some would remain effective, others, the weaker ones, must inevitably slow. King felt that two broadsides from each battery would be sufficient, then the individual gun captains could be given their heads, and independent fire ordered. But it was important that the first barrages were powerful enough to knock the stuffing, and most of the fight, from the Frenchmen.

Rose raised his hand, and King thought he saw the shadow of the second enemy ship's bow loom through the starboard gun port. From above they could hear the sound of the marines as they started to take pot shots. It would be long range for their muskets, but there might be psychology involved there as well, and it was faster to reload a Bess than an eighteen pounder carriage gun. Barrow's hand was also up, and both were peering out intently; it could not be long, and some of the gun captains were standing to one side, eager to hear their weapons speak.

"Hold it, hold it..." King repeated, willing the ship on. It could only be a matter of seconds now. A crack came from above, clearly the leading enemy had stern chasers, and was firing on them. Someone shouted and one of the British forecastle carronades went off. Then both lads brought their hands down at almost the same time and King bellowed the command for his guns to open fire.

The cacophony of a double broadside was deafening, even to men who had been used to the sound of cannon fire for most of their working lives. *Scylla* trembled dreadfully beneath their feet, and as the emptied barrels were sponged out, reloaded and heaved back, King even worried that they had caused some major internal damage to the frigate's fabric. But all such thoughts were soon wiped away as the first gun captain signalled his piece ready. King could have no exact idea of the reload time, but knew that it was fast. Rose and Barrow had rejoined him; clearly Banks had brought the ship to a halt, and *Scylla* was ideally placed for another onslaught. The larboard battery was ready first and he despatched it. Two guns from starboard joined in, but that mattered little now. Soon the rest were ready, and the second starboard broadside was released. Then he gave the command for all to fire at will, and the race was truly on.

* * *

The wounded had started to appear on the orlop deck and both surgeons were at work. Mr Clarkson, assisted by two loblolly boys, had a member of the afterguard on the operating table and was attempting to stitch a gash to his calf. The man was clearly terrified, and quite convinced the surgeon wanted to cut the leg off. Meanwhile Manning, his assistant, was examining a marine who had been struck on the head and appeared concussed. The women had three more waiting for them, none of whom seemed to be in any great pain, and Sarah was just getting used to the idea of tending to injured seamen when the casualties from the last broadside began to be delivered.

These were of a different order; the wounds were horrific and demanded immediate, if not necessarily expert, attention. Mrs Porter applied a tourniquet to the leg of a man who was surely about to lose his foot, and soon moved on to comfort a lad with a large splinter in his right thigh with all the assurance of his own mother. Betsy Clarkson was also occupied with a seventeen stone gunner who had lost an ear and was crying like a child. But Sarah hesitated. There could be no denying it, she found the patients intimidating, and was suddenly aware both of what everyone expected of her and how hopelessly inadequate she was to the task.

"If there is bleeding, try to stop it," Betsy called across while her current charge began to shake uncontrollably. "For those that need dressings there are bandages a plenty, and you can use one of these if it is a limb," she said, pointing to a pile of tourniquets. "But make sure you chalk a mark on the forehead, in case they gets left for too long."

Sarah knew she was being a fool, but Betsy understood. "Look, we only got to keep them alive, nothing more," she said, in a softer voice. "The surgeons will deal with them proper later."

She nodded; she felt weak and her hands seemed unusually large and clumsy, but still she looked at the nearest man and tried to smile reassuringly. He was bleeding badly from a cut on his left shoulder. Blood had already soaked into the canvas flooring, and showed no signs of stopping. The wound was unsuitable for a tourniquet, but the flow was significant and might be hard to check with just bandages.

Sarah was about to go for help but stopped when she caught the man's expression. He was clearly frightened; his eyes stayed fixed on hers and carried a desperate plea for help. She looked away, feeling both unworthy and undeserving of his trust, but the look remained with her, and she collected a roll of bandages and returned to him.

"Well then, you seem to have been a little unlucky," she said, her voice sounding unusually loud as she braced herself to pull back his shirt. The cloth came apart in her hands, and the sight of the mangled flesh was almost too much to cope with. But the man was still watching closely, considering her almost, and she felt embarrassed, knowing he deserved far more than her inept ministrations.

"I'm going to make you more comfortable," she said, now confronting the seeping wound while reaching for a bundle of cotton waste, "and will try and stop that dreadful bleeding." She placed her hand upon his shoulder and examined more closely. In fact it was not as bad had she had feared, though quite a large flap of skin had been torn back, and a piece of what might be wood was lodged against his shoulder blade, holding the cut open and doubtless encouraging the haemorrhage. At first she considered pressing the injury closed, but guessed it to be a waste of effort as the wound must eventually be re-opened to have the object removed. A loblolly boy was waiting while Manning attended to the concussed marine and looked across in her direction when he felt her eyes upon him.

"Can you fetch a pair of tweezers?" she asked, feeling mildly ridiculous as she closed her forefinger and thumb together in mid air. The man, who was far older than she was, appeared unsurprised at her request; he collected something from the instrument box and came across.

"You gonna stitch him, ma'am?" he asked.

"No, I want to clean his wound," she said, as if it was the most natural thing in the world. The loblolly boy passed across a pair of bright brass forceps. Sarah took them and noticed the patient was still watching her.

"What is your name?" she asked.

"Jeffreys, miss," the seaman told her.

"Very well, Jeffreys, are you happy for me to do this?"

"Yes, miss."

She glanced at the loblolly boy. "Can you help Mr Jeffreys forward?"

"Very good, ma'am." he grasped Jeffreys's good shoulder and heaved him upright, rather roughly, Sarah thought.

Jeffreys gave a groan, but the wound was much easier to reach, and was even in a shaft of light from the lanthorn. She brought the forceps closer, and eased the skin back with her other hand. Yes, it was wood: a wedge shaped piece about three inches long and almost half an inch square at its thickest end. She grasped it in the forceps, and eased it gently free of the muscle. The blood continued to flow, but the loblolly boy saw to that with a handful of tow, and as she removed the piece completely, the skin flopped back neatly enough. Sarah sighed, and felt the tension leave her to be replaced by a deep and heady feeling of success.

"You have to check the wound, ma'am," the loblolly boy said, as if stating the obvious.

"I have to what?"

"Check to see there ain't no bits left behind," he told her patiently. "They can cause it to go bad later, else."

It made sense, she supposed, although part of her felt that Jeffreys had already suffered enough. She returned to the injury and, as carefully as she could, lifted it open again. The man stirred, but the loblolly boy was holding him still in expert hands. There looked to be nothing untoward, and she was about to release the skin once more when a small piece of black attracted her attention.

It was another piece of wood, far shorter, and very much thinner, almost insignificant looking. She reached forward with the forceps and removed it.

One more the wound closed itself, and she felt ready to apply a dressing. The loblolly boy passed a piece of tow to her, and she smoothed the skin flat before beginning to wind a strip of coarse cotton cloth about the chest. Jeffreys was breathing hard; she could feel his warmth on her neck, but she continued to work, keeping the bandage as tight and even as was possible. Then, reaching the end of the roll, she tied it off with a simple knot.

"Nicely done, ma'am," the loblolly boy told her. They lowered the man back onto the deck, and Sarah arranged a bundle of canvas behind his head to act as a pillow. "I seen a deal worse, and that done by doctors," he continued, then added meditatively. "But then doctors ain't surgeons: most are too full of learnin'. They might know all about humours an' the like, but few would care for a wounded man in the normal way. They ain't got the sensitivity, you see. Hardly any could close a body, not with any feelin', not as you jus' did."

* * *

Scylla was keeping all her promises. She had already proved herself an excellent sea boat, fast and biddable; now she was showing just how fine a gun platform she could be. And her cannon were well worth the mounting; already the eighteen pounders on her main deck, supplemented in no small way by the forecastle and quarterdeck carronades, had made a visible impact on both enemy ships. Banks had backed the main and they were maintaining position reasonably enough, just in line with both frigates. Fire from the great guns was almost continuous, and Westwood and Adshead had organised their marines along the starboard bulwark. The crisp bank of red and white stretched almost the entire length of the ship, and under the stoical command of Sergeant Rice the men were working like automatons, buffeting the nearest Frenchman with volley after volley of deadly musket fire. The starboard ship had begun to turn when fortunate shots from *Scylla*'s main battery brought down both her jib boom and the fore topmast, making the manoeuvre clumsy and incomplete. A trail of line, canvas and spars now trailed from her foretop; she hung in temporary suspension with her starboard bow exposed to the British frigate's broadside, and most of her cannon either covered by wreckage or unable to bear. There was a solid pencil of smoke winding up from her waist and at times a tongue of flame could been seen. Banks knew that if he were to remain much longer she would strike, although strangely that was not in his plans. The frigate that was third in line was a good way back but coming up on her stern. She was without damage; his next task must be to engage and disable her.

Meanwhile, to larboard, the leading French ship had received a proper pounding. Her stern lights and quarter galleries had been almost completely knocked in, and it was only luck that had left her with a mizzen and any means of steering. Quite what conditions were like below deck he could not tell, but no ship survives two comprehensive stern rakings and emerges undamaged. She had limped on and was now only just in long range of their cannon, and clearly intended to wear. Doubtless her captain proposed turning back on her tormentor, and Banks was quite prepared for just such a move.

"Bring her to the wind, if you please."

The quartermaster strained at the wheel, and *Scylla* eased gently to larboard as the braces brought the main back to the breeze once more. There would be an uncomfortable moment when her stern was presented to the starboard frigate. But she was still in such disarray from the downing of her spars that

Banks considered the risk worth running. The larboard ship had caught his intention, and was coming round as fast as she could, but would be in no position to deliver a broadside while their bow was vulnerable.

For a moment there was blessed silence as the guns were stilled. All stood waiting while the British frigate picked up speed, then the yards were adjusted further, and *Scylla* began a tight and tidy turn. Her starboard battery fired halfway through the manoeuvre, and the leading enemy ship was nicely straddled. Little material damage could be seen, apart from the forecourse, which took fire and was consumed within seconds. Banks watched with satisfaction; doubtless the flames would be quickly contained, but the ship would lose speed, and her crew confidence. Then *Scylla* was round and heading seemingly on a collision course with the bow of the second frigate.

The quartermaster was clearly following his captain's train of thought, and had the ship aiming at a point just ahead of the Frenchman's bowsprit. *Scylla* was gathering speed all the time and should pass her with ease and in ideal range for a sound broadside, although Banks had a different target in mind.

Beyond, the third in line was on the starboard tack and closing. She had slowed following *Scylla*'s intervention, and was now setting to clear the disabled ship. Banks knew then that he must be prudent and not waste shot on an enemy that was already badly damaged. There would be no time to reload; they must be ready to face that third frigate with something more than empty barrels.

"Tell Mr King to ignore the first target," he said, turning about for a messenger and remembering that Parfrey was absent. Crouch, a reliable hand, was standing at a nearby carronade and took the instruction without question. Banks watched him as he made for the quarterdeck steps. King might find it hard to contain his gun crews; their blood would be up, and some were bound to protest at being ordered to leave the exposed bow of an enemy unattended. But the third in line was fresh, and liable to deal them a nasty blow; he had to meet her with some degree of retaliation.

"Hot work, sir!"

Captain Westwood was beaming at him from the starboard bulwark: the man's face glowed almost as red as his tunic. He mopped at his brow while a private fed fresh shot into the loading chamber of his rifle and Adshead began to regroup the men on the opposite side.

"You have been busy, Captain?" Banks asked as the marine followed his men across the deck.

"Aye, sir," he said, regarding the rifle with obvious affection. "The piece is truly a marvel. I reckon to have bagged three Frenchman already, and those from quite a distance."

It must have been seeing young Parfrey wounded, that or lowering his defences enough to allow Sarah to get close, but Banks felt a sudden surge of revulsion well up inside and was quite unable to reply. He wondered for a moment; they were both fighting officers after all, and the fact that Westwood was taking pleasure in his work should not count against him: such dedication might even be applauded. And Banks had both ridden to hounds and shot for game; was there anything so different in the satisfaction the marine was currently exhibiting to that felt at the end of a successful day in the field? Banks supposed not, but even as he gave a curt acknowledgement he could not ignore the chill that stayed long after he had moved on. Then it came to him: Westwood was taking all this far too personally; he should be attending to the direction of his entire force, not allowing himself to become entrapped with the detail of one single weapon. He watched as Westwood eagerly collected the rifle and stood waiting for further sport. He was an officer yet seemed content to behave like a private, and it was that, Banks finally decided, as much as any enthusiasm for the task, which particularly grated. The revelation came as something of a relief and he tried to empty his mind of all further distracting thoughts.

The next French frigate was a large one, probably bigger than *Scylla*, and liable to be carrying more guns. They would meet almost head on; he had to plan some way of gaining the upper hand, and random musings on the function of officers and men would not help.

"We're missing a prime target there, sir."

And now it was Caulfield's turn to interrupt him. Exasperated, Banks swung round to see his first lieutenant pointing at the bow of the nearest Frenchman. But he could not deny, it was a tempting mark, and any gunner could hardly be blamed for sending his shot into that frail and beckoning prow. A solid broadside from *Scylla* would settle her for good whether she chose to strike or not. It would be a satisfying blow and Bank's fame was certain to rise one notch higher in consequence.

But then he must not fall into the same trap as Westwood. The men beneath him were there to fight, it was his responsibility to organise their efforts without regard to personal satisfaction. Besides, there would be little gained if he took out the nearest frigate, only to be beaten to a wreck by the fresh ship that was steadily growing closer.

He forced himself to speak lightly, knowing that any other reaction might be misinterpreted "Aye, Michael, she is a tempting prize, but first we must account for her sister." He indicated the third frigate.

"Of course, sir." Caulfield agreed readily enough, even if there remained a taint of longing in his eye as his attention strayed back to the nearer target.

But Banks could not afford such a luxury; he must set his mind to the job in hand. The next ship was indeed large, and she would also be prepared for them. *Scylla* had already sustained a fair amount of damage from the first two, and it was likely that this one would deliver a good deal more, and may even account for her completely. But he had been ordered to stop the line, and his task was not yet done.

Beyond the approaching frigate there were more Frenchmen, although they appeared to be turning. And beyond them he could see the enemy flag, surrounded by several British ships, while *Foudroyant* and *Canada* were creeping steadily closer to leeward. He told himself he had this one further ship to disable. Wound it sufficiently, and he could make for the safety of other friendly vessels, or steer away from the fight completely and nurse his wounds; *Scylla* would have done more than her share that day. He might not be credited with taking a prize himself, but could feel content that they had played a pivotal part in the action. And if he failed to become a hero in the eyes of the mob, there were naval officers a plenty who would recognise the part that he had played.

They were about to pass the disabled Frenchman now, but Banks was concentrating solely on the oncoming frigate. He ordered *Scylla* two points to starboard. Ideally he should clear her by a cable to give his gunners a reasonable chance while not letting the enemy send her boarders across. He was considering this when he noticed the oncoming ship had also altered course a fraction. It was possible they intended to allow their wounded comrade a wide berth; maybe the smoke had spooked them, and they were fearing fire or even an explosion. But that faint change in direction was all that Banks needed to envisage a further opportunity.

He looked at the stricken ship again as his thoughts, now free of all distractions, ran on unbidden. King had been firm; no shots had landed on the vulnerable prow, although Westwood's marines were regrouped on the larboard side and sniping at the men on her forecastle. But the very fact that *Scylla* had ignored the chance to fire her larboard broadside had indicated his intentions plainly enough. And now, now that he had seen another way, he would benefit from his caution in quite an unexpected manner. He turned to the sailing master, who had been standing by as a mute witness throughout the action.

"Mr Fraiser, would you say it were possible to lay us alongside the approaching enemy to windward?" His voice was soft and purposefully restrained.

"To windward, sir?" The older man eyed him cautiously. "Why, that should be relatively easy."

Banks hesitated for a moment; the sailing master's pacifist views were well known, yet what he was to ask must place them in an invidious position. "Indeed, but I wish them to think otherwise; they are to believe we intend to engage to their lee, with our larboard battery."

So, *Scylla* was not heading for a long range duel but would be taken into the very teeth of the action once more. Massive damage might be expected from the Frenchman's guns, and equally terrible destruction doled out in return. Banks hoped that Fraiser would be dispassionate enough to disregard this, and simply answer his question.

"You are thinking to make a hasty turn and engage their windward side?" Fraiser confirmed, but even as he spoke he seemed to understand the possibilities. "We may well have the speed, that is, if the ship were capable of such a manoeuvre..."

Banks waited while the older man considered the breeze and what was left of their sails.

"Yes, sir," Fraiser said finally, his voice soft and level. "I think I can do that, but it will be a close thing, and we shall need to act swiftly."

There was no arguing with that; in fact they should really be altering course now. But for the plan to succeed he must also leave it until the very last moment. It would have to be fast enough to take the enemy off guard, when most of their gun crews were manning their larboard battery. Snipers and boarders would not be so easy to catch unaware, but if he timed it right *Scylla* could deliver a crushing blow that would probably knock at least half the fight from the Frenchman. Even if no major spars were affected, she would be badly shaken and must, at the very least, be slowed sufficiently to fall victim to one of the approaching British ships.

But if he failed, if he left the moment just a little too late, if some fluke of wind meant they were unable to pass to windward, and must choose between falling to leeward under the guns that would be primed and ready, or ploughing head first into the enemy ship itself, then it would be a disaster. His men would be taken aback, there would be confusion and probably panic. And when the French released their own, heavier, broadside at a far closer range than he had anticipated, all the terror and devastation planned for them would be delivered straight onto his own dear ship.

Banks's eyes remained on Fraiser; there was much wisdom stored in that grey haired head, and although he knew the man could not approve of his actions he had to ask. "Do you think it will work, Adam?"

The sailing master gauged the wind once more, and looked back at his captain. "I'd say it has a fair chance, sir," he said evenly, understanding far more than Banks would ever know. "And I certainly think you would be right to try."

CHAPTER FIFTEEN

"What the hell do you think you are doing, girl?"

Sarah glanced up to see the greatcoated figure of her father standing over her. He looked angry, extremely angry, although that faint trace of fear that she had come to recognise so well of late was also present.

"I am taking care of this gentleman," she said, brushing the hair from the face of the young topman who had broken his right arm and was waiting patiently for it to be set.

"Well, you can leave him be and tend to your mother. She is worried sick, and will not take kindly knowing you are mixing with such rabble."

He moved off, clearly expecting her to rise and follow, but the seaman was in pain, and Sarah had no intention of going anywhere.

"Are you to come, or must I have you taken?" he asked, when her intentions became clear.

"I am staying, papa," she replied softly. "There are those here who need help, and I will not leave them."

"So be it, Missy; then you allow me no choice." The man was clearly exasperated, and began looking about for a likely servant.

"I would let her be," Betsy Clarkson spoke from across the deck. "Your daughter is doing good work, and should not be interrupted."

"And there are some who would stop it, should you try and take her." Mrs Porter's voice rang out with natural authority. She had already formed an opinion of Sarah's father and been keeping an eye on matters from her place next to the drugs cabinet. Monroe looked from one to the other, and was not oblivious to the gaze of the wounded men who lay about him. They might be his social inferiors, but there was no doubting the intent in their stares, nor the sullen silence that had suddenly descended upon the cockpit.

"You shall hear further of this," he said, mustering all his well practised self-regard.

A whistle came from somewhere far off, and was quickly joined by a series of jeers and hoots. Standing alone, puffed up and pompous, amid the clamour of wounded, belligerent men, he cut quite a comical figure. Her father might be a magistrate and accustomed to having his way, but there was little he could do in the face of such opposition, and Sarah almost felt sorry for him as he gave one final menacing glower before stomping angrily out of the cockpit.

* * *

Crowley had drifted away for no more than a few seconds, but his mates shouted at his lack of attention and he quickly hurried back to work with the rammer. He had seen enough, though. The three frigates ahead of *Hoche* were wearing out of line and would be coming to their aid. Positioned as they were, they should meet the British head on and were bound to cause damage and confusion. If the French captain grabbed the opportunity and set what sail they could manage, there might still be an end to this mess. The fresh ships could deal with both the liner and the frigate: *Hoche* had done enough. He pressed the rammer into the warm barrel and felt the round shot bed in against the charge. The procedure had become so automatic that he could do it blind; just as well: acrid smoke had found its way into his mouth, nose and eyes, yet he barely squinted as he worked. But the memory of the frigates stayed with him. He glanced across at Tone as the man tapped yet another charge into the touch hole. If there was only a chance to pause, a moment or two to gather breath, he might be able to speak with him. He, of all present, would see the need to move on. *Hoche* had already taken severe punishment; her canvas was all but shredded and Crowley did not like to think of the damage the British had inflicted upon her hull. Unless she extricated herself soon, she would become totally unmanageable and must inevitably be surrendered. He noted by a second crafty glance that the French frigates were almost in position now; it was time for *Hoche* to benefit from the reprieve. That or wait and be taken.

"We have support from for'ard!" he chanced as MacArthur and Doyle brought the cannon back to the firing position. Tone looked up, but did not appear to understand Crowley's words.

"*Loire, Immortalité* and *Bellone,*" he screamed in desperation. "They're coming back for us, and will be raking the British afore long."

Tone considered this for a moment, then took a step forward through the smoke, while Doyle collected a charge and waited for Crowley to finish sponging out the barrel. He was having a good look, and failed to return to the piece even when the ball was in place. Doyle swore, and snatched the priming horn from Tone's hands, but still he remained watching the course of the battle. Crowley felt a wave of hope break over him. For all of his fanatical ideals the man was no fool; he must understand the situation they were in, and he was bound to speak with the commodore. Doyle discharged the cannon and almost simultaneously a British shot hit the *Hoche*. A server from the next gun screamed out and fell to the deck, his hands clutching at his torn face. This business was far too warm to last very much longer; they must be moving and without delay. As it was, that single frigate that had thrown herself at the French van would have to be passed, and already the two bigger ships, approaching on their larboard bow, were growing dangerously close.

"Michael, will you look to your work, there?"

He jumped at MacArthur's rebuke, but still Tone was absent, and Crowley was becoming more and more convinced that sense would prevail. Yes, he was returning now, and even made eye contact as he approached the cannon.

"Aye, it's a mess and there's no mistaking." Crowley waited as he collected the priming horn back from Doyle, but there was no more.

"We can move on," Crowley insisted, when he realised Tone had no intention of doing anything other than continue to fire the cannon. "The three frigates are fresh and will silence these two," he waved his hand dismissively at the British ships that were competing to stay alongside *Hoche*. "We can be away from here, maybe even get as far as landing some troops." It was an indication of Crowley's state of mind that he actually tried to appeal. Tone sensed this, and stopped in the act of filling the touch hole.

"Now why would you be wanting to do that, Michael?" he asked. "You who have never shown any inclination to free your country, yet now speak like the hardest of all revolutionaries." Doyle and MacArthur were also watching him, and Crowley felt himself wither slightly under their combined gaze. "Is it possible you would rather be out of here? That you were never really so committed in the first place? Or would you prefer be across the water," he looked in the direction of the British seventy-four. "Fighting your friend's battles once more, even if it goes against your own kind and the country of your birth?"

A shot landed against the frame timber almost next to them, creating a ball of dust and splinters that showered down about the carronade's crew.

"There isn't the time for this," MacArthur said sullenly as he brushed the debris from his shirt.

"Aye, and there's a true word," Tone agreed, his eyes still fixed firmly on Crowley. "There isn't the time, and the chance is now there never will be."

* * *

Further to the west, the two frigates were closing on opposing tacks. *Scylla* had sustained a fair amount of damage; all of fifteen minutes back the carpenter had reported three feet in the well. Numerous shrouds and stays hung loose, and the larboard mainchains were weakened. But she was still sailing tight enough for now, Banks reassured himself; and as the enemy grew closer, and the enormity of what he proposed became clear, his confidence actually increased. He had already taken *Scylla* further to starboard to signal his apparent intention and gain a little more sea room. Now he guessed there was a minute and a half, maybe two, before he need act again; scant time, but just about enough for what he had in mind.

He stepped forward to the break of the quarterdeck and called for attention. Below him, in the waist, he could see King and young Rose waiting on his word. Something of what he had planned had probably been communicated to the two, and Banks felt King might guess the rest. Likewise with Chilton over on the forecastle. But it was still a good idea for him to speak; that way no one could be in any doubt both of his intentions, and the whole ridiculous caper was completely his responsibility.

"We shall be passing the yonder enemy frigate," he said, his voice firm and rising powerfully over the distant sound of battle. "They will expect us to do so to leeward, but I intend to claim the windward gauge." There was a brief muttering from the nearest gun crew, and the marines began to lower their muskets in preparation for moving to the opposite side of the deck. "Should we be successful it will be close, almost touching distance in fact. I do not intend to come alongside, however, as they are liable to be better manned than us." That was an important consideration, and he looked to the tops where there were men ready with grappling hooks, and received a wave of acknowledgement from one of the midshipmen.

"Mr Westwood, Mr Adshead, you will oblige me by retaining your men to larboard." The younger officer appeared confused, whereas Westwood looked positively angry at missing the opportunity of bagging a few more Frenchmen. But it was necessary for the enemy to be fooled for as long as possible, and nothing would give the game away more effectively than the marines taking up station early on the starboard side. "How are you loaded, Mr King?"

"Double round, sir. Both batteries"

"Mr Chilton?"

"Round on canister, sir."

"Very good. You will both hold your fire until the enemy are at their most vulnerable." The guns on either side were already run out, so there was no room for confusion there. "We may need the larboard at some point, but I would suggest you combine both crews to starboard in case we get two bites of the cherry." He glanced up to where Chilton had control of the forecastle. "Mr Chilton, you may do likewise, but retain both crews until we open fire." The crews manning the forward carronades would also be visible to the French, so again, he must not signal his intention. The enemy was growing closer by the second. Banks cast a glance about once more; all seemed to be in order. Now everything depended on the next few minutes. If he was right, and *Scylla* could make the move to windward successfully enough, they may yet see an end to matters. He was still confident that a single broadside, coming from both an unexpected quarter, and far closer range, would deal a crushing blow to the enemy. And if he failed, if his frigate was more badly damaged than he had judged and fell short, either ploughing prow on, or dropping meekly to leeward, they might still delay them long enough to ensure her subsequent capture. It would be at the cost of his ship, but then he had been prepared for just such an outcome before the plan had first come to him, so really nothing would be lost.

"We have to make the move, sir," the sailing master prompted him quietly from the binnacle. He was right, but Banks delayed a second or so longer, enjoying his ship for what might well be the last time. Then he turned back almost stiffly, and caught the eye of Caulfield and Fraiser.

"Very well, gentlemen," he said. "We shall begin."

* * *

On the forecastle Surridge had listened to the captain with ill concealed disdain. He was totally in charge of his cannon, and didn't need officers telling him what to do with it and when. The starboard carronade had already acquitted herself well, and Surridge had not been slow in pointing out the speed of his crew and the accuracy of the piece to any that would listen. But now it looked as if she was to be presented with an absolute pearl of a target. A prime French frigate, and what sounded like the ideal range. His gun could throw a twenty-four pound round shot with remarkable accuracy; certainly, if his shouted commentary could be believed, it had scored several important hits already that morning. But there would be no need for sharp shooting in what was to come. They had already doubled the load, adding cannister to the round shot, and were bound to create some true mischief. With luck he felt they might get two or even three broadsides in, and Surridge was more than ready. Now that he had become accustomed to the piece he was truly enamoured with it; the carronade was so quick and light to serve, and the rate of fire was far faster than anything he could have achieved with his old carriage guns. He slapped at the cascabel and grinned at Cox.

"Likely we're to give the old bitch a touch more practice," he said. Cox smiled awkwardly in return. Surridge in a good mood was possibly more disconcerting than Surridge in a strop. Both conditions were likely to change at any time, and Cox was rather hoping that action would not be delayed for too much longer.

Chilton, watching from his vantage point next to the galley chimney, had been keeping a wary eye on the carronade captain throughout the morning and his thoughts were running on very similar lines. There could be no arguing that Surridge was a born fighter, but his strength of mind and purpose were almost those of a lunatic, and the lieutenant was quietly relieved that such emotion had a plain and clear target to hand in the form of the French. Then the ship heeled as if suddenly mishandled, and all thoughts for the men were instantly dismissed.

They were turning. The yards creaked as they tried to keep pace with the breeze, while the helmsman brought the ship round in a way that would not have impressed many. But then all knew that this was for speed, not elegance; they had to gain fifty, sixty, maybe even eighty feet almost directly into the wind. And they had to gain it fast, so that the enemy, however alert or practised they may be, would not have the chance to claw any back. Chilton looked across and was faintly reassured. So far there was no sign of movement from the oncoming frigate; she was continuing on her way, still apparently expecting to meet *Scylla* in the accepted manner. He held his breath as he waited. Their speed was steadily dropping, but already half the distance had been covered. Now all that mattered was what the French intended to do.

They could retain their present course, come up on *Scylla*'s leeward side, and attempt to rake her stern, or make a race of it, and turn likewise, vying for the windward gauge as they closed on the opposite tack. Every second was vital and he realised then that Banks was depending heavily on the French not being either as fast or agile as the equivalent British vessel. He only needed to be unlucky, to have found an opponent in better practice than the norm, and his bold plan would end in ignominious failure. Then they began to react.

She too was altering course; the braces and sheets were released and canvas began to billow, but for several seconds it was impossible to say where she was bound. Would she fall off to leeward, creating a greater distance between the two ships and allow *Scylla* valuable sea room? Or also come up to the wind, fight for every inch of space, and hope to win the ultimate race to cross the other's prow? He watched as the helm was put over and the Frenchman turned. She clearly intended to compete, and with a full suit of sails and undamaged rigging, was far better set to do so than *Scylla*.

Chilton thought they might have forty feet on the Frenchman, but needed to maintain that room in order to complete the turn in front. It was certainly going to be tight; nothing more than the wind changing by a point or two would probably decide. Should it back, *Scylla* would take the advantage, and gain a corresponding increase in speed: should it veer the reward would go to the French. And should it stay constant, he decided, well then it was anyone's guess.

* * *

Banks considered matters from the quarterdeck. So far his plan was working; the French had decided to follow, and it was now a simple sailing contest. They had a slight lead that he felt he might maintain and even improve upon if the wind would only hold. He glanced up at the weather vane once more: if the wind would only hold – aye, there's the rub. For the last two minutes the breeze had grown fickle and even dropped and was now playing an odd catch-me game that had *Scylla*'s sails alternating between board tight and shivering in a way that must be infuriating to the quartermaster.

Banks took a turn across the deck, his eyes low, not wishing to meet those of Caulfield or Fraiser. Despite the circumstances he felt this to be a very private battle. Even if every seaman on deck knew the situation it was he and he alone who had instigated matters. And whatever the outcome, be it complete victory, or devastating defeat, he would be accountable. Men would be dead tomorrow who might otherwise have survived because of his actions: such responsibility cannot be shared.

"We're gaining on her," Caulfield said suddenly, and Banks came back from his self-imposed isolation. The first lieutenant was not known for bold statements; there would be something worth seeing. Yes, the lead had increased, and as the enemy frigate pounded towards them it was obvious that the time to act was close.

Banks looked to the weather vane again: the wind had even backed slightly. The French frigate was barely more than two cables off their quarter, yet *Scylla*'s lead was sufficient to blank almost all of her broadside guns. As he watched smoke erupted from her forecastle, to be whipped away by the breeze. Shots whistled overhead, and there was a loud crack as the trunk of their mainmast was struck a glancing blow, but it would have taken a lucky shot indeed to have stopped them now.

"Are you ready, there?" Banks called to the quartermaster. The man grunted without taking his eyes off the sails. Men at the starboard battery rose, unbidden; all knew what was about. More shots came from the Frenchman, but these were musket balls. A line of soldiers could be seen manning her side, and volley after volley of small arms fire came screaming over the bulwarks. The sight triggered something in his mind and he glanced across to Westwood. The marines were still lined along the larboard rail, and only now were being ordered into position. For a moment Banks wondered if the man was sulking from the earlier instance, but could spare little time for anyone with wounded feelings.

"Take her across!" It was the time; Banks instinctively knew it, even though some later might say he made his move too soon. But he wanted it tight; he wanted to maintain the surprise he had created less than three minutes ago. *Scylla* heeled as her helm was put across, and the afterguard strained desperately to keep what wind they could. She had inertia aplenty though, and was cutting across the enemy's bows before any had truly realised it.

He ran forward and to the leeward side, watching the men at the guns in the waist below. King was out of station; he had climbed from the gundeck to the starboard gangway and was holding his hand high for all to see, as marines swarmed about him trying to take up their positions and gun captains frantically adjusted their elevation to allow for the ship's heel. The two forward mounted long guns on the enemy's bow were fired almost simultaneously, and one shot smacked into the hull just below where Banks stood, but he barely noticed the impact, nor the sound that came immediately afterwards. And now they were round; *Scylla* corrected like a professional and there was no longer a risk of collision as she began to run down the length of the enemy's windward side.

There was no time to back sails, but *Scylla* was not sailing fast, due to her apparent mishandling. King brought his arm down, and a deep and mighty rumble began from her hull as the double shotted barrage started to bite.

It was not the hard crack of a simultaneous discharge, nor even the regular wave of disciplined ripple fire, but a slow and considered attack, with each gun captain waiting until he had a definite target in sight. The French main channel and chains dissolved into their component pieces when two eighteen pound round shot buried themselves in the mounting, and several banks of snipers vanished as furrows of canister cut through their tightly packed ranks. The carronades next to him were firing now, and Banks saw French officers brushed aside by the terrible power of the overloaded guns. The enemy quarterdeck must have been all but swept clear, he guessed, as men at the wheel fell to the withering onslaught. About him musket balls began raining down from the Frenchman's tops like so many hailstones, but it was not until they were all but past that the first of the enemy's great guns fired in return.

They did little damage. Either the men were untrained, or such panic had been induced that they fired indiscriminately, without troubling to aim their weapons to any degree. Caulfield was still looking back at the Frenchman when Banks finally turned to him. There was little either of them could say, and both knew the other well enough to resist any of the trite platitudes that came to mind. It had been a bold plan, one that proved successful. That single broadside had knocked much of the fight from the French. They might continue to run, but they would be caught, that was now a certainty; as would the others that lay disabled in their wake. *Scylla* had carried out Warren's orders to the letter: the enemy line had been halted.

"Beggin' your pardon, sir." Banks looked round to see the carpenter knuckling his forehead as Caulfield ordered the ship back on to an easterly course. "There's another two feet taken in the well. I put patches to a couple of nasty leaks, but would reckon there to be a plank or two stove in below the waterline."

"The pumps are in operation?" he asked.

"Jus' the one, sir. Mr King said he can spare me more men when we are out of action."

"Very good." Over five feet in the well was a good deal of water, but King had been right in keeping his gunners at their posts, and Banks must also think of the action in hand. Behind them *Foudroyant* was already exchanging long range fire with the first of the frigates, and Warren himself in *Canada* lay close behind. *Melampus* was off their starboard quarter and beating up against the wind. Then he switched his attention to the *Hoche* for the first time in what felt like ages. The ship was besieged, with *Magnanime* and *Robust* competing for position to one side, and the smaller *Amelia* off her stern. "Very well, he repeated. "Mr Fraiser, can you lay us alongside the enemy flagship?"

The sailing master peered through the smoke and glanced up at the sails before nodding. "Aye, sir. There should be little difficulty."

Badly holed as she was, *Scylla* was in no fit state for high speed sailing, but could still continue to make her mark in the action, and while she was so able, Banks had every intention of using her to the full. "Then you will oblige me by doing so without further delay," he said.

CHAPTER SIXTEEN

Hoche was little more than a wreck. Crowley and the rest were still tending their gun, but those on either side had grown silent due to a lack of trained men. And the supply of powder, previously brought by a succession of soldiers, had slowed until they were left waiting for each charge to appear. But the enemy seventy-four was also severely damaged, as was the heavy frigate on their quarter, and even the fifth rate now to their stern. In the pause Crowley noted a further British ship heading for them, and the frigate that had done so much to initially halt the French column was also bearing down from the west. He wiped the back of his arm across his forehead. Shot and splinters continued to fly about the quarterdeck but the small group had remained unharmed since Doherty and Walsh had been accounted for. Now, deafened by gunfire and apparently immune to the rigours of action, it was doubtful that any even noticed the carnage that was being wrought about them.

A fresh charge came by way of a new face, a young lad who looked no more than twelve. He passed the deadly package across and waited, panting, while it was inserted into the mouth of the carronade.

"Be gone," Doyle told him roughly. "We need more; bring back at least two, I don't care about the regulations."

The boy looked at him blankly and stayed where he was. Tone translated, but still he did not move, and eventually replied in a series of short sentences delivered in a thick Bretton accent.

"He says they have no cartridges," Tone told them. "They are sewing more as fast as they can, but have resorted to using powder ladled straight into the guns on the lower deck."

Crowley heard, but said nothing. The earlier incident, when he had all but revealed his private thoughts, was still with him. Whatever his reasons, he maintained that moving on would have been the right strategy, but in saying so he had clearly earned the universal disdain of his fellows. He might feel no particular claim on any country, but even a temporary loss of friends was surprisingly painful to him, and he longed for a way to make amends.

The gun roared out yet again, and they went through the routine of clearing the spent charge and sponging out the barrel, but there seemed less need for haste now, and hardly any to even continue fighting. The soldiers, still formed in ranks along the deck, were maintaining a steady rate of musket fire, but all seemed to know instinctively that defeat could only be a short wait away. A further charge eventually arrived, this time carried by a different lad, and the cannon fired again. Her crew went through the motions of clearing once more, and fired without even bothering to look for a result. Then they waited for more powder, but none was forthcoming. Crowley caught the eye of MacArthur; the man sighed and pursed his lips.

"Reckon we're done for, Michael," he said sadly.

Crowley nodded, stupidly grateful for even this small amount of human contact. "Aye," he replied. "Reckon we are."

* * *

It was yet another gamble, but Banks, still mildly elated from delaying the three frigates, felt there was little he and his ship could not achieve. Of course *Hoche* was far larger than *Scylla*, and boasted two full gun decks containing cannon half as large again as any his fifth rate carried. And she would be packed with men; in addition to a compliment of seamen that probably outnumbered the British by more than two to one, there would be soldiers: the nucleus of a small army. But then the *Hoche* had been under constant fire from another line-of-battle ship, with a heavy frigate and a further fifth rate also joining in. And she was visibly sitting lower in the water, with her tophamper all but destroyed. Banks was betting that *Scylla*'s arrival would come at a time when her commander was considering surrender and his frigate, already demonstrably successful against three of her kind, should be excellently placed to deal the final blow. With their flagship gone, the remaining French could hardly hold out for very much longer and the entire action would be over. A gamble it may be, but he was growing increasingly certain it was one worth the taking.

But, damaged or not, there was still some bite in the two-decker. Fraiser had set a course that would see them closing on her starboard bow and they were just sweeping in ready to join the fight when the Frenchman's entire forecastle appeared to erupt in a cloud of smoke and fire. The guns had clearly been without a target for some while, and were despatched with deadly efficiency on *Scylla*'s prow. Round shot rang about her foremast and bowsprit, bringing down her jib and smashing the martingale rig. Banks cursed, and for a moment even considered laying off and commencing a long range bombardment, but the satisfaction derived from dealing with those frigates was still with him and more than anything else in the world he wanted an end to things.

"Keep her as she is," he muttered as *Scylla* continued to cut through the water. The present angle meant that none of her broadside guns were bearing, but as soon as she was wedged in alongside Banks would order another thunderous barrage to be unleashed. Then Westwood and Adshead would lead their marines across, followed by any seamen detailed as boarders and probably a few extra following out of pure devilment. Banks reckoned they would have control of the forecastle and upper deck within minutes, and it could not be much longer before additional men came. *Robust* was almost touching; and the other two were not so very far off. It would be a short, if bloody fight, and then all would be done: the battle ended, and they could look to securing the prizes and licking their wounds.

Scylla's boarders were grouped about the forecastle and starboard gangways, the marines still crisp in their splendid uniforms, bayonets gleaming in the morning sun. The seamen were far more ragged in comparison and diversely armed with cutlasses, pistols and pikes; some also carried hatchets, others belaying pins, and there was one amongst them who appeared to be wielding a butcher's cleaver. *Scylla* was slowing, the loss of jib, together with what must now be a considerable amount of water in her hull, was finally taking effect. But she only had to be good for the next fifty yards or so, and she had served them so well that Banks felt she would provide that much more at least.

* * *

Surridge, on the forecastle, was certainly ready. His gun was to be used just one more time during the action, then he would abandon it and get to grips with the enemy in a proper manner; in a way that he truly understood. And even Cox by his side, usually a man who preferred to be led rather than lead, even he was looking forward to the forthcoming *mêlée* with a relish that was almost primeval.

Chilton, the senior naval officer present, was perhaps not quite so certain. This was his first true action, the only previous time he had heard a shot fired in anger having been when *Scylla* chased down a privateer off the coast of France. On that occasion the enemy was lightly armed and gave little resistance, a dramatic contrast to what had taken place that morning. He felt he was holding up well enough, but the last thirty minutes or so had definitely taken a toll on his nervous energy. And now he was to lead men in actual hand to hand fighting: he would never dream of shirking such a responsibility but knew in his heart that it was not the ideal task for him.

Captain Westwood, on the other hand, was extremely keen and could not have felt fitter for the fray. His trusty rifle that had proved itself so many times was freshly charged and would soon be tested further in the close confines of hand-to-hand combat. He also wore a sword of course, but the weapon had remained in its scabbard all morning, and there seemed little likelihood that it would be drawn that day. What he had achieved with the *Windbüchse* had convinced him of the superiority of such a weapon, and the marine was determined to see that his experience was properly reported. Just how much damage a unit of men so equipped might do could only be imagined; it was a devastating tool, and one that the British must take full advantage of.

They were closing now, and further enemy shots began to reach them. They were merely small arms fire, however, and most were efficiently absorbed by the hammock-packed netting. Chilton waited, listening to the men as they muttered amongst themselves. No one apparently expected more than token resistance, the consensus being the enemy were all but spent and this was going to be a walk over. The young lieutenant had a soul far too sensitive for such an assumption, and was starting to wonder if he could even take part in an attack, even though he knew that Westwood would assume overall charge when the time came. Then, with a great feeling of relief, he noticed King and Barrow, along with Johnston, the master's mate, make their way up to the forecastle.

"Rose has the guns," King said, grinning broadly at his friend. "Reckoned not much would be needed from them after we touch, so he is to despatch what will bear, then send the crews to join us."

Chilton went over to speak. As the only senior naval officer he had felt very alone on the forecastle for a good while, and was grateful for someone to confide in. "Tell me, Tom," he said, his voice soft and barely audible, "the ship, does she not feel a mite low?"

"Aye, we've taken some nasty knocks; carpenter reports nearly six feet of water in the well." Despite this news the older officer appeared quite cheerful, and his ready acceptance was like a tonic to Chilton. "But we have both pumps in action now, and this little lot should not take too long to finish."

He was unusually casual, and Chilton regarded him carefully. "You make it sound like a jaunt," he said suspiciously.

"Oh no," King hastened to reassure him. "No, I think it will be anything but." His eyes flashed suddenly. "This would be your first time, Peter?"

"It would."

"Then you shall quickly realise that much will be down to luck." He drew closer, speaking as privately as the crowded conditions allowed. "There is not a man present who is not afeared. Any that say otherwise are liars or fools. But it will help if you do not wear your concern on your sleeve; it hardly encourages the people."

Chilton saw the sense in that and felt his body relax for the first time in what seemed like hours. It was far easier now that he was not alone.

"Stand by!" Westwood had mounted the starboard catshead and was holding his rifle high, every bit the ancient warrior waving a spear.

King considered him thoughtfully as he eased the pistol in his belt, and adjusting the hilt of his cutlass. "Of course there may be some who take their bluster a little too rich," he said. Chilton laughed, then King bent to peer down the barrel of the nearest carronade.

"Wait 'tils we touch," he growled as the ship grew closer. There was a snapping of wood and tearing of lines as *Scylla* slowly and unceremoniously ploughed into the Frenchman's starboard bow. The two hulls drew apart momentarily but joined again a little further down. Then, with a deadly groan from the timbers, the warships finally locked.

Without waiting for an order, *Scylla*'s carronades were fired, and all but wiped the waiting Frenchmen from their forecastle and gangway. Then, following Westwood's mighty shout, the boarders left with a rush.

Despite the impact there was still several feet to clear before the enemy deck could be gained, and the battleship's freeboard was higher than the frigate's. King found himself tottering on *Scylla*'s side, conscious of the body of men behind, and actually jumped before he could plan a suitable place to land. He was lucky, and fell against the flagship's main rail. It took no time to clamber across and pull himself up. Cox, immediately behind, was less fortunate. He leaped, but missed his footing, and disappeared into the dark void between the two vessels without a sound.

King recovered himself and took his pistol from his belt. He brought the hammer back to full cock and drew his cutlass as he looked about. The forecastle was all but clear, yet there were enemies a plenty, far more than any of them had realised. The entire waist was filled with soldiers, most of whom would soon be swarming up to meet them. For a moment he wondered about returning, but a glance at the number of British still coming across revealed the folly of such a thought. There was no way any of them could leave now.

Westwood had landed further along the forecastle and was still swinging that ridiculous gun and shouting as he made his way down the ship. But it was a compelling example and several were already following. To their left another group of seaman had just come from *Scylla*. Amongst them King noticed Johnston, alongside Surridge, the quarter gunner. The latter was already in the fight and wielding a boarding cutlass against a French army officer who was trying to reclaim the forecastle.

The man was swept aside by Surridge's heavy blade as if he were a mere puppet, and Johnston casually pressed the body back down to the waist with his foot. Westwood advanced into the space they had created, and more followed. As King watched the marine looked back to him.

"Make for the quarterdeck!" he shouted, indicating the enemy's starboard gangway. King nodded. Westwood had the right of it: the waist was tightly packed with soldiers; it would take an age to cut through such a mob, but the gangway ran several feet above, and had been all but cleared by *Scylla*'s carronades. It also acted as a direct line to the command point of the ship; if they were to force the French to strike, the order must come from there.

One of the marine privates fell, shot in the chest by a group of marksmen on the opposite gangway. Westwood called his men's attention to the threat and aimed his own rifle. The rank of Frenchmen collapsed amidst a volley of musket fire, and Westwood grinned, clearly satisfied.

King started for the gangway and joined it about ten feet behind Westwood's group, with Barrow and Chilton close behind. Another Frenchman fell to the marine officer's piece as the forward party advanced. The thrust of a pike came up at them from the waist, but Johnston was alert and grabbed at the shaft before it could do any damage. A downward slash of Surridge's cutlass followed, then the pike was unceremoniously plunged backwards into its owner's face, and they continued.

The British were just over half way along the gangway when the French fully realised their position. Soldiers on the quarterdeck took aim with muskets, and the man next to King was sent spinning as a ball hit him in the arm. The lieutenant caught the body instinctively, and realised it was Barrow. His face was stretched in pain, but the wound did not appear critical. King heaved him to one side, telling the lad to keep still. There was little he could do to help, but at least the midshipman would be safer propped against the bulwark than if he had fallen to the mob below. They moved on, Surridge pushing past Westwood as the officer paused to pick off a man on the French quarterdeck. Chilton came level with King; he was gripping an ornate hanger and grinning like a madman.

"All well, Peter?" King asked.

"Splendid, Tom," the lieutenant replied through gritted teeth. "Splendid."

Two Frenchmen joined the gangway from the quarterdeck, and ran down towards the advancing British. Westwood's rifle fired, and Surridge swung his cutlass, pausing to finish both his and the marine's victim off with unnecessary zeal.

Then they reached the quarterdeck proper, and Surridge immediately laid into a group still working a carronade. There was an officer amongst them, or at least a man wearing an officer's decorated coat as well as a pair of rather dandy pantaloons, and the British seaman was clearly in the mood for some upper class sport. He advanced, his cutlass at the ready, but the man was armed with a short sword, and parried the strike expertly. Westwood also fired, hitting a seaman with vivid red hair who shrieked like a startled rabbit. The marine was raising his piece to reload, when a musket ball fired from the poop struck the weapon.

There was a loud crack and Westwood's precious rifle seemed to fly from his grasp. The officer's head rolled back, both hands went to cover his face, and he began a long and agonising scream as he sank to his knees at the very end of the gangway. King bounded forward and rolled him aside, gasping as he saw the terrible wound. The rifle was lying on the deck; its butt had exploded and was now nothing more than a tangle of jagged, twisted metal. King kicked angrily at the weapon, sending it down to the waist below. There was nothing for it, he must take command.

He glanced back. More men from *Scylla* had followed them along the gangway. King saw Chilton hesitate as he noticed the prone and moaning body of the marine ahead of him. The young lieutenant looked more astonished than frightened and King figured his nerve would be good for a while longer. Further forward Surridge still seemed locked in combat with the French officer and a British marine was swinging his musket by the barrel like a club. King pressed on, and Chilton followed, stepping carefully passed the groaning Westwood.

A Frenchman fired a pistol; King instinctively ducked even though he could not tell where the shot had been directed. Rising up he almost casually hacked the man back with his cutlass. Then he was free of the gangway and safely on the quarterdeck, although there now seemed to be men everywhere. From one side a madman was waving a wooden handspike with no obvious intention, while the pantalooned officer and Surridge were totally absorbed in what was fast becoming a private battle. King struck wildly at two soldiers who were attempting a bayonet charge; one fell to the blade, the other dropped his musket and drew back at the sight of his colleague being butchered. Chilton was in the fight now, and slashed wildly at a soldier who desperately tried to fend off the blows with his musket. The man was retreating, the weapon held in front of him like a staff, as the lieutenant stepped forward, steadily gaining ground like any professional. Then there were more men from *Scylla* swarming about them, and King knew it could not last for much longer.

A seaman came towards him with a cannon rammer in his hands and a look, almost of enquiry, on his face. For a moment King sensed recognition but in the nightmare that was the *Hoche*'s quarterdeck, reality and conscious thought were effectively suspended. The heavy tool would make a serviceable weapon and instinct told him to defend himself. His sword was ill placed to parry, but the pistol remained unused. He raised it and squeezed the trigger in one fluid action. The gun fired and the face, that strangely familiar face, took on an expression of mild surprise and shock, before disappearing entirely from view. Then a French soldier was charging at him with a musket. There was no bayonet fixed, and King was able to dodge effectively enough, but already another moustachioed seaman was advancing with a sword and deadly intent. King blocked and struck him down, but he knew his luck must soon run out.

He glanced about in desperation, eager for any sign that the French might be beaten. *Amelia* was visible off the larboard quarter. She was clearly intending to come to their aid but remained some way off. And there was *Robust*, nearly alongside, although her boarders still lined her rails. Then he noticed a French officer standing, almost aloof, next to the ship's wheel. Their eyes met, and King nodded in his direction. The man appeared tired, exhausted actually. King advanced towards him, thoughtfully lowering his cutlass as he went. He had little French, and could not begin to explain what was in his heart, but it must be clear to all that nothing more would be gained by fighting. The day was won, or would be within minutes. In that time more men would be killed, more injured; it might as well be acknowledged now as later.

On seeing King approach the man went to raise his sword when he seemed to have a change of heart. His shoulders slumped slightly, the blade was returned to its scabbard and, instead, he reached into his jacket for a small silver whistle. There was one loud, solid blast, followed for a second by almost silence. Then the note was repeated and men actually paused to draw breath. The officer spoke in a commanding voice and looked towards King. Someone called up from the waist, and there was a chorus of angry protests. But soon the Frenchmen were lowering their weapons and slowly the nightmare began to fade.

* * *

The scene on the orlop deck was one of contained confusion. Sarah had long since banished any foolish horrors about dealing with the injured and was tending each man with a newly discovered competence and understanding. And while doing so she had acquired a loyal friend; one who was helping her attentively as any child might their mother.

Parfrey had already been seen by Mr Manning, who closed the gash that ran from his nose to his ear with light horsehair stitches. It was a neat enough job and the bleeding had stopped almost immediately, even if for the rest of his life no one would ever be in doubt of the injury. But at that moment there were other matters far more important to attend to and with his head bathed in bandages the boy followed Sarah about, ready with swabs, instruments, lemonade or rum as the situation demanded. Together they had removed at least eight small splinters and tied three tourniquets, while the number of temporary dressings she had applied, with Parfrey passing the rolls of linen and deftly supporting the patient, were countless. And the men were quieter for the couple's very presence; none were in any doubt as to their medical qualifications, but the attention of other caring beings was in many cases worth as much as any bandage.

Occasionally she would glance across to Mrs Porter, carrying out a similar task on the opposite side of the deck. Betsy was currently assisting Manning, who had the complex job of removing several deeply embedded metal fragments from a gunner's torso. The patients had been coming at a steady stream from the start of the action, with the backlog gradually growing as the medical team fought to keep up with the flow, but in the last ten minutes there had been just one man with a minor cut. The great guns had also been silent and all in the cockpit were wondering if the action had finally come to an end.

Their hopes were roughly crushed when a commotion at the hatch heralded the start of a fresh tide of injured. Mrs Porter rose to meet the new intake, swiftly followed by Sarah and her shadow. The new patients were mainly marines, and there were none of the splinter injuries and shot mangled bodies the medics had become inured to. Instead they were presented with the effects of heavy cutlass blades, small swords and pike heads, with the occasional bullet wound to add variety. A marine officer had been savagely wounded in the face and was shouting for laudanum; there were several who had shed their life's blood on the journey down, and could only to be placed amongst the growing pile of corpses. Some were French, and there was one, a well built bearded man, who was clearly Irish and struggled with the loblolly boys as if they were his sworn enemy. Sarah was attending a seaman wounded in the chest by what she guessed to be a musket shot. The injury was deep and many were in the queue ahead. It would take time to find and extract the bullet, and even then the chances of severe internal damage meant there was little hope for him. She was examining the wound and speaking softly while he watched her with the air of one not fully aware.

"Is there anything we can get you?" she asked as Parfrey applied a light dressing. "A drink, maybe?"

The man shook his head almost sadly but said nothing. Then, as Sarah and the boy stood up to leave, he whispered. "What ship is this?"

Of all the questions asked of them that morning, his was certainly the strangest. And it was spoken in another Irish accent, although this was softer, and there was clearly no malice. Parfrey bent down to him.

"*Scylla*," he said. "She's a fifth rate."

"A frigate?" The man considered the fact for a moment.

Parfrey nodded. "Captain Sir Richard Banks," he added.

"Banks?" The name seemed to cause physical pain, and he closed his eyes. Sarah touched Parfrey on the shoulder; there was little that could be done and they were needed elsewhere, but the lad stopped for a second, as if conscious that more was required of him. Then the eyes opened, and the Irishman's expression softened.

"So what happened to the liner?" he asked.

Parfrey shook his head. "I'm sorry, I know little of the battle."

"It matters not," the man smiled again, this time as if in resignation. "Let it remain a mystery to us all," he said. Then they left him.

* * *

King knew his hands were shaking. He glanced about; everywhere there were casualties: many lay moaning and grasping at an injury, while others were sprawled in the varied abandoned attitudes of death. Some of those still standing were staunching minor cuts with neckerchiefs and shirts. There was Barrow, lying up against the starboard bulwark with Chilton tending to him. And Johnston, the boastwain's mate, was standing quietly while Surridge tied a strip of canvas about his wounded left arm with uncommon delicacy. King went to return his cutlass to its scabbard and noticed, with a wave of disgust, that the blade was running red with blood.

"Steady there!"

He turned to see an unknown marine lieutenant at the head of a group of men that were currently filing down the larboard gangway. The man reached the quarterdeck, then stopped to order a sergeant to secure the prisoners.

"There are wounded that should be dealt with as well," King said, interrupting him. The officer looked up; he was roughly of the same age, although his face appeared unnaturally pale.

"They will be accommodated, sir," he said. "You will be from *Scylla*, I'd chance?"

"I am."

"Name's Masterson, of *Robust*," he said. "Your captain took one deal of a risk, did he not? A frigate to board a battleship is a rare feat indeed."

"We managed well enough," King replied stiffly. "Though your help would have been more welcome a touch earlier."

Masterson smiled. "We was concerned the Frenchie might blow. As still she could. Come, we had better see that order is restored."

There was a Captain and a Commodore to deal with. Neither could – or were willing to – speak English and King knew his French to be limited. For an unaccountable reason he found himself reminded of Crowley, and how useful his ability with language had been. A vague image of the man suddenly came to him, as if he was actually close by, or they had recently met. But the effects of the battle were still with him, and doubtless affected his thoughts. He glanced down; he was still holding the soiled cutlass in one hand. And there was his pistol in the other; it had been fired, although for the life of him he could not remember when, or at what. The red coated lieutenant was speaking in an unnaturally loud and clear voice as the two French officers were taken under the care of a marine guard. There was much to be done and wounded aplenty to care for, as well as ensuring the ship was not suddenly re-taken by the unsecured crew below. He should also report to Banks as soon as possible. He started as Chilton approached, and rather formally extended his hand.

"A fine show, Peter," he said, noting that the younger man's grasp was surprisingly firm. "Tell me, how is Barrow?"

They both looked back to where the midshipman was being helped to his feet by two seamen. "It is a wound to his upper arm," he said. "I dare say not serious; the bullet appears to have passed through and the bone is unbroken, though it pains him deeply."

"Best let the surgeons take a look," King grunted. Barrow was made of solid stuff and would be more than capable of surviving a minor injury. Providing there was no infection he might even return to general duties within a week. And within a week they should be back in harbour; in dock as well, if there were any justice. There was bound to be much to put right in *Scylla*; but it would be strange if some shore leave were not allowed him, and when that time arrived he would send for Juliana, of that he was oddly certain. Whatever it took, and however much the cost in effort, time or money, he wanted her beside him.

As far as he was concerned it was just a matter of chance that he was alive; alive and completely unhurt, when he could so easily have been wounded like Westwood, Barrow and Johnston, or even dead like many others. The brush with death had unleashed such a barrage of irrelevant thoughts that he had difficulty in organising the remains of the boarding party, and when Caulfield came across to assist and congratulated him on his success, it was hard to find suitable words to respond. But in his own mind he was quite set. He had been at sea for all of his adult life; now he was owed a little time ashore. Time to organise a world beyond that of the Royal Navy. Time to get married, to watch while Kate and Robert's child grew up, and maybe seek out the few friends he had made. And it was odd that, once again and for no apparent reason, he found himself thinking of Crowley.

* * *

The Irishman was still alive by the time they took him to Manning's operating table, even if it was clear to all that there was little strength left in him. Betsy deftly removed Parfrey's bandage, revealing a bruised and weeping mark below the left shoulder. The surgeon pressed gently on the wound that had already started to swell, and Crowley winced. Manning glanced at his face and visibly started.

"Michael? Michael Crowley?" he asked, amazed. The last time he had seen the man was almost a year ago on the deck of *Pandora*.

Crowley nodded slightly. "Aye, it's me," he said, his tone one more of resignation than surprise.

The surgeon stepped back and brought his hands apart. "I don't understand, how did you..?"

"That would be a long story," the Irishman replied. "And I don't think I have the time left to tell it."

The words reminded Manning of his duty, and he hurriedly returned to the wound. "I shall have to probe, and it may hurt." He hesitated as a thought occurred. "Tell me, were you on a French ship?"

"I was," Crowley murmured. "And you can save your time looking for the shot, we both know it to be badly placed."

"I would chance it worth the effort, if you are willing." Manning noticed Betsy was ready with probe and bullet retractor. "There are many old Pandora's aboard," he said, almost conversationally as he wiped a swab across the wound, "Tom King amongst them. We shall get you through this and then you may meet up."

Crowley sighed. "Mr King and I have already met," he said. Then his body tensed suddenly as the probe was inserted. There were several seconds of intense pain, before Manning mercifully removed the tool.

"I shall send for him," he passed the probe back to Betsy. "You were friends, and he would wish to know, I am certain."

There was a finality in his words that was not lost on anyone present. Betsy accepted the probe, along with the retractor. Clearly the surgeon had no intention of trying further.

"It were Tom what set the bullet so," the Irishman muttered. "And I don't think we shall be meeting again."

Manning paused, guessing much. Despite his time in

Pandora, Crowley had clearly sided with the enemy. After all, he was present in a ship bound to retake his home country, and had been mortally wounded actively fighting against the British. He found it hard to believe of one who had been so sound, but clearly Crowley's patriotism was greater than any feelings for his former comrades. "Was he aware?" he asked, despite himself. "I mean did he recognise you?"

"I don't believe he did," Crowley's eyes flickered. "It were a mite confusing."

"And I am sure he would not have done so if he had," Manning said, strangely eager to reassure himself as much as anyone. "You two were such good friends, and..."

"Aye, we were that," Crowley agreed; there was little more to be said.

"Let me send for him." Manning repeated. "There has been scarcely any gunfire for some time, the battle must be all but over."

"No." Crowley spoke the word quite loudly, even though the effort clearly gave him pain. "No, you will leave him be, and not mention our meeting."

"I am to say nothing?" Manning regarded him doubtfully. "But he would wish to know, and be sorry, I am sure."

"It is better that he does not," Crowley replied firmly. "Better that he remembers me as a friend. If he should have any regret, no good shall come of it."

"Not a single word?"

"Not one." His eyes flashed over to Betsy suddenly. "And you as well, miss. I am dying; you would not deny me that."

"Very well," Manning conceded. Crowley was quite right, he was done for, and already too much time had been wasted when there were others requiring a surgeon's attention. "We will move you to a place where you can rest," he said, looking up for a loblolly boy.

"And you will say nothing?" Crowley insisted.

"I will," he replied. "If that is what you wish; though I think it to be a mistake."

"Do you swear?"

Two men were approaching, ready to carry Crowley off. "Do I what?" Manning replied.

"Swear." Crowley repeated, his voice now noticeably softer. "I would hear you do so and be content."

Manning watched sadly as they collected him. "I swear," he said clearly, while they carried him away. He glanced across to Betsy who had been a mute witness to all that had been said. "What else could I have done?" he asked.

"Nothing," she said, and laid a reassuring hand upon his arm. "You did what was right." Her eyes seemed suddenly bright. "As I was told once: the truth can be dangerous. It must be handled with caution, and sometimes is best used sparingly."

THE END

Author's Notes

The Battle of Tory Island took place on the 12th of October 1798, and in reality Sir John Warren managed quite well, even without *Scylla*'s intervention. At the time there was some speculation as to why he delayed attacking Bompart's fleet and attempted to form his ships into a line of battle when a general chase might have seen a swifter and more complete resolution: certainly his tactics were old fashioned. It should be remembered, however, that the more aggressive stance favoured by Nelson and other contemporary commanders had yet to be widely accepted. The Battle of the Nile, probably the best example of what can be achieved when individual captains are trusted to make decisions, had only been fought a few months previously. Besides, many commanders would remain disciples of the old fighting tactics until the end of their careers. And Warren's victory was decisive, with nearly all of Bompart's force captured and more than two thousand men taken prisoner, even if the original fleet action dissolved into a series of single ship engagements that carried on for a considerable time afterwards.

Wolfe Tone was indeed captured on the deck of the *Hoche*, where he had been serving a cannon. He was taken in irons to Derry gaol and tried, in Dublin, on the 10th of November. Using his own admission, combined with overwhelming evidence against him, conviction, followed swiftly by a death sentence, was inevitable. His wish to be shot was not granted, however, and he was due to be hanged two days later. A rebel to the end, Tone cheated the executioner by cutting his own throat with a razor left behind by his brother when he had been held in the same cell. The wound was not immediately fatal, but he finally died on the 19th of November.

The *Windbüchse* air powered rifle was moderately successful and saw service with the Austrian Army for many years, although difficulty in manufacturing the reservoirs, (which also took considerable effort to charge) and a general vulnerability in action finally caused it to be withdrawn. It has been credited with being the first repeating rifle to see military service, and a version was carried by the Lewis and Clark Expedition of 1804.

The Battle of Tory Island (often referred to as Warren's Action, or the Battle of Donegal) was the final major action of the 1798 Irish Rebellion, and marked the last of several attempts made by the French to land a large body of men in support of a rising. British losses were relatively slight; 13 killed and 75 wounded, as opposed to 270 casualties in the French flagship alone. The *Hoche* was repaired and taken into British service where, renamed HMS *Donegal,* she served for many years, finally being broken up in 1845.

The cost of the rebellion, in terms of lives and money, has been calculated many times, with almost as many different results. In March 1799 the government reported that eighty-one men had been executed since Cornwallis took command, four hundred and eighty-one transported, and "great numbers" sentenced separately at the assizes. At that time the total number of casualties was thought to be roughly twenty thousand, fifteen hundred of which were loyalists. Later estimates placed the initial figure far higher at seventy thousand deaths, (twenty thousand being government troops), while more recent research puts the total nearer to thirty thousand. The British government received claims for just over one million pounds in compensation from loyalists. Obviously no figures are available for rebel losses; the vast majority had less to lose, although being as they were far greater in number, it is thought that their cost was considerably higher. But figures, however accurate, can never hope to indicate the suffering caused by such a conflict. At least ten towns were heavily affected; some, like Kildare, being razed to the ground by the military, with at least two others similarly destroyed by rebel forces. In 1799 Dublin was reported to be filled with the widows and orphans of those who had fallen in battle, and on both sides whole families were effectively wiped out.

As a direct result of the 1798 rebellion, union with Britain became official on the 1st of January 1801, just six months after the Irish Parliament had effectively voted itself out of existence.

SELECTED GLOSSARY

Abercromby(Ralph) – Scottish lieutenant-general in charge of British forces in Ireland until mid 1798.

Able Seaman – One who can hand, reef and steer; well acquainted with the duties of a seaman.

BackWind – Change, anticlockwise.

Backed sail – One set in the direction for the opposite tack to slow a ship.

Backstays – Similar to shrouds in function, except that they run from the hounds of the topmast, or topgallant, all the way to the deck. Serve to support the mast against any forces forward, for example, when the ship is tacking. (Also a useful/spectacular way to return to deck for topmen.)

Backstays,running – A less permanent backstay, rigged with a tackle to allow it to be slacked to clear a gaff or boom.

Barkie – *(Slang)* Seaman's affectionate name for their ship.

Beetle headed – *(Slang)* Dull, Stupid.

Belaying pins – Pins set into racks at the side of a ship. Lines are secured to these, allowing instant release by their removal.

Bight – Loop made in the middle of a line.

Bilboes – Leg irons, or iron garters. Bilboes were supposed to have originated in Spain – Bilbao – and were used to restrain prisoners on the punishment deck; a sort of pedal handcuffs.

Binnacle – Cabinet on the quarterdeck that houses compasses, the log, traverse board, lead lines, telescope and speaking trumpet

Biscuit – Small hammock mattress, resembling ships rations. Also Hard Tack.

Bitter end – The very end of an anchor cable.

Bitts – Stout horizontal pieces of timber, supported by strong verticals, that extend deep into the ship. These hold the anchor cable when the ship is at anchor. Also Jeer bits.

Blab – *(Slang)* Gossip.

Block – Article of rigging that allows pressure to be diverted or, when used with others, increased. Consists of a pulley wheel, made of *lignum vitae*, encased in a wooden shell. Blocks can be single, double (fiddle block), triple or quadruple. Main suppliers Taylors, of Southampton.

Boat fall – Line that raises or lowers a ship's boat.

Boatswain(pronounced *Bosun*) – The officer who superintends the sails, rigging, canvas, colours, anchors, cables and cordage, committed to his charge.

Bolt rope/line – Line sewn into the edge of a sail, at the bolt.

Boom – Lower spar to which the bottom of a gaff sail is attached.

Bootnecks – *(Slang)* Marines. Also Gallouts, Guffies or Jollies.

Bower – Type of anchor mounted in the bows.

Bowline – Line attached to the middle of the leech that keeps the leading edge of a sail forward when sailing close to the wind.

Braces – Lines used to adjust the angle between the yards and the fore and aft line of the ship. Mizzen braces, and braces of a brig, lead forward.

Breach rope/line – Heavy line to stop the recoil of a cannon, (7" for 32 pounder).

Brig – Two masted vessel square-rigged on both masts..

Broach – When running down wind, to round up into the wind, out of control usually due to carrying too much canvas.

Bulkhead – A wall or partition within the hull of a ship.

Bulwark – The planking or wood-work about a vessel above her deck.

Bumboat – *(Slang)* A shore based vessel that approaches large sea going ships to sell luxuries, etc. Often contains money lenders (who will give a mean return in cash for a seaman's pay ticket). Frequently crewed by large masculine women, who employ far more fetching girls to carry out the bargaining with the seamen.

Bunt – Middle upper part of a sail, next to the mast.

Bunting – Material from which signal flags are made.

Button – Top of a mast or extreme end of a cannon, (on the Blomefield model, carrying a loop to take the breach rope) See cascabel.

Canister – Type of shot, also known as case. Small iron balls packed into a cylindrical case.

Carronade – Short cannon firing a heavy shot. Invented by Melville, Gascoigne and Miller in late 1770's and adopted in 1779. Often used on the upper deck of larger ships, or as the main armament of smaller.

Cascabel – Part of the breach of a cannon.

Caulk – *(Slang)* to sleep. Also Caulking, a process to seal the seams between strakes.

Channel – Projecting ledge that holds deadeyes from shrouds and backstays, originally chain-whales.

Channel Gropers – *(Slang)* The Channel Fleet, when under blockading duties.

Cleat – A retaining piece for lines attached to yards, etc.

Close hauled – Sailing as near as possible into the wind.

Coaming – A ridged frame about hatches to prevent water on deck from getting below.

Companionway – A staircase or passageway.

Cornwallis (Charles) – Viceroy and Commander in Chief of Ireland during 1798.

Counter – The lower part of a ship's stern.

Course – A large square lower sail, hung from a yard, with sheets controlling, and securing it.

Crimp – *(Slang)* One who procures pressed men for the service.

Croppy – hunter*(Slang)* One who persecutes rebels.

Crown and Anchor – A popular shipboard dice game.

Crows of iron – "Crow bars" used to move a gun or heavy object.

Cutter – Fast small, single masted vessel with a sloop rig. Also a seaworthy ship's boat.

Cutting out – The act of taking an enemy vessel while it is in a supposedly safe harbour or anchorage.

Deadeyes – A round, flattish wooden block with three holes through which a lanyard is reaved. Used to tension shrouds and backstays.

Ditty bag – *(Slang)* A seaman's bag. Derives its name from the dittis or Manchester stuff of which it was once made.

Dollond – Maker of optical instruments; slang for the instrument itself.

Doxies – *(Slang)* Shore based prostitutes or temporary wives. Usually reasonably attractive as by tradition they do not pay the ferryman's fair unless they find a "Fancy Man". (Also the officer allowing them on board will only admit pretty women, for the honour of the ship.)

Driver – Large sail set on the mizzen in light winds. The foot is extended by means of a boom.

Dunnage – Officially the packaging around cargo. Also *(Slang)* Seaman's baggage or possessions.

Eight bells – The end of a normal 4 hour watch. The bell is rung every half hour, the number of rings increasing with the passage of time.

Fall – The loose end of a lifting tackle on which the men haul.

Fat head – *(Slang)* The feeling one gets from sleeping below on stuffy nights.

Fetch – To arrive, or reach a destination. Also the distance the wind blows across the water. The longer the fetch the bigger the waves.

Fife rail – Holed rail to accept belaying pins.

First Luff – *(Slang)* First lieutenant.

Flexible rammer – Gun serving tool made of thick line, with rammer to one end and sponge to the other. The flexibility of which allows a gunport to remain closed while the gun is served.

Forereach – To gain upon, or pass by another ship when sailing in a similar direction.

Forestay – Stay supporting the masts running forward, serving the opposite function of the backstay. Runs from each mast at an angle of about 45 degrees to meet another mast, the deck or the bowsprit.

Frapping/Frapped – To make secure by binding.

Frizzen – Striking plate of a flintlock mechanism.

Futtock shrouds – Rigging that projects away from the mast leading to, and steadying, a top or crosstrees. True sailors climb up them, rather than use the lubber's hole, even though it means hanging backwards.

Gaff – Spar attached to the top of the gaff sail.

Gangway – The light deck or platform on either side of the waist leading from the quarterdeck to the forecastle, often called a gangboard in merchant ships. Also, narrow passages left in the hold, when a ship is laden.

Gammoning – Wrapping line about a mast or spar *e.g.* the lashing that holds the bowsprit against upward pressure, to the knee of the head.

Gasket – Line or canvas strip used to tie the sail when furling.

Gig – Medium sized boat.

Glass; – Telescope. Also, hourglass an instrument for measuring time. Also barometer.

Go-about – To alter course, changing from one tack to the other with the wind crossing the bows.

Gratings – An open wood-work of cross battens and ledges forming cover for the hatchways, serving to give light and air to the lower decks. In nautical phrase, he "who can't see a hole through a grating" is excessively drunk.

Grappling-iron – Small anchor, fitted with four or five flukes or claws, Used to hold two ships together for boarding.

Grog – Rum mixed with water (to ensure it is drunk immediately, and not accumulated). Served twice a day at ratios differing from three to five to one.

Gunpowder – A mixture of charcoal, salt petre and sulphur.

Half deck – Area immediately between the captain's quarters and the mainmast.

Halyards – Lines which raise yards, sails, signals, etc.

Handspike – Long lever.

Hanger – A fighting sword, similar to a cutlass.

Hawse – Area in bows where holes are cut to allow the anchor cables to pass through. Also used as general term for bows.

Hawser – Heavy cable used for hauling, towing or mooring.

Head – Toilet, or seat of ease. Those for the common sailor were sited at the bows to allow for a clear drop and the wind to carry any unpleasant odours away.

Head braces – Lines used to adjust the angle of the upper yards.

Head rope/line – Line sewn into the edge at the head of a sail.

Headway – The amount a vessel is moved forward, (rather than leeway the amount a vessel is moved sideways), when the wind is not directly behind.

Heave to – Keeping a ship relatively stationary by backing certain sails in a seaway.

Holystone – *(Slang)* Block of sandstone roughly the size and shape of a family bible. Used to clean and smooth decks. Originally salvaged from the ruins of a church on the Isle of Wright.

Hounds – Top of a section of mast, where the shrouds run from.

Hulled – Describes a ship that, when fired upon, the shot passes right through the hull.

Idler – One who does not keep a watch, cook, carpenter, etc.

Interest – Backing from a superior officer or one in authority, useful when looking for promotion to, or within, commissioned rank.

Jape – *(Slang)* Joke.

Jeer bits – Stout timber frame about the mast, these extend deep into the ship.

Jeers – Thick lines which raise the lower yards.

Jib-boom – Boom run out from the extremity of the bowsprit, braced by means of a Martingale stay, which passes through the dolphin striker,

Junk – Old line used to make wads, etc.

Jury mast/rig – Temporary measure used to restore a vessels sailing ability.

Lading – The act of loading.

Lake (Gerard) – English lieutenant-general who took charge of British forces during 1798.

Landsman – The rating of one who has no experience at sea.

Lanthorn – Lantern.

Lanyard – Short piece of line to be used as a handle. Also decorative tassel to uniform.

Larboard – Left side of the ship when facing forward.

Launch – Large ship's boat, crew of 40-60.

Leeward – The downwind side of a ship.

Leeway – The amount a vessel is pushed sideways by the wind, (as opposed to headway, the forward movement, when the wind is directly behind).

Legs and wings – *(Slang)* A surgeon's 'offcuts'.

Liner – *(Slang)* Ship of the line or Ship of the line of battle (later battleship).

Linstock – The holder of slow match which the gun captain uses to fire his piece when the flintlock mechanism is not working/present.

Lobscouse – A mixture of salted meat, biscuit, potatoes, onions and spices, minced small and stewed together.

Loblolly men/boys – Surgeon's assistants.

Lubberly/Lubber – *(Slang)* Unseamanlike behaviour; as a landsman.

Luff – Intentionally sail closer to the wind, perhaps to allow work aloft. Also the flapping of sails when brought too close to the wind. The side of a fore and aft sail laced to the mast.

Main tack – Line leading forward from a sheave in the hull allowing the clew of the maincourse to be held forward when the ship is sailing close to the wind.

Martingale stay – Line that braces the jib-boom, passing from the end, through the dolphin striker, to the ship.

Master-at-Arms – Senior hand, responsible for discipline aboard ship.

Midshipman – Junior, and aspiring, officer.

Open order – In fleet sailing, 3 - 4 cables apart.

Ordinary – Term used to describe a ship laid up; left in storage, with principle shipkeepers aboard, but unfit for immediate use.

Orlop – Deck directly above the hold, and below the lower gun deck. A lighter deck than the gun deck (no cannon to support) and usually level or below the waterline. Holds warrant officers mess, and midshipmen's berth, also carpenters and sail makers stores. Used as an emergency operating area in action.

Over threes – *(Slang)* Referring to a captain of over three years seniority, and entitled to wear both epaulettes (after the uniform changes of 1795)

Palaverer – One who attempts to fool or con through clever wordplay.

Pariah-dogs – *(Slang)* Men who change mess so often they are forced to mess alone, or with others of their kind. They are usually unpopular for a variety of anti-social reasons.

Peach – *(Slang)* To betray or reveal; from impeach.

Peter Warren – *(Slang)* Petty Warrant Victuals, fresh food sent from the shore to ships staying in harbour.

Pinance – Ship's boat powered by oars or sail. Smaller than a barge.

Pissdale – A basic urinal.

Pointing the ropes – The act of tapering the end of a line to allow it to pass easily through a block.

Poop – Aft most, and highest, deck of a larger ship.

Pox – (Slang) Venereal Disease, Common on board ship; until 1795 a man suffering had to pay a 15/- fine to the surgeon, in consequence, many cases went unreported. Treatment was often mercurial, and ultimately ineffective.

Protection – A legal document that gives the owner protection against impressment.

Provisions – Naval rations.

Pumpdale – Gully carrying water cleared by a pump.

Purser – Officer responsible for provisions and clothing on board.

Purser's dip – Tallow lantern allowed below deck.

Pusser – (Slang) Purser.

Quarterdeck – Deck forward of the poop, but at a lower level. The preserve of officers.

Queue – A pigtail. Often tied by a man's best friend (his tie mate).

Ratlines – Lighter lines, untarred, and tied horizontally across the shrouds at regular intervals, to act as rungs and allow men to climb aloft.

Reef – A portion of sail that can be taken in to reduce the size of the whole.

Reefing points – Light line on large sails which can be tied to reduce sail in heavy weather.

Reefing tackle – Line that leads from the end of the yard to the reefing cringles set in the edges of the sail. It is used to haul up the upper part of the sail when reefing.

Rigging – Tophamper; made up of standing (static) and running (moveable) rigging, blocks *etc. (Slang)* Clothes.

Roach – The lower edge of a sail, usually scalloped, in the case of a main or fore course. In warships the roach is deeper (more round). Also Gore.

Rondey – (Slang) The *Rendezvous* location where a press is based and organised.

Running – Sailing before the wind.

Sailor's joy – *(Slang)* A home made drink so potent that even men accustomed to drinking grog on a regular basis soon become intoxicated.

Schooner – Small craft with two masts.

Sconce – Candle holder, made of tin, usually large and flat for stability.

Scotch coffee – An infusion of burnt biscuit thought, by some, to resemble coffee.

Scran – *(Slang)* Food.

Scupper – Waterway that allows deck drainage.

Sennight – Seven days.

Shako – Marine's headgear.

Sheet – A line that controls the foot of a sail.

Sheet anchor – Heaviest anchor (although often not much bigger than the bower). Also slang for the seaman's last hope - if the sheet doesn't hold...

Shrouds – Lines supporting the masts athwart ship (from side to side) which run from the hounds (just below the top) to the channels on the side of the hull. Upper run from the top deadeyes to the crosstrees.

Sick Bay – An area permanently set aside for the accommodation of sick and wounded, as opposed to

Sick Berth – Any other place reserved for invalids.

Skylarking – *(Slang)* Unofficial exercise aloft, often in the form of "follow my leader" or other games.

Slab line – Line passing up abaft a ship's main or fore sail, used to truss up the slack sail.

Sloop – Small craft, usually the command of a commander or junior captain.

Slops – *(Slang)* Ready made clothes and other goods sold to the crew by the purser.

Slush – *(Slang)* Fat from boiled meat, sold by the cook to the men to spread on their biscuit. The money made was known as the slush fund.

Slushy – *(Slang)* The cook.

Snow – Type of brig, with an extra trysail mast stepped behind the main.

Spring – Hawser attached to a fixed object that can be tensioned to move the position of a ship fore and aft along a dock, often when setting out to sea.

Sprit sail – A square sail hung from the bowsprit yards, less used by 1793, as the function had been taken over by the jibs, although the rigging of their yards helps to brace the bowsprit against sideways pressure.

Stag – *(Slang)* To turn against your own.

Stay sail – A quadrilateral or triangular sail with parallel lines, usually hung from under a stay.

Stern sheets – Part of a ship's boat between the stern and the first rowing thwart, used for passengers.

Stood/Stand – The movement of a ship towards or from an object.

Strake – A plank.

Swab – Cloth, or *(Slang)* officers' epaulette.

Sweep – A large oar, often used to move bigger vessels, such as brigs or cutters.

Tack – To turn a ship, moving her bows through the wind. Also a leg of a journey; relates to the direction of the wind. If from starboard, a ship is on the starboard tack. Also the part of a fore and aft loose footed sail where the sheet is attached or a line leading forward on a square course to hold the lower part of the sail forward.

Taffrail – Rail around the stern of a vessel.

Tarpaulin – Tarred cloth or *(Slang)* used to describe a commissioned officer who came from the lower deck.

Tattletale – *(Slang)* Gossip.

Thwart – (Properly ATHWARTS). The seats or benches athwart a boat whereon the rowers sit to manage their oars.

Tie Mate – A seaman's best friend, one who ties his queue, and attends to his body should he die.

Tight ship – In good order, watertight.

Tophamper – Literally any unnecessary weight either on a ship's decks or about her tops and rigging, but often used loosely to refer to spars and rigging.

Tow – *(Slang)* Cotton waste.

Traverse board – A temporary log used for recording speed and headings during a watch.

Trick – *(Slang)* Period of duty.

Turnpike – A toll road; the user pays for the upkeep. Usually major roads.

Under threes – Referring to a captain of under three years seniority, and only allowed to wear one epaulette, on the right shoulder (after 1795).

Veer – Wind change, clockwise.

Waist – Area of main deck between the quarterdeck and forecastle.

Wales – Reinforcement running the length of the ship, under the gunports.

Watch – Period of four (or in case of dog watch, two) hour duty. Also describes the two or three divisions of a crew.

Watch list – List of men and stations, usually carried by lieutenants and divisional officers.

Wearing – To change the direction of a ship across the wind by putting the stern of the ship through the eye of the wind.

Weather helm – A tendency to head up into the wind. A well trimmed ship is often said to have slight to moderate weather helm. The opposite of lee helm.

Well – A deep enclosure in the middle of the ship where bilge water can gather, and be cleared by the pumps.

Windward – The side of a ship exposed to the wind.

Wormed, parcelled and served – Standing rigging, which has been protected by a wrapping of canvas and line.

About the Author

His Majesty's Ship
The Jackass Frigate
True Colours
Cut and Run

Alaric Bond was born in Surrey, England, but now lives in Herstmonceux, East Sussex, in a 14th century Wealden Hall House. He is married with two sons.

His father was a well-known writer, mainly of novels and biographies, although he also wrote several screenplays. He was also a regular contributor to BBC Radio drama (including Mrs Dale's Diary!), and a founding writer for the Eagle comic.

During much of his early life Alaric was hampered by Dyslexia, although he now considers the lateral view this condition gave him to be an advantage. He has been writing professionally for over twenty years with work covering broadcast comedy (commissioned to BBC Light Entertainment for 3 years), periodicals, children's stories, television, and the stage. He is also a regular contributor to several nautical magazines and newsletters.

His interests include the British Navy 1793-1815 and the RNVR during WWII. He regularly gives talks to groups and organizations and is a member of various historical societies including The Historical Maritime Society and the Society for Nautical Research. He also enjoys Jazz, swing and big band music from 1930-1950 (indeed, he has played trombone for over 40 years), sailing, and driving old SAAB convertibles.

LINDA
COLLISON

BARBADOS
BOUND

BOOK ONE

Patricia MacPherson
Nautical Adventure Series

For the Finest in Nautical and Historical Fiction and Nonfiction

WWW.FIRESHIPPRESS.COM

Interesting • Informative • Authoritative

All Fireship Press books are now available
directly through www.FireshipPress.com, amazon.com
and via leading bookstores and wholesalers from coast-to-coast

"OLD IRONSIDES" AND HMS JAVA
A STORY OF 1812

A highly recommended must-read for every naval enthusiast—indeed, for every American!

Stephen Coonts
NY Times best-selling author

HMS *Java* and the USS *Constitution* (the famous "Old Ironsides") face off in the War of 1812's most spectacular blue-water frigate action. Their separate stories begin in August 1812—one in England and the other in New England. Then, the tension and suspense rise, week-by-week, as the ships cruise the Atlantic, slowly and inevitably coming together for the final life-and-death climax.

The Perfect Wreck is not only the first full-length book ever written about the battle between the USS *Constitution* and HMS *Java*, it is a gem of Creative Nonfiction. It has the exhaustive research of a scholarly history book; but it is beautifully presented in the form of a novel.

WWW.FIRESHIPPRESS.COM
Interesting • Informative • Authoritative

For the Finest in
Nautical and Historical
Fiction and Nonfiction

www.FireshipPress.com

Interesting • Informative • Authoritative

CPSIA information can be obtained
at www.ICGtesting.com
Printed in the USA
BVHW091656200121
598206BV00003B/30

9 781611 792386